The Path to
Kitty Islet

by Nancy Pekter

*To Chloi —
another story of mine
for you to "hear"!*

Nancy Pekter

◆ **FriesenPress**

Suite 300 - 990 Fort St
Victoria, BC, Canada, V8V 3K2
www.friesenpress.com

Copyright © 2016 by Nancy Pekter
First Edition — 2016

The Path to Kitty Islet is a work of fiction. Any references to historical events; to real people, living or dead; or to real locales are intended only to give the fiction a setting in historical reality. Other names, characters, places, and incidents are the product of the author's imagination or are used fictitiously, and their resemblance, if any, to real-life counterparts is entirely coincidental.

Kitty Islet/Adirondack chair photo-Christina Aitchison-Photographer

All rights reserved. No part of this publication may be reproduced, in any form, or by any means, electronic or mechanical, including photocopying, recording, or any information browsing, storage, or retrieval system, without permission in writing from FriesenPress.

ISBN
978-1-4602-7792-8 (Hardcover)
978-1-4602-7793-5 (Paperback)
978-1-4602-7794-2 (eBook)

1. Fiction, Sagas

Distributed to the trade by The Ingram Book Company

To my daughter, Marilla,
and my mother, Dorothy, with all my love.

With special thanks to my superb and supportive editor,
John Eerkes-Medrano, gone too soon.

Tell all the truth but tell it slant,
Success in circuit lies,
Too bright for our infirm delight
The truth's superb surprise;

As lightning to the children eased
With explanation kind,
The truth must dazzle gradually
Or every man be blind.

~ Emily Dickinson

When You Are Old

When you are old and grey and full of sleep,
And nodding by the fire, take down this book,
And slowly read, and dream of the soft look
Your eyes had once, and of their shadows deep;

How many loved your moments of glad grace,
And loved your beauty with love false or true;
But one man loved the pilgrim soul in you,
And loved the sorrows of your changing face.

And bending down beside the glowing bars,
Murmur, a little sadly, how Love fled
And paced upon the mountains overhead
And hid his face amid a crowd of stars.

~ W.B. Yeats

"But true love is a durable fire
In the mind ever burning..."

~ Sir Walter Ralegh (also spelled Raleigh)

ROSALIND

1991
VICTORIA, B.C.

Some decisions don't matter, but others change our lives. We make a hundred decisions every day, most small and unimportant. And yet—and yet some of our choices can truly change everything.

Since my grandmother, Minnie—or Grandmama as we called her— shared her life story—all of it—I can't stop thinking about her decisions. There were so many moments when she could have chosen another path, another life, simply by deciding differently.

It makes me wonder—how did she choose? How do any of us choose, really? Sure, we'd like to think that we always weigh our options, consider the alternatives, but in reality, how many of us just close our eyes, choose something in the heat of the moment, and then spend the rest of our lives making up the stories we tell ourselves and others about why we made those decisions?

I do wonder how she chose—and perhaps I always will.

Part One: Water

MINNIE

JULY 1908
MID-ATLANTIC

Greetings my dearest Emily!
I have tried to start this letter to you a hundred, no, a thousand times. Yet each time I begin it seems my words never say enough, contain enough, to share my experiences with you. It is very selfish of me I know (especially since I am on this ship and know just how horrible this has been), but I do so wish you could be here with me. I am sad without your support, your friendship, and your love.

Things have happened so very quickly, haven't they? As you know so well, it has been mere months since we two were together plotting and planning for another Christmas. Tormenting Graham and Edward—threatening a double wedding that would forever tie our families together. But then the advent of Harry. I owe you so much, Emily! The way you protected me, encouraged our love, and persuaded Mother to look on him favourably.

We are still happy, dearest Emily. It is simply that the heaving of this all too small ship drives most thoughts of love, indeed most thoughts of any kind, from my mind. I have never been so ill and so frightened. The waves threaten to engulf us at times, and most of us who have been so very sick almost wish for the ocean's oblivion. It seems blasphemous to write, but it has been on my mind. Harry, however, is my anchor. The swell affects him not at all. His cheeks are as ruddy as ever. I call them my roses, for it is as if his cheeks transport me back to terra firma and I can smell again the warmth of newly dug earth on solid ground.

I must admit, though, that I am improving—hence this letter. I will mail it from my new country (how odd that sounds, though of course the Dominion is still part of Britain) the first possible chance I get. Harry has promised that the crossing will not endure much longer. We were lucky, he says, to take passage in the summer, as winter crossings are almost unendurable for poor sailors like me.

You would laugh at the deprivations aboard, Emily. And probably go marching to the captain's quarters to demand that the situation be improved. I, however, am not made of such stern stuff. I have simply given up performing all but the most modest toilet most days. Many around us have abandoned all pretence of washing, and the stench is quite unbearable. But with the Lord's strength and my Harry's roses, I too will bear up to these inconveniences. Harry has been telling me more of the great land we will farm in the west—it seems that the arable land stretches on forever across the Canadian prairie. In my mind's eye, I picture a small, neat house, a garden, and a small pond. And it will come to pass; I can just feel it in my bones! Our own land, Emily! Hard to imagine! And it will be our decisions that will make our farm prosper!

All my love,
Minnie

The Path to Kitty Islet

LATE JULY 1908

    I haven't much time. Emily, we made it! The ship arrived in Quebec a few days ago. We disembarked and made it through customs quickly (though some are detained in the quarantine area). Harry knows ways of dealing with people—I was enthralled and amazed. Soon, he had engaged a taxi of sorts and we were taken to the train station. Most of the cars were crowded, but we found a corner. We travelled through at least one day and night. (I'm afraid I'm rather muddled when it comes to time. I have never felt so tired in my life!) The heat is oppressive and close—it always seems to threaten a storm, but so far we have not had any refreshing rain.

    We stopped in Ottawa briefly—a fine city with some elegant buildings—and then left immediately for Harry's hometown—Kingston, Ontario. There are brick buildings here and some wooden farmhouses. And land! The fields seem to stretch for miles. Harry's parents were not as I expected (but how could they have been? I had expected at once so much and so little!), though Harry is a younger reflection of his father. I do hope that Harry keeps more of his fine black hair, however! Oh Emily—I need your humour and your hand in mine. I feel such a stranger. Harry's mother has been kind, perhaps too kind. I will try to explain that in my next letter.

    But onward now! Harry is eager to put hidebound, settled Ontario behind him, behind us. He has booked us train passage from Port Arthur, in Northern Ontario, to Edmonton (in the real west) and now we must take ourselves quickly across most of Ontario to get the train. It seems we will take a boat much of the way but I am not to dread the necessity of this, as we will be on huge, calm lakes (or so Harry promises!). Ontario is a huge territory, but much of it lies along these immense lakes. It is apparently much easier to go by boat than to try some sort of land transportation. His mother has been crying and begging us to stay; she plies me with tea and tears almost every hour of the day, seeming to think I have some ability to stem Harry's enthusiasm. For my part, I am not anxious to remain with Harry's parents too long. I feel that I have disappointed them and ruined a scheme favoured by Harry's mother and her good friend—a mother to a young, ill-tempered, unmarried girl. Harry had hinted at something of the sort, as I'm sure you recall. I must stop now—I will post this at once. It's teatime (again) and I'm being rounded from our sanctuary.

All my love,
Minnie

AUGUST 2, 1908

We are embarked on the second stage of our journey. Harry obtained passage on one of the paddle wheelers that plies what they call the Great Lakes. We left Kingston not long after my last letter was written. Jane (Harry's mother) was bereft. She kept imploring us to stay the winter with them and start out fresh in the spring. I still cannot comprehend the depth and breadth of these Canadian winters if we must concern ourselves with them in August! It truly seems impossible that this humid heat, these terrific thunder and lightning displays, must give way to hoarfrost, snow, and bitter cold. Of course, everyone we've met has been at great pains to tell the "fragile English miss" of the fierce Canadian season, the blasts of Arctic air, the restless cabin fever—they assure me, one and all, that they are not exaggerating in the least. I look to Harry for guidance in this regard, as his kind face soon betrays a telltale smile when the stories are simply preposterous.

The Path to Kitty Islet

As we made our way along Lakes Ontario and Erie, Harry seemed to withdraw into himself. I tried to draw him back out at first, but have determined that it is best to leave him alone. I have made friends with one of the other women aboard; she is a little older than me and emigrated to the Dominion when she was just a girl. Her family lives near Winnipeg now, and thus she will share most of the first leg of the journey with us. She has been most kind in suggesting the types of provisions we will need to purchase for our first Prairie winter. You would like her too I'm sure; she has a fire in her eyes and a quick tongue. It seems the other women are scared of her and keep their distance, for she is not afraid to tell them how to discipline their young ones or tend to their babies. She is studying to be a nurse, and it seems to me that she has found the perfect profession for her talents.

How odd that though I am travelling through alien territory, I keep describing the people rather than the place. You, I am sure, would remember your purpose and would act as the "eyes of the Empire." I simply feel that no words can possibly encompass the contradictions we see daily. Around Kingston, the land was settled, contained. There were dairy farms and schools and churches. Parts of the city felt not unlike England—there were even spreading oak trees and the flowers found in every British garden. But along the Lakes, all is different. The towns remain civilized—for the most part—and it cheers me to see the church spires offering ready praise to the immense Canadian sky. We have seen natives too, though; Indians clad in a strange assortment of traditional garb and ordinary attire.

Some of the people on board are here simply to see the Lakes and experience the Indian way of life. One fellow plans to be taken by an Indian guide in one of their boats, a canoe, to the wilds of Western Ontario. He informs me that there he will experience the true spirit of the land and will be able to conquer his fear of solitude by matching wits with nature. I hesitated to point out that his Indian guide would provide all the food and knowledge of the local terrain, as I could not ruin his obvious pleasure. It is an odd thing, though.

We have stopped at several small towns where the wharves are thick with Indian families selling trinkets of all sorts. After seeing my interest, Harry bought me a pair of beaded moccasins—tiny shoes for a small infant. The handiwork is at once exquisite and coarse. I later learned from another passenger that the correct way to purchase items from these people is to barter. Harry had simply paid the price asked, despite his usual business acumen in other instances. In my heart, I am glad that he did not argue about the price.

Toronto, a loud and rambunctious upstart of a city, did not impress. All that seems to recommend it is the lake and its sense of importance. Harry scathingly calls it a frontier town without a frontier. As yet, I am struggling with such references. In this, as in so many things here, I know I am sadly naïve. The shores of all the lakes seemed to me at first to be enough of a frontier, but now that we are on Lake Superior, I think I begin to get a sense of what he meant.

It is a huge inland sea, and it appears often as if it has no end and no beginning. There are waves too, but so far they have remained small and unthreatening. It is not always so. We have watched squalls come out of nowhere and then disappear to our left as our route continues to follow the shore. The shores here are generally completely empty of any human imprint. If the ship were to suddenly disappear, one could easily be certain of being the very only human on earth. It is frighteningly majestic.

It is getting late, and my hand and eyes tire. I will try to paint a better picture in my next letter.

All my love,
Minnie

The Path to Kitty Islet

Carefully putting away her writing paper and pen and ink, Minnie straightened up their tiny cabin. It was absolute luxury compared with the space they had occupied on their Atlantic crossing, and Minnie, for perhaps the hundredth time, thanked Providence for its care. Above the washstand and basin hung a smeared and cracked mirror. Leaning close, Hermione Worthing, née Sinclair, inspected her face. As she regarded herself, she noticed that her brown eyes, usually large, now seemed enormous and frightened. Her letters to her dear friend, Emily McCrindle, often had a soothing effect on her nerves. But not tonight, as tonight her descriptions of the land had seemed trite, evasive. And she hadn't dared to mention just how dark Harry's moods had become. In truth, he frightened her at times.

She lowered her lids, refusing to meet her own wide-eyed stare any longer. She began pacing—two steps to the washstand, turn, two steps to the bed, turn again. Unconsciously, her hand rose to her throat. The collar of her dress seemed too tight, the lace trim scratchy. Perhaps minutes, perhaps hours later, she sat down on the edge of the bed. Her best black boots protruded from beneath her second-best dress. She felt that she needed to be doing, to be occupied, active. She could of course take a turn about on deck, seek out her friend, the soon-to-be nurse, or try to find Harry. But none of these options seemed to be enough. Her toe scuffed back and forth rhythmically, in time to something she couldn't quite hear. And then she must have slept.

Harry Worthing, Jr. had been pacing too. The late summer sun was not interested in sinking below the horizon quickly, and Harry had promised himself a sunset before he would return to their tiny cabin. Like Minnie, he felt caged, contained, and therefore restless. He also felt the burden of her trust and hope grow ever heavier as they made their way to their final destination. Those qualities had brought them together. Now Harry feared them.

He leaned on the rail, the breeze lightly playing across his features. His brow was clear, unlined, not daring to reveal the turmoil inside. His eyes reflected the dark water beneath him, however. Usually they sparkled like waves in the sun. Lately, though, they had clouded over. His hands were work roughened, tanned, strong. But were they strong enough?

As a small boy, he had sat at his Uncle Samuel's feet, soaking up the wild stories, the tales of virgin forest, beckoning gold, and daring adventure. Samuel, inspired by his nephew's bright inquisitiveness, had embroidered his stories lavishly: two feet of snow became twenty, one old sick black bear become a sixteen-foot-tall Kermode bear subdued by Samuel's strength alone, and Vancouver became a sort of Pacific coast Shangri-La populated by pretty girls and wily, slant-eyed Orientals.

When Samuel passed away, ironically in a pristine white hospital bed in downtown Toronto, all his worldly possessions had passed to his favourite nephew. Harry inherited directions to several wonderful tracts of farming land near Grande Prairie, in the newly created province of Alberta, a share in a lumber mill on Vancouver Island, on the very western edge of the Dominion of Canada, some money, and his uncle's duffel bag. Ignoring his mother's pleas and his father's silence, Harry packed a few of his own belongings in the duffel bag and set out. He went west first, across the Prairies, and up to see this land, which could be his own if he wanted to homestead. His own land: the words tasted of strength and purpose. He liked what he saw. But the duffel bag was still packed. He went north to the Yukon. He was relatively immune to the pull of gold; rather, he focused on the crush of disappointed humanity and the burning weight of dwindling

The Path to Kitty Islet

optimism. The goldfields could not hold him. He went west again, to the mill on Vancouver Island. The smell of pitch, green wood, and sweat affected him unexpectedly. It was all too new, too raw, and, if he'd been honest with himself or paying attention, too real.

Back east he went. But he avoided Ontario, the known world. He set sail from New York instead. The noise and effusion of the Americans on board infected him. He adopted a swagger, a broad wink, and a captivating grin. Now Europe was old enough. He toured much of the continent: Berlin, Munich, Rome, and finally, Paris.

Realizing that his supply of money was finite, Harry worked at odd jobs. He worked in vineyards during the harvest. He drove a taxicab, sleeping in the barn with the horses. He laboured in warehouses. He had discovered that he had an affinity for foreign languages, particularly profane words, and acted as an interpreter at a train station for a few francs. France was good to him. His swagger appealed to the French men he met, while his captivating grin secured him the affections of many a mademoiselle.

He dutifully wrote home but never bothered to include a return address. Harry's life would have impressed and appalled his Uncle Samuel; his father simply refused to mention his name. His mother, Jane, hoarded his letters, placing them carefully in the bottom of her hope chest. Harry's younger brother, Arthur, began to help out in the family's dry goods store. The pitch had stopped running, and the family tree had mended itself. The lost limb was simply a knothole now: a cache for a canny squirrel, and an almost forgotten reminder of what had been.

Finally, in the winter of 1907, Harry tired of France. He longed for home but did not have enough money for his passage. So, he crossed the English Channel. The sea was angry and violent, and Harry was morose. The swagger was all but gone. Portsmouth was a shock. Garish and British, it was everything

France was not. But it did manage to restore Harry's spirits through its incredible belief in sheer frivolity. Shaking his head, Harry wondered how anyone could survive Portsmouth in the summer at the height of its madness.

He caught a train to London. It was Christmas Eve. There were decorations in shop windows, people carrying parcels. Harry had nowhere to go, no one to see. He found a seedy-looking pub that had rooms to let above. He took one. Then he began to wander. He found the Tower of London, Kensington Palace, and Westminster Cathedral. His feet hurt. Outside the cathedral, he sat down. And Minnie came into view.

Her dark hair was loose (was it supposed to be?) and tumbled down her back. Her snapping brown eyes glowed, and her laughter filled him like warm brandy. She and another girl were arm-in-arm, sauntering slowly along the street in front of the cathedral. They had eyes for no one but each other. And somehow, they put Harry in mind of his sisters, Sarah and Anne, and his own loneliness. And he began to weep. The tears coursed down his cheeks. He didn't bother to wipe them away nor did he hang his head. He simply cried.

It had been a remarkable December for Minnie as well. It seemed as if the whole world were impregnated with the same sense of expectation that moved her. Her brown eyes glowed like rocks on the bottom of a golden stream. Conversations were richer, deeper. She and Emily were closer than ever, and Graham had finally begun to notice her. She was no longer simply a pest or his sister's playmate. She felt his eyes follow her as she crossed the room bent on some trivial errand. And he no longer called her Minnie. He had begun using her full name, lingering over its syllables to make it sound like a poem in and of itself, or so Emily assured her.

All that month, she and Emily had much to discuss. They had decided that they must have a double wedding, for what could be more perfect than best friends marrying on the same day? And marrying into each other's family? Long a favourite fantasy, it now seemed to be a likely reading of their future: shared always.

And then December 24, 1907, arrived. Both mothers, sensing their daughters' eager restlessness, proposed a walk. Malcolm had pleaded to be taken too, but they had adroitly avoided such baggage. "Another day, my boy," soothed Minnie as his lip pouted and his eyes filled with tears. Seconds later his sadness was forgotten as, arm-in-arm, Emily and Minnie sauntered forth. They hardly registered where they roamed, so engrossed were they in their shared plotting.

Suddenly, the air changed. The air vibrated. The tenor had been broken. Minnie stepped forward of her own accord, removing her arm from Emily McCrindle's, to help ease the man's obvious sorrow. Later she would say that she felt rather than heard his sorrow. Had she not invited him home, she would never have been able to describe him. For she had not seen him as a person; instead, she had reached out, instinctively, to touch his sadness. In that simple movement, had she but known it, she incorporated the same daring hopefulness that attends the pleading Catholic intent upon stroking divinity into reality by soft fingertips on a marble Mary. Her gesture spoke grace. Harry felt its purity. Emily, for a brief moment, felt bereft.

And one gesture was all it took. It wasn't love at first sight or a falling away of pretence. It simply was. Minnie extended her gloved hand and introduced herself and her friend to this man. He did not take her proffered hand; instead, he raised himself up to his full height—close to six feet—and bowed low before them. Emily, standing farther back, noticed his height and his controlled strength. Minnie, closer, noticed only his eyes and his calloused hands.

Moments later, they were a threesome. Few words had been exchanged, but they had been the right ones. Then all was as before, except now they were three. The evening passed in a blur for Minnie. Her eyes saw the world through a sort of veil. Only Harry's face came into some sort of focus—and stayed there.

Harry accompanied the girls to Minnie's home. And Minnie's parents, Ephraim and Amelia Sinclair, welcomed Harry almost as easily as their daughter had. Harry felt as if he had come home, and the evening passed far too quickly. Christmas carols had been sung by the entire family, and duets too, performed by Minnie and Emily. Minnie's older brothers, Albert and Edward, had plied Harry with questions about his travels. Edward, in particular, seemed fascinated by the stories of the great Canadian prairie and the multitude of acres awaiting cultivation. Emily had stayed close to Edward all evening, just as Minnie orbited Harry, and soon their foursome was engaged in an animated discussion. The girls sparkled while the men smoked, thoughtfully weighing each other's words, and worth, with care. The Christmas candles burned down, young Malcolm fell asleep beside the pianoforte, and the evening was at an end. And yet, it had also just begun.

Harry took rooms closer to the Sinclair household. He found work as a store clerk. In the evenings he and Edward squired Minnie and Emily around town. It seemed both natural and permanent, as if the situation had never been anything but as it was. They went to plays and, afterward, they adopted poses, speaking in what they hoped was an elevated, slightly risqué, manner. Laughter was their constant companion. In the beginning, Edward and Graham had come too, and sometimes Elizabeth. But their circle really seemed to have room only for four: Minnie and Harry, Emily and Edward. Both girls blossomed under the

The Path to Kitty Islet

attention, and both turned their attentions ever more resolutely to their respective suns.

Minnie's family was unconcerned and indeed, after a slight hesitation by Minnie's mother, encouraged the relationship. But when, on more than one occasion, Graham found himself to be simply a bedraggled afterthought, he made sure that Emily's parents regarded all this "gadding about" in an appropriately negative light. William McCrindle, a well-to-do barrister, was only too happy to curtail what looked to be an unseemly and too common pleasure. His wife, Nellie, tried to temper his ponderous pronouncements, but she managed to win her daughter only one social evening a week.

Soon enough, Minnie and Harry had become a twosome out of circumstance and desire. The courtship began in earnest. Emily, privy to all of Minnie's thoughts and yearnings, still found she was being left behind. Minnie had, overnight it seemed, taken huge steps to womanhood. She and Harry had begun to plan a future together. Young and determined, Minnie found that she wanted what she sensed she'd been lacking: adventure.

That spring, after a long afternoon of shared confidences, Emily turned to Minnie.

"You've decided then?" she asked brightly, too brightly. "The double wedding's off?"

No other words needed to be said. The two girls looked at each other, the low table spread with tea things between them, and they knew. The step taken in December had borne early fruit. Both girls blinked, used crisp white handkerchiefs, and then chattered inconsequentially about a hundred other things.

The shadows in the room lengthened as they talked. The fine old McCrindle grandfather clock boomed the hour. Minnie jumped. She felt startled, as if she had been caught napping inappropriately. Emily was watching her face. All triviality was erased and the two sat silent, but not alone. It was still there, the connection they had had since they were youngsters of six or seven. The familiarity that had been there in December remained. They still had the sense that, even with the dismantling of the shared dream, somehow the friendship would endure.

Soon after that, Minnie and Harry's wedding was announced. Both houses became bastions of "wedding fronds and frippery," as Emily's father sniffed. He and Graham reacted as one man: both felt the slight—losing out to an upstart colonial—no matter how much older than Minnie he was. And yet neither William nor Graham could articulate their hurt. William retreated to his study and his port. Graham abandoned the house for long periods at a time, spending days or weeks with friends in Surrey, Hampshire, and Kent—somewhere away. When he was home, and in the presence of Minnie, he regarded her reproachfully and made cutting remarks about the colonies.

While Minnie steadfastly ignored Graham's comments, Emily tried to be bridge and quiet peacemaker. It saddened her that her brother, Graham, and her father were angry, especially when it was so utterly obvious that Minnie was absolutely, completely happy. Though she had always been attractive and bright, since Harry's declaration of love, she seemed taller, older, fuller. Full as the moon at its zenith, she was, but full with an intensity and brilliance never possible while simply reflecting another's light.

But the old Minnie was still there too. At times her hand went unconsciously to her throat, and she fingered the locket she wore. Worry lines fanned across her forehead, tracing and retracing her decision: to marry and to go to Canada, to begin life anew. In these moments, when she was no more than a frightened, though love-struck, fifteen-year-old, her other hand stretched out and grasped Emily's. A fleeting touch, a petal of warmth, and the fitting could continue, the trousseau could be inspected once more, and her breathing could resume its usual calm rhythm.

Harry's parents would not come to the ceremony, as there wasn't time for them to travel to be there. But Harry assured his young bride-to-be that they would regard her in the same light as he did; they too would love his "English rose." Her cheeks coloured delicately whenever he called her this, and she would be forced to look away or the tide of red would not subside. Harry would laugh delightedly. Minnie's mother would rock contentedly, complacent in the face of her daughter's good fortune, believing her to be in good hands, while Emily felt the nick of sadness on the edge of her own overflowing heart.

—

They'd only been together just over six months before their wedding. Harry shook his head, as he approached their cabin. He loved Minnie, truly he did, but how could he be so selfish, tearing her away from all that she had known? Could he possibly take care of her as he had promised her father that he would? What had he done?

Closing the door quietly behind him, Harry regarded the sleeping figure of his wife. That same dark hair was again loose, cushioning her head better than any pillow could. She had not undressed and was sprawled diagonally across the bed. His mouth curved into a slight smile. It was foolish to think of her or her trust as a burden. She was simply a gift: generous and glorious. Bending over Minnie, he softly pressed his lips to her cheek. The living warmth of her skin always startled him somewhat. He spent so much time watching her beauty, examining it, that it shocked him anew every time he realized it was alive. She was not a painting. But when she slept and her eyes were closed, it was so easy to imagine that she was some sort of art that he had had the foresight to get close to. His lips touched in turn the central curve of her brow, the slight outward arch of her nose, the delicate wing of her ear.

The rain of tenderness brought animation and Minnie's eyes opened wonderingly.

"You've come back."

"Yes," he said, moving to sit on the edge of the hard bunk.

"I've been sleeping," her words were tentative, partly a question. He nodded.

"Has there been rain? I feel as though the air is fresher."

Again he shook his head. "No storm, a sunset, though. You would've liked it, I think."

"Why didn't you come and find me?"

He regarded her for a long moment. "I was afraid you mightn't want me to find you."

Minnie's hand played with a section of her skirt. She pleated it then let it go, then pleated it again. His tone of voice was laced with a thick sense of seriousness, almost like maple syrup. She felt he was offering her a test, and she didn't want to fail it in his eyes. But she was unsure of the correct answer. Finally, she raised her head, looking at him squarely. Her hand stopped its movement.

"I have never gone away from you. And I will not." Her words came out barely above a whisper, but her gaze had the intensity of a shout.

He nodded, satisfied.

"We should undress, and sleep."

Her breath caught as he stood up with one lithe movement, and took off his shirt, pants, and undergarments quickly. He sat down again, then, completely naked and gently touched her face.

"Minnie?" His voice made that one word encompass everything, all of it. She nuzzled his strong hand, and inhaled the wonderful scent of him; something of the lake still, combined with peppermint, and something she couldn't define but would now recognize anywhere, she was sure. He slid his hand down her face, along the side of her neck, fingers tangling a bit in her hair, then, slowly, ever so slowly, slid his fingers across her covered breasts, down the rest of her rib cage, along her waist, over her hips, and down the outline of her legs. His hands slid up, pushing aside the layers of her skirts.

By now, her breathing had intensified, quickened. Before she was married, she would never have imagined how wonderful it was to be physically loved, wholly and completely, by a man. She had had no real idea what to expect; she had mostly been afraid, and thought that it would be something to bear, to force herself to endure; although quite what she would be enduring, she could not have explained. But now, now that the first few awkward times were long past, those times when making love had been somewhat odd still, and a bit frightening, and yet also desirable, now a part of her was almost laughing at herself as she struggled to help Harry raise her skirts and lower her undergarments. Now she was desperate to be held by him, to encompass his beautiful manhood inside herself, to breathe him in from within and without.

He was so beautiful. A funny word for a man; but it was true, he was. Intense, yes, full of darkness sometimes, yes, and yet when he was completely with her, focused on her, touching her down there as he was now swirling his fingers around and across her most private parts, she could hardly stop from crying out. Before she knew it, she was begging him, in an intense whisper, to move more quickly, to come closer, to bring himself nearer to her, closer to her, faster, faster. She needed him to be with her, to be inside her, as only he had taught her anyone could be.

Suddenly, he was inside. He was kissing her face, stroking her breasts through the thin material left covering them, and he was moving, rhythmically and ever quicker, trying to match her movements, her pleas. Her hands wove themselves into his hair, pulling him closer to her, biting on her lip and then his, before they both settled down into giving each other deep fiery kisses; she was matching his intensity inside her with quick thrusting movements of her own. He was closing his eyes, waiting, waiting, and then looking down at her, with an incredible smile on his face. As his back arched, he thrust deeper, lower, and she suddenly found herself rippling along her own Great Lake, eyes pressed tightly closed, breaths ragged and deep, floating through an intense blue that was like nothing she had ever seen or felt before.

Moments or hours later, she could never have told which, they lay side by side together. The bunk was narrow, but Minnie didn't mind. She leaned back into the cradle of his arms. A glimmer of moon appeared, and then faded away. Their breathing slowed. The real boat continued on its way. They slept.

SEPTEMBER 15, 1908
EDMONTON

Dearest Emily,

I promised that I would describe this land. But I am always hampered by my words—they are not enough. But I will try. But, oh, how I wish you could be here with me, dear Emily!

The greatest lake of them all, Lake Superior, took forever and a day to cross. We finally experienced a lake storm too. It was not the Atlantic, but I was frightened. Harry was too. I had been afraid of his quiet, of his black moods, of the distance that seemed to be forming between us. But the lake brought us together again. And for that, I will always think of it fondly—but with respect. Our boat bucked and turned and fought to stay upright. And in the end, the storm moved on—to find larger prey, I suspect.

We landed at Port Arthur none too soon. It is an odd town, braced up against the lake on one side and a forbidding territory on the other. Fort William broods nearby, quintessentially British, yet also completely other. It had its day, apparently, and now sits remembering past tales of glory. I admit—it seemed romantic!

The Path to Kitty Islet

We packed up our belongings and prepared to wait for the train. They are not quite as regular as we are used to in Britain. My nurse friend was determined to catch the same train, as we had become fast travelling companions. After a wait, we were once more on our way. Sometimes I fear that I will never remain in one place for any length of time again!

First we made our way through dismal, swampy country. They call it muskeg. And the weather was ugly too. I felt the old familiar shiver of doubt crawl up and down my spine and wondered what I had let myself in for. Polly, the nurse, took pity on me—and poor Harry, as he was just about worn out trying to dissuade my growing despair—and kept telling me of the great prairie sky, the prairie crocus with its heart of purple passion, and the neighbourliness of the folks in the small communities. I clung onto her words, Em, but I could hardly believe them—what the windows revealed was dark and dreary.

And then, like a promised miracle, the land changed. And it seemed all the more beautiful in contrast to the swampy, desolate land we had seen before. Though I had feared we would never see hospitable country again, I was, happily enough, proven wrong. We were now in Red River country, where Lord Selkirk first brought honest farmers and settlers, or so Polly told me. And what a beautiful spot! The sun came out too—casting its glorious rays on neat farmhouses, painted white, with brilliant red barns and outbuildings. The soil looks unimaginably rich—even I could sense its worth. And then we reached Winnipeg.

It is a bustling, busy town. There are signs in a number of languages and churches of all sorts. I am beginning to understand the hold this country has on Harry. Even though he was not brought up out here, it just seems so much more alive than Ontario. Even religious belief seems more necessary, more valued, and simply more obvious. The odd onion-shaped domes belong to Galician churches. Polly assures me that they are quite lovely inside, although also a bit overdone and garish compared to a Presbyterian church.

    Oh Emily, it was hard to part with Polly. We have become close and I feel that she is my first real friend in this new, and often overwhelming, land. We exchanged addresses—well, she gave me hers and I have promised to write. It is a good thing you gave me so much paper before I left home. The way I ramble on I use up page after page. Polly's family had come to meet the train, and she was soon swept up in their warm embraces. There was no chance for introductions, as she had to collect her baggage and we were requested to move into another car. How I envied her their welcome, though. For, as I keep reminding myself and steeling myself, we will have no one to greet us at the end of our journey. We will need to make our own happiness.

    I cannot write more at the moment.

Ever yours,
Minnie

    The train wheels clattered rhythmically. Minnie's head bobbed in time as she tried desperately to stay awake. They had left Winnipeg only an hour or so ago, and she had wanted to pay close attention as they crossed Manitoba and entered the next province, Saskatchewan. Their car was full of farmers and their families. Some had made the trip to Winnipeg to visit family, while others had gone to the city to purchase equipment or household items, as well as a few frivolities such as small wooden toys for the children, and a brightly coloured fabric or two for the womenfolk. The atmosphere was festive and the spirits of the children especially could not be dampened, not even by the gusts of wind that carried the train's ash and dust directly into the crowded cars.

Minnie nodded on and off, sometimes waking momentarily because the children across from them laughed particularly loudly and at other times waking because of a moment of unusual quiet. Eventually she shook herself completely awake and made a determined effort to look around. Harry was beside her, reading a paper he had purchased in Winnipeg. Though he seemed oblivious to her presence, his hand occasionally touched her arm lightly, as if to say, "I know you're here." After his dark moods on Lake Ontario, Minnie was relieved that the Harry she had fallen in love with had been returned to her—they now shared a comfortable, easy silence.

Minnie returned Harry's gentle touch and let her attention be captured by the view outside her window. The land was not uniform by any means, and sometimes it undulated like the waves on Lake Superior, with acres of green gold giving way to patches of dried grass. There were animals too, sometimes—cattle and birds of all sorts, and sometimes a horse or two. The train stopped frequently at small towns, and at tall grain elevators, and, occasionally, out in the middle of the sweeping prairie—at all of these stops people got on and off, bags of supplies were exchanged, packages were left or picked up. It was all very organized and yet seemed entirely without premeditation to Minnie. It was as if, she thought to herself, the people or the packages or the trainmen simply looked around and said, "This is the spot," and the people or the packages agreed, and got off.

She wondered idly when it would be her and Harry's turn. Would the trainmen recognize their connection to the place called Grande Prairie? To the place where Harry was determined to own land? Where she and Harry were going to build their own happiness? She told herself that of course they would know—if the train actually went that far. And she herself would look at the land and it would call to her, and she would have come home.

The seats grew more uncomfortable. The children became whiny and irritable. Harry had long ago finished his newspaper and had slept as fitfully as Minnie had. The stops seemed to occur both more frequently and less often. There were always too many when Minnie was trying to rest, and never enough when she needed diversions to keep her awake.

The city of Saskatoon came and went. Minnie had been charmed by its stone buildings and its location on the gently flowing river. Harry had been asleep. The train ran alongside the river now, mostly anyway. A man a few seats in front of her told his wife that the river was dangerously low for this time in summer. Minnie had no idea—and no idea how or why that could be dangerous. To her it looked simply peaceful, quiet. She wished they'd been able to take a riverboat. By now Harry was alert again and laughingly pointed out the shallows in the river—and the fact that it ran west to east, so she would not simply be able to float with the current, quietly, gently.

Minnie's head ached. Her eyes were sore and scratchy. The sun seemed to beat down upon the train with the intent of heating all the passengers like so many fried eggs. Minnie told Harry this and he guffawed, which annoyed her. But just as her patience and hope were evaporating, Harry seemed to access reserves of humour and optimism that she couldn't believe possible. Perhaps he really knew something she did not. Perhaps it was all still an adventure. And perhaps they would finally get there.

A few hours west of Saskatoon, the land changed yet again. First there were acres and acres of scrub brush, some taller trees, and small boggy areas. These sections eventually gave way to gently rolling hills. Some were quite steep, and Minnie realized how much she had missed seeing real changes in elevation. Farmhouses cowered in sheltered valleys, with only a few built near the crest of the hills. Minnie promised herself that if their land had even a hill, or a rise, or a small incline, that is where she would demand that their house be built. She regarded the farms in the valleys as lowly and mean-spirited. "Why wouldn't those farms want to drink in the sky?" she thought.

They saw a few church steeples and some more onion domes marking the Galician settlements. Small ponds and little lakes began to dot the countryside. Minnie watched the waterfowl in amazement. There seemed to be so many different kinds of ducks and geese. And she had seen deer-like creatures a few times, especially where the land was flatter. But they were always too fleet of foot for her to get a really good look. She felt they were teasing her, daring her to stay awake—and alert.

When they finally arrived in Edmonton, Minnie was shocked. Unlike Saskatoon, Edmonton looked as if some angry giant had just flung it at the North Saskatchewan River, not caring how it landed. The river cut deep into its own valley, refusing to acknowledge the city above it, as if it hoped that if it just kept to itself, the city would too. The streets were dusty, unkempt. Scorched grass seemed to be the most common ground cover.

Minnie and Harry found a hotel that had, despite its relative youth, seen better days. They carried themselves and their belongings up the rickety, uneven stairs and into a room.

The bed at least looked clean. Tired and disappointed, Minnie used the washstand and rubbed ineffectually at her face and neck. It was hard to see in the dim light coming from the grimy window, but the mirror seemed to show a young woman with skin the colour of the Indians they had seen on the street corner just below the hotel. Minnie didn't know whether to laugh or cry, so she did neither and kept scrubbing.

When she was done, she turned and started to say something to Harry. But she realized it was no use. With his boots on, and his new broad-brimmed hat cradled in his arm, he was sprawled across the bed, fast asleep. Watching him, Minnie felt her own deep tiredness. She bent, undid her boots, slipped them off, and surveyed the bed. With a sigh, she climbed carefully across his legs and tucked herself between Harry and the wall. And while she considered undoing her hair, her eyes closed and she too was sound asleep.

A faint rustle tapped at her consciousness. She was dreaming of London, and Emily was standing over her, shaking out her wedding dress from among its wrappings. Only after a few moments did she realize that she was not in London, or at least not at home. She looked around the room feeling out of sorts. She wondered where she was, thinking that the answer was near at hand—if only she could reach out and grasp it. Finally, she moved her right hand, got it out from under the bed cover and reached up to touch her hair. It had been up and was still pinned in places, but much of it had come loose and was curling of its own accord. As she was trying to gather the strength to get up—why did her limbs feel so sore and achy?—the door opened and Harry came in. And then she knew. She knew it all: the wedding, the crossing of the Atlantic, and then Canada. And now they were in Edmonton.

With a swift petulance she moved her arm back under the covers. Harry regarded her in the soft lamplight.

"Are you hungry?" he asked.

She shook her head for no.

He put the tray down on the washstand and dragged the only chair in the room close to the makeshift table. Then he sat down, facing her. She could smell the food now, but could not identify what it was. It smelled gamey, or perhaps rancid. Her stomach did a slow, angry flip-flop. She turned her head and examined the wall.

It had been papered at one time, and now only patches of the stuff remained. She concentrated on recreating the pattern, willing her nose to stop working and her stomach to stop moving. Now it felt as though her stomach were still on the train while the rest of her body was completely stationary, able only to look on as her stomach moved farther and farther away. It was not a pleasant feeling, and she resented Harry for putting her in this horrible position.

She turned and stared at him angrily. "Surely you could have found somewhere else to eat that—that slop," she said.

Harry regarded her, continuing to chew rhythmically, carefully. He had a few more spoonfuls of what Minnie guessed was some sort of stew. Her stomach continued to lurch in protest. She felt hurt and angry. Why was he making her so uncomfortable?

Harry put his spoon down. He wiped his mouth with the back of his hand. "I didn't want you to wake up without me," he said quietly. "And I figured you'd be hungry too. Are you not feeling well, then?" A shadow of concern was evident in his face.

"No, I'm not," Minnie replied. She considered turning her head to the wall and avoiding his worried expression, but thought better of it. "My stomach feels like it's still travelling. And that stew, or whatever it is, it smells vile, Harry. I don't think I can stand smelling it much longer."

"Well, why didn't you just say so? Here, I'll take it downstairs again. But I'll be back. Quick as a wink, I promise." With that, Harry scooped up the tray and was gone. The door didn't quite close behind him, and Minnie could see out into the dark hallway. Someone had lit a lantern there, and it was smoking. The shadows it cast seemed ominous, threatening. Minnie felt small, tired, frightened.

"He said he'd be back, quick as a wink," she whispered to herself. "He always keeps his promises. I know he'll be back. And I'll be fine. Just fine."

NOVEMBER 11, 1908
GRANDE PRAIRIE

Dearest Emily,

I must, must apologize to you. I am sure you think me the worst correspondent on two continents. I have not forgotten you—but life has taken some unexpected turns. I can't even remember when I last wrote or what I last told you. I believe I told you a bit about our train trip to Edmonton. Well, our stay in Edmonton turned into more of a trial. We had not been there more than a day or so when I came down with some sort of horrible lung infection. Harry was so concerned! And the doctors all had that look—the solemn faces, the serious frowns, and the low speaking voices. I knew, at once, that they feared tuberculosis. Strange as it may seem, though all around me were alarmed, and I was sick enough to be in and out and often unaware of my surroundings, I was calm.

My first real time of lucidity came after I had been in the hospital for some days. I was given such care there, Emily. The Grey Nuns, as they are called, were kindness itself. And Harry came by daily, telling me funny anecdotes to entertain me and encourage my continued progress. I really wanted for nothing except the best friend in the world. But it was almost as if you were there, Emily—at times I swear that I could hear your dear voice telling me to buck up and try harder. It was a comfort to me to imagine you there—even if it was only my fevered imagination.

As I got better inside the hospital, Harry was busy outside plotting and planning. He realized we would not be able to get out and onto any land—as there are no buildings of any substance—before the weather changed and so he began to make inquiries in Edmonton about staying on here through the winter or possibly renting some small house in Grande Prairie. When he came to visit me, he would not tell me about the choices he was being forced to make on account of my silly sickness, but he did help me make sense of the impending fall and winter. Once the nights get chill, Em, though the days may remain warm—in fact, quite hot and muggy—all the inhabitants here—human, animal, bird, and plant alike—seem to brace themselves, to stand up taller, and inspect the skies more frequently. Even I have joined in and perform this Dominion occupation.

And what one often sees is stunning. A double line of geese—the beautiful Canada-type goose, native to this continent—form a V and then play follow the leader across the sky. Their black heads and dark grey bodies cleave through the now often chill air. And their piercing, haunting, quite unmusical honking sounds better than any choir I've ever heard. They seem so filled with longing. Some days they fuel my feelings of homesickness and I find their cacophony almost unendurable. But other days, I just want to drop everything and stand and watch. There is real magic in their flight, Emily. I wish you could see them!

Harry finally met up with a young man whose family lives not far from Grande Prairie. It's not much of a settlement, actually—not yet. This family has several quarter sections of land and are in the process of "proving up"—making the necessary clearings and plantings, and putting up permanent buildings. When these improvements are judged acceptable, then one actually gains title to the land. We will have to do this too. This fellow was about to travel back to visit his parents, so Harry sent a letter with him asking if we could possibly room with them once I was well enough to travel. I am not sure how I would have reacted to this proposal had I not been sick, but my stay in the hospital has given me much time to myself and I have been able to reconsider what this new life will require of me. I am determined to be the support that Harry will need, and he is determined to make a go of our farm.

So, a few days before my release from hospital, the young man—Steve is his name—returned to Edmonton. His parents, he said, would be delighted to rent us their spare room for the winter—as long as we could also bring some wood to contribute to the family heating. Harry was greatly relieved, I think, as taking rooms in Edmonton for the winter would have diminished our savings quite dramatically.

I was finally given a clean bill of health and was released from the hospital on a stunning fall day. The sky was a glorious blue, and my spirits were buoyed by the tang in the air and the smell of freedom. We spent a night in a small hotel—not the one where I fell ill when we arrived, thank goodness—and then made ready to travel to the north and west. Harry had managed to find us some places in one of the delivery wagons—great huge lumbering things—as the train does not yet reach our destination. Everyone assures me that it soon will—when it does, travel to Edmonton will become relatively comfortable! We seem to have accumulated a great number of belongings already, and it was interesting to watch Harry and a young boy load it all into the wagon.

Then we set off. What a trip, Emily! Just west of Edmonton the land becomes much more rolling. We saw many prosperous-looking farms, and the earth seems dark and almost succulent. We went past some pretty little lakes and small communities too. Many of the trees had turned colour, and their leaves were like moving, breathing gold. In a few places, the route went perhaps too close to the watery areas—we were stuck in mud on more than one occasion. We were even forced to unload most of the supplies, struggle with them through the bog, and heave them up onto higher ground, all the while being pestered by mosquitoes (it may have been fall, but it has not been cold enough to rid the air of these pesky, noisy, noxious creatures!) before the poor horses could pull the wagon free.

You would not have recognized me at the end of our trip. I was covered in mud from head to toe and had acquired more mosquito welts than I could possibly count. At least the mud kept the bites from being quite so itchy. But, despite the discomfort and the fear of being stuck or possibly even sucked into the muddy bogs, for the first time I felt that I too was ready for this adventure. It was no longer intimidating, or simply Harry's choice. I am not simply the extra baggage along for the ride. It seems I have truly decided to make this new beginning mine too.

We camped out overnight several times en route. We were lucky we had no rain or early snow. The stars, when seen away from the lights of a city, are simply beyond description. I think I spent more time lying awake simply looking up at the heavens than I did sleeping (slapping at mosquitoes had a little to do with my wakefulness as well).

We finally reached our destination. Both Harry and I were a bit taken aback when we met the Chiruks—though their son, Steve, speaks English as if it is his native tongue, neither of his parents are very fluent. It seems that they came here from Galicia originally, homesteaded near Winnipeg in Manitoba, but then suffered some serious setbacks there, gave up that land, and came west. Or at least this is what Harry and I have been able to make of their story. Their homestead is at least a day's travel—by horse—north of Grande Prairie. The original house that they built, a sod and mud affair, now houses their eldest daughter, her husband, and their children. The main house is quite large, by prairie standards, and is built of sturdy material with incredibly thick walls. It frightened me at first, for there are very few windows and the rooms are sometimes filled with smoke from the stoves and ovens. But, as I began to realize the logic behind the design, the house didn't feel as dark and foreboding.

We have been given the best room—it is hung with multi-coloured tapestries and has newly whitewashed walls. There are also a few religious pictures—nothing that I have ever really seen before—suffering figures surrounded by glorious halos of gold drawn as fantastic crowns. In one corner is a huge earthen kiln cum woodstove. It heats the room and does the cooking as well. Our bed is actually above this stove and the warmth permeates our bedclothes, keeping us very cosy. The Chiruks senior and their other children occupy the other half of the house, which is constructed in a similar fashion though it lacks the wall hangings. (There is a large hallway in between, with ladders that give access to the huge storage area directly beneath the thatch roof.) All the Chiruks sleep in the one bed above their stove. Harry says that the fact that this house has two stoves proves how unusually well off they are.

They have been quite welcoming, even though our understanding of each other is often imprecise. Mrs Chiruk is always incredibly busy, but she still takes the time to make sure that I have got our fire going, that I have brought water inside to heat on the stove, and that I am happy. One of the few phrases she knows is "You happy, yes?" And I nod yes, giving her great pleasure it seems. I cannot tell you how many children she has at home because the children of her eldest daughter are always here as well, and I cannot yet tell which child belongs to whom. Everyone disciplines the children if and when it is required, and generally the children are kept far too busy to get up to much mischief. One of the smaller girls—we have taken to calling her Helen, as I cannot get my tongue around her Galician name—has taken a particular fancy to me and follows me around everywhere. She is actually quite good company and has helped me adjust to their ways of managing their farm and household. She has such large expressive eyes—it is easy enough to tell when I have done something they consider extraordinary (like wearing an extra pair of

The Path to Kitty Islet

Harry's trousers when helping to collect wood—I thought I was being a little daring too).

And now, we are firmly in the grip of old man winter. The small windows have become a blessing, as it is easy to cover them up and prevent such a loss of heat as would occur with more glass. Harry helps with some of the barn chores and is learning more about keeping livestock warm in such bitter cold. Apparently the snow and the north wind have been particularly unkind to this region in the past few years, so we must hope for an easier time of it this year. I do not venture outside hardly at all—I only go when it is absolutely necessary. The whiteness of the snow is incredible, especially on the clear days when the sun glares down—in anger, it seems, for there is no warmth, only a bright light that seems to threaten blindness at any moment.

But we are here and we are fine. Helen, my shadow, has learned quite a bit of English from us and has also taught me a few words in her native tongue. She is a quick little thing, with deft and nimble fingers. She is already able to darn thick work socks and is eager to learn how to print and write (she is fascinated by my letters to you and my parents!). Teaching and learning helps to pass the time. As for the rest, Harry and I spend hours every day planning our own farm and looking forward to "proving up" our own land. Harry or Mr Chiruk will post this letter the next time the supply wagon comes past. I do hope it gets to you before the New Year, or you will think that I have broken my promise! I am truly well now, Em, and I'm liking this adventure more than I thought I might a few months ago. I will write to you again soon.

With love,
Minnie

—

Minnie looked up from the table and her writing as Harry came in and quickly closed the door behind him.

"Brr!" he said as he stomped his feet. He made his way closer to the oven, holding his still-mittened hands close to the oven door. "It's going to be much colder tonight than it has been, I think. Chiruk put extra straw out for the animals and kept pointing to the clear sky and shaking his head. I just hope the wind doesn't come up again, like it did the day before yesterday."

Unconsciously Minnie shivered, remembering that wind as she put her writing paper and pen back in the small leather case that had been a gift from Emily. She came and stood behind Harry, pressing the warmth of her body against the sharp cold that still lay on his outer garments. The cold had such a presence here that it seemed as if it had a definite smell too, she thought.

Slowly, Harry turned until he was facing her, holding her loosely. She tipped her head back, waiting expectantly. When her expression began to change from expectancy to worry, Harry bent forward and kissed her, forcefully. Minnie pulled away and he let her go. The cold seemed to bring out a devilish streak in him, a streak she both loved and feared. Almost childishly, she rubbed the back of her hand across her mouth and Harry laughed.

"I'm not about to apologize," he said. "You're my wife. We're alone. And you asked for a kiss. Not in so many words, perhaps. But you wanted it."

Minnie took a deep breath. "I didn't say I didn't want you to kiss me. It's only that I . . . " she stopped, mid-sentence. She didn't really know why she had wiped her lips. Sometimes, when he was in this kind of playful, forceful mood, she loved him more than at any other time. Yet at others, she almost feared him or—she couldn't really put her feelings into words.

"Never mind." Harry's voice was almost as cold as the air that had come in the room with him. "I'm too tired to talk about this for hours. You want to be left alone. So be it." He retreated to the far corner of the room and began to take off his outer clothing.

Hesitating, Minnie felt her hand reach up to her throat. She knew it was already too late to say anything else. Harry was angry now, and perhaps, she thought, he had a right to be. Before she could reflect further, there was a light knock at their door.

"Come in," Harry said without even looking at his wife. "We're not busy," he added as the door swung open. Helen and one of the youngest boys came in, their eyes looking at Harry with some trepidation. Harry was much taller than the adult Chiruks, so the children seemed to find him intimidating. Helen let go of her brother's hand and sidled over to Minnie without taking her eyes off Harry. She slipped her small hand into Minnie's. The boy, thus abandoned, seemed to consider his options with grave attention for a few moments. Finally, without looking at Helen or Minnie, he walked slowly over to Harry, who by this time had sat down on one of the low benches that ran along the far wall. With a barely suppressed giggle, he scrambled up. Before Harry could speak or move, the boy was proudly sitting in Harry's lap.

Later, Minnie could never quite recall which was funnier—the look of amazement on Harry's face or the self-satisfied yet frightened look on the small boy's face, the expression of a child who only at the moment of contact seemed to comprehend the enormity of his action. As Minnie began laughing, Harry bent forward, hugged the boy close to him, and started to chuckle. Helen looked back and forth at both Minnie and Harry, and then, in a fine imitation of her mother's voice, inquired, "You happy, yes?"

Harry, still holding the boy tight, looked at Minnie and Helen and said, "Yes, I am happy. Impulsive too often, but happy."

Helen nodded in agreement, as if she had understood every word. She tugged on Minnie's hand. "You happy, yes?" Her big, brown eyes searched Minnie's face for the answer. Unwilling to meet Harry's gaze—for now her behaviour seemed childish and unwarranted—Minnie said softly, "Yes, lambkin, I'm happy."

Meanwhile the little boy had struggled out of Harry's bear hug and was leaning to one side, peering at one of the religious drawings suspended almost directly above the end of the bench. Harry turned to look at it too.

Helen, clearly not interested in the picture, tugged at Minnie's hand. "We print?"

Minnie smiled at her and drew her over to the table. "We print." Pulling out several sheets of lined paper, Minnie set them in front of Helen and retrieved a pencil from her writing case. Helen's eyes were as big as small moons and, in her excitement, her breath came in hard, heavy gasps. She sat demurely, though, despite her anticipation. Minnie drew a large capital "H" on the paper. "Here, you try," she told Helen. Grasping the pencil carefully, but firmly, as if it might try to run away, Helen laboriously copied the letter. Minnie then wrote out, in large capitals, Helen's first and last names—Helen Chiruk.

As Helen continued to copy the letters, Minnie looked across the room. Harry had helped the boy to stand on the bench and had his arm around him. They were both looking at the poster with deep attention. The boy said something softly, but Minnie was too far away to determine whether he had said it in English or Galician. She left Helen to her printing and approached Harry and the boy. "What is it that he finds so fascinating?" she asked.

Without turning his head, Harry responded, "I'll be darned if I know. He keeps repeating the same thing over and over, but I can't make heads or tails of what he's saying."

Minnie touched Harry on the shoulder. "I'm sorry about before," she said softly. "I don't know how to explain it exactly. It's as though—it seems as if you bring in the wild cold with you, and though it's you there's something in your face, something in your grip sometimes—it frightens, no, it catches me off guard." Her voice petered out a bit. Harry still wasn't looking at her. All his attention was focused on the boy in his embrace and the picture of the Virgin Mary. Minnie tried again, "I'm sorry, Harry." She let her hand drop.

Harry, startling both her and the boy, suddenly turned and plopped the boy back onto the floor at Minnie's feet. "It's a good thing these two came along when they did," he said, ruffling the boy's dark hair. "Else we probably would have had our first cabin fever fight. It's all right, Minnie. I do wish that you wouldn't be so scared of me, though. I'm still the same bloke I was in England—nothing more, and nothing less." The little boy watched Harry's face the whole time he was speaking. Then he looked at Minnie. Carefully, he repeated his sister's phrase: "You happy, yes?"

With that, all the tension in the room vanished. Minnie knelt down, looked into the boy's eyes, and nodded yes. A slow grin spread over his face until his eyes were crinkled up like his mother's and all his teeth showed. "I happy!" he responded, delighted with his own, innovative phrase. He spun around and scurried over to the table, where he clambered up beside his sister. He made no attempt to disturb her or get too close. He watched her careful movements, which became slightly more careful as she played to her new audience.

Once more Harry took Minnie in his arms, from behind this time. She relaxed her whole body so that he was forced to support most of her weight. Minnie felt that somehow they had survived another squall, a leftover from their trip across the Great Lakes. "Strange how someone I know, someone I love so well, can suddenly seem more foreign, more frightening, than a complete stranger," she thought. "Is there something wrong with me? Do all women feel this way? Or is it Harry? Does he really change sometimes?" She shook her head a little at the thought. Harry, feeling the movement, tightened his grip around her waist. His lips grazed the side of her ear and Minnie closed her eyes.

Perhaps it was simply cabin fever. Perhaps she had imagined the whole silly thing.

Another knock sounded at the door. This time it was Mrs Chiruk who opened the door, and she came in quickly and apologetically—ducking her head several times as if to prove that she hadn't meant to disturb. Though it was her house, once she had finished wordlessly apologizing she looked lost and uncomfortable. Minnie moved out of Harry's hug and gestured for Mrs Chiruk to take a seat at the table across from the children. Then Minnie moved the kettle of water toward the burner and took down her tin of tea, smiling and making motions with her hands to indicate that Mrs Chiruk should stay. Mrs Chiruk nodded and smiled and settled herself more comfortably on the wooden bench.

Helen pushed the piece of paper she had been working on across the table to her mother. The two spoke quickly in Galician and the small boy giggled, whereupon his mother looked at him reproachfully and he hung his head. Helen got up and came round the table to sit by her mother. Hesitatingly, looking to Minnie every so often for support and confirmation, she sounded out the letters in English, and then read her name. When she had finished, both Minnie and Harry applauded. Helen bobbed her head slightly, looking both proud and embarrassed.

As Minnie served the tea in large tin cups, Mrs Chiruk asked her usual question: "You happy, yes?" But this time she didn't wait for the reply. Glancing at Harry, she seemed to make up her mind. Pointing to the children and then to Minnie's belly, she said, quite distinctly, "Baby." Minnie thought she understood at once. She coloured a bit, but said clearly, "No." Mrs Chiruk looked frustrated by Minnie's answer. She tried again, this time pointing both to Minnie's belly and to her own. Minnie was perplexed. What was this woman trying to say?

Then Harry's voice boomed out, no doubt a little louder than he had intended. "I think maybe it's she who's in the family way, Minnie dear. What would that be then? Number seven?" He pointed at Mrs Chiruk's stomach and held up seven fingers. Mrs Chiruk nodded, looking relieved. But she held up eight fingers, and then patted her stomach carefully.

Helen had gone back to her original spot at the table and once more sat beside her brother. She looked at Minnie and pointed at her brother, saying, "Name?" Minnie looked helplessly at Harry, who came over and squatted near the boy. He pointed at himself and said, "Harry." Then he pointed at Minnie and said, "Minnie." Then he pointed at Helen and Mrs Chiruk in turn. Finally he pointed to the boy. The boy grinned and said, quite clearly, "Billy."

"Well now, that's a fine Galician name, I'm sure," Harry said with a smile. "Here, Minnie'll write it out for you."

Minnie took the pencil and wrote, in block letters, "BILLY." Billy took the pencil and, with his tongue protruding slightly, tried to make his small hand do his bidding. Mrs Chiruk beamed at them all. Minnie felt closer to Harry again, as if they had always belonged together, as if they had long resided with the Chiruks. Billy's pencil scratched across the paper. The wind raged outside. But not one of the five people in that room paid it any heed.

—

FEBRUARY 1909

Emily dearest,

Do tell me that another world exists besides this one—it has been so cold and so overwhelmingly white. I am almost unable to convince myself that the world I used to inhabit still bides its time across the ocean in a world of dreary rain! I would dearly love to hear rain again. We are warm, mostly, and dry, it is true.

And the Chiruks continue to provide us with companionship. But it is so desolate, Em, so very stark. All the time. Night. Day. Always white. And the chill.

Both Harry and I seem to be suffering from the thing many had warned us about—cabin fever. It is not a true fever—it is more of the mind, heart, and soul than of the body proper. It is created because of our caged circumstances. I pace. I think. I read. I write. And then I pace again. Some days I fear I will go mad. Other days I wish I could, so I could then escape the endless sameness. The silly squabbles, the silences, the talking. Nothing is ever enough, and everything is too much. Harry is affected by the fever too. He can be so bitter and harsh. I fear sometimes that he will never be the same again, and then his mood breaks, and I catch glimpses of the man I knew in London. This cabin fever is a terrible thing. How I long for our walks, Emily—striding arm in arm. How lucky we were.

The wind has ceased. Its voice must feel as dry and cracked as my hands—both of us exposed to the cold. Harry has gone out to the barn with the Chiruks. There is a move afoot to bring the animals into the house—to the hallway area between the two rooms—as the weather does not improve. Their body heat would help us, just as the stoves would help them. I never thought I would look forward to rooming with a horse or two and several cows!

It seems that our own family is starting to expand. Mrs Chiruk's belly grows ever more obvious, and she was the first to realize that I too am now on the same path. She knows so little English, though—I only wish I could ask her the many questions I have in mind. I have not told Harry yet—at first I wanted to be certain, but now I feel as if I need to keep this secret to myself for a while. It is a tiny affront to the cold, a breath of the promise of spring and new life. I sound all romantic, don't I? I'm much more scared than that, I assure you. I haven't told Harry for another reason—I'm not sure how he'll take the news, since it will further complicate our ability to get on a farm and make a go of it. I am rather afraid that perhaps he'll be somewhat angry, as the timing is not the best.

Don't tell Mother anything, Em. I'll tell her in my own time and in my own way. Pray for me as I pray always for you. And think green, warm thoughts.

Your friend,
Minnie

MAY 1909

Dear Emily,

We are just about ready to truly start our new life. Harry and Mr Chiruk have been up to our hoped-for property on numerous occasions—despite the wetness of the spring melt—and they have chosen a spot for our own dear house. Steve Chiruk will return from Edmonton in a few days, and he will help build the house. Harry has learned much during this long winter and feels quite sure that he is ready to be responsible for his own farm, land, and wife! He is a bit like a proud papa robin when he struts around our room, planning aloud. You'd laugh, Em, I know, and sometimes it is all I can do not to laugh either, except that I know how absolutely serious he is.

I have been busy too while he has been away. Mrs Chiruk had her baby (I don't think Mother's confinements were ever as short!) and I have been both helping out and watching. She keeps that baby girl with her most of the time, as the child is in a sort of holder slung over Mrs Chiruk's shoulder and back. As a result, I suspect, the baby never cries and simply sleeps placidly even while her mother is engaged in her chores. It seems somewhat scandalous, I know, but it works so well. The older children, particularly the girls, help out and know what is expected of them, even before their mother asks. They really act as one.

I have found that I tire more easily and I have begun taking naps in the afternoon. When I wake, though, I tend to feel rested and strong, so I am certain that all is well. Harry knows now. In the end, I didn't find the right time to tell him—it was little Helen who said something to him. At first he was quite surprised, almost disbelieving, but then he seemed happy enough. I try not to sleep too much when he's home, as I don't want him to think that I won't be able to help on our farm.

Do talk about the news with Mother, Emily. I have sent a long letter to her too, but I know she likes to see you since she misses "girlish chatter" now that both Lizzie and I are married. It will warm my heart to know that you and Mother are together and thinking of me. When will it be your turn to marry? Surely Edward will not keep you in suspense much longer? If he weren't my brother—I'd give him a good tongue-lashing by letter! Perhaps I will nonetheless. Take heart, my dearest chuck. I know you will soon be happy.

Yours as ever,
Minnie

JUNE 1909

Dear Emily,

Again, I have let so much time lapse between letters I must apologize. You will be sick of my apologies soon, won't you, Em? But now for the news—we are in our own house!

It is nothing grand—in fact it is not much more than a small cottage—but it is ours! Harry and Mr Chiruk and the oldest

The Path to Kitty Islet

boys—including Steve—put it up in just a few days' time. Harry decided to copy some of the design elements of the Chiruks' homestead, so we have a log home—partly—and a sod and mud affair—partly. The barn leans up against the back of the house, sharing one of the walls and hopefully making both the house and the barn in that corner warmer and sturdier. We have also created a big warm stove/oven, topped with our sleeping platform, so that in winter we will be as cosy as possible.

Harry splurged a bit too and we have four real glass windows. I think he had Steve bring them up from Edmonton. How they didn't get broken during the trip I'll never know! Our house is on a tiny knoll, overlooking a small lake that straddles both our property and the neighbour's. There are a few farms around—last year was the first harvest they had here in Grande Prairie. So we will not be the first, but definitely a close second.

Once the house was put in place, Harry and I began clearing away the scrub, getting ready to till the soil. Harry was somewhat leery about my offer to help, but I know from watching the Chiruks that much more can be accomplished if all hands are brought to bear on a task. And my hands, once small and delicate, are proving they can be useful. I hardly recognize any part of my body these days. My hands, arms, and face are as brown as the sod in our house. My stomach is protruding mightily now, and makes my back ache if I spend too much time on my feet. But otherwise I feel so strong. I never really knew what I was capable of before, and now I feel that I am finally learning.

We have not had much contact with our neighbours as of yet. I had expected that they would come by once they saw we had moved in and gotten our house up and running. Even Mrs Chiruk and the baby have come by for a visit—she brought a beautifully embroidered cloth with her, Emily. It is wonderful and bright. I had so hoped to make friends with some of the few other women, especially since I suspect my time is not far off. I am disappointed that the sense of community that Polly spoke of existing in the rural areas hasn't yet extended here. Harry thinks I'm being too cynical and impatient. Of course, he has spoken to some of the men, and even visited our neighbour to the north—the one who shares our lake—so he doesn't feel the loneliness as much as I do. He feels that once the early harvesting and berry picking and the like are complete, then the women will pay a visit. I hope so. Without Helen's company and the company of all the Chiruks I feel uneasy.

Perhaps it is simply that I am pining for my dear, dear friend. You are truly missed, Emily. I must close now though. It is late—past eleven in the evening—but still the sun lights the land. Unfortunately, we pay for this long day with huge bugs—they too seem to lap up the sunshine growing bigger, stronger, and more annoying every day. It is time to hide beneath the mosquito netting—and sleep.

God bless.
Minnie

The bright morning light found its way into the house through the polished windows. Harry had been too restless to sleep much. He found the long days invigorating. As he worked outside, it was as if the sun beat a melodious message into his mind. But it was only at night, lying awake in bed beside his pregnant wife, that he was able to consider the sun's message. He was full of plans and wild enthusiasm, and sleeping simply interfered. Today was Sunday, though, and Harry had promised himself and Minnie a day of rest. He forced himself to stay in bed, to watch the sun mount higher in the sky, and to lie still so as not to disturb his wife.

The Path to Kitty Islet

Minnie often slept fitfully now too. Her distended stomach forbade certain positions, and sometimes the baby seemed to feed off Harry's energy and become restless and energetic after the sun had disappeared. But last night, Minnie had slept as deeply as during her sickness. When she opened her eyes, she was both surprised and pleased to find that Harry still lay against her, and she was happy to feel truly refreshed. She stretched her toes and shifted slightly so that her belly rested against Harry's hip. He turned his head and smiled—that same slow, full smile that had won her heart. She snuggled as close as her stomach would allow and he turned slightly himself, folding her warmth against him.

"It seems such a long time since we've been close like this," Minnie murmured against his chest. "We've been so busy."

Harry nodded, pulling her even closer. "It will get better, I promise. Once the land is cleared and we get a few crops in, we'll have a pattern, a routine. And we can plan to hire some men too—once we get in the first crops." He hugged her tight, and then moved away from her as if to get up.

"No. Not yet," she insisted. "Just hold me a while longer, Harry. Just for a while?"

He relaxed and readjusted his position so that he could see her face. It was nut brown, almost as brown as her eyes. Though it was the same face he'd first seen in London, in some ways Minnie now bore barely a passing resemblance to that other self. Pregnancy had changed her, as had the manual labour. Harry took one of her weathered hands in his own. She had a palm crossed with calluses and veined with ground-in dirt. Their hands were now two of a kind.

Minnie watched Harry through the screen of her lashes. There were times when he frightened her still. Times when that dark mood descended and he became more frightening than a stranger. He was even more alarming then, because she knew his features, his voice—but not him. At moments like these, she half-convinced herself that she imagined those fits. The silence. The rage. How could those soft blue eyes, the same colour as forget-me-nots, ever be anything but gentle? As his hand traced a pattern on her bare arm, she allowed herself to believe in the softness again, to trust it; she allowed it to envelop her, softly, sweetly. There was no darkness. There was nothing but this.

―

Later, with the sun high overhead, they emerged, blinking rapidly, from their dark house. They were surrounded by a pulsating heat, a heat moved into gathering eddies by the half-hearted breeze. Minnie shaded her eyes and slowly turned. The lamb clouds had scurried away today, leaving behind them the same blue to which she had again surrendered. Harry went around the back of the house and began hitching the horse to their small wagon. Minnie started to follow him when she realized that the moving speck a ways along the trail seemed to be a person. Using both hands to shade her eyes, she stood up on tiptoe trying to make out who or what it might be.

By the time Harry brought the horse and wagon around to the front, Minnie had determined that it was a person: a person walking and wearing a dress.

"Harry! Look!" she could barely contain her excitement. Both she and her voice were shaking. "Do you think she's coming here? Who do you suppose it is? Could it be Mr Wright's wife? Could it?" Her words rushed out. "Do I look presentable?"

Harry looked at his wife. Sometimes, in the midst of his own excitement at building and creating a farm, he remembered how foreign all this was to Minnie, and he remembered how well she was taking it. And he would remind himself to take her visiting. But then another job would present itself, another setback would occur, and days and weeks passed when Minnie had no company save his own. Her eagerness now, at the prospect of a visitor, smote him. What had he been thinking, never taking a day to convey his pretty wife around to the neighbours, no matter how far away? Even today he had not planned that they should visit with anyone. No, he had intended to take Minnie south to show her the good arable land that he hoped one day to add to their holdings. His guilt made him gruff and short: "Why don't you go in and inspect yourself, if you're so concerned? I doubt she's a high society lady."

The words hung in the air for a moment, buzzing like a small cloud of mosquitoes. Then they descended, and each word bit separately at Minnie's heart. She turned and went inside, carefully taking down her small mirror. She no longer bothered putting her hair up every day; instead, as now, she often wore it in a single braid. Her eyes were bright, all the brighter because she was angry. She tucked the few wisps of hair behind her ears, smoothed her skirt, and put the mirror back onto its hook. If this woman was coming to visit her, Harry was not going to belittle such a visit, or whoever the visitor was, by his usual means. He could say rude things to her, or be as dark as he could be; but she was not going to let him be rude to a guest.

She cast a quick glance around the room. Everything was neatly stored away, save for Mrs Chiruk's embroidery, which, as the Chiruks' did in their home, Minnie had proudly put on display. It was a far cry from her home in London, but it was not a home to be ashamed of. She went back outside, completely ignoring Harry, who was now unhitching the horse. He seemed subdued, so she took that as a sign that he would behave. The woman was much closer now, and it was plain that she too was in the family way. Minnie walked down their rutted path. Even if the stranger were not planning on stopping in, she would speak to her in a neighbourly fashion.

Both Minnie and the visitor reached the end of the Worthings' drive at the same moment. The woman, like Minnie, was tanned and dressed for comfort rather than fashion. Her blonde hair was pinned high atop her head, and her hands kept flicking at the mosquitoes that were trying to settle on her bare forearms and neck. She looked searchingly into Minnie's eyes. The young woman's eyes were a pale watery blue, the blue of a sky scudded over by wispy, greyish clouds. Her face was unlined, fairly pale, and striking.

Realizing she'd been staring, Minnie did a small curtsy, bobbing her head slightly, and extended her hand. "I'm Minnie. Minnie Worthing. I live just up there. Would you like to come up for a drink of water perhaps? Or were you—?"

The young woman smiled broadly, shook Minnie's outstretched hand, and then spoke. "Some of the folk round hereabouts almost had me convinced you were a foreigner. Your Old Country accent is strong indeed, but I doubt that that would qualify you to be counted as foreign in the Dominion of Canada now, would it?" she asked, followed by a light laugh.

Minnie's brow furrowed. "People think we're foreign?"

"I suspect it has something to do with your house." The young woman gestured toward Minnie's home. "It's not exactly standard 'Last Best West,' is it?"

Minnie glanced back over her shoulder to look at her home from the other woman's perspective. Of course, as she realized now that the woman pointed it out, their house would seem odd compared to the more common shanties around, since Harry and the Chiruks had constructed it to follow a more Galician pattern. Caught up with the daily round of chores, and the time spent clearing the land, she had almost forgotten that their house would seem odd. No wonder their few neighbours hadn't stopped by.

As she regarded the house in this new light, she also noted that Harry had disappeared, leaving only the wagon standing

The Path to Kitty Islet

forlornly in their yard. The few flowers Minnie had planted bent under the weight of the heavy summer sun. "Come on," she said to her first visitor. "It's so hot out here. Let's go inside. Did you set out without a hat?"

Once they entered Minnie's home, the woman looked around her approvingly, then sat at the table while Minnie busied herself with getting cups and ladling cool water into them. Minnie passed the woman a blue tin cup and the woman bobbed her head in acknowledgement. Lifting the cup high, she drank lustily, letting the liquid sluice down her long throat. She was truly beautiful. Her hair was like spun gold and her face was fascinating to watch. Minnie, starved for female companionship for so long, couldn't stop staring.

The woman put her cup down on the table and ran her tongue around her lips, moistening them. Folding her hands carefully in her lap, she settled back in her chair, regarding Minnie with amusement. "That's much better. I think you and I are going to be friends." Her voice was melodious and full of barely contained mischief.

"My name is Callie, by the way," she continued. "Callie Lloyd. Our homestead is just a few miles down the road. I think we're probably your nearest neighbours in that direction. Your husband—Harry, isn't it?—anyway, he was talking to Tim in town and mentioned you were on your own out here without kith or kin to keep you company. I felt guilty for I should have come earlier, but I've been a bit under the weather with this little burden." She patted her belly. "As for the others round here, well, some are standoffish at first, but most are just plain tuckered out by all the work that homesteading involves. We tend to visit more in the winter, before it gets really cold. You'll likely see more people after the autumn harvest. I hope that you and I will be able to see each other often though, won't we?" For the first time since Minnie had laid eyes on Callie, the other woman seemed slightly unsure of herself and her welcome.

Minnie put her head to one side, pretending to consider, causing Callie to bite her lip as she waited for Minnie's decision. But Minnie already felt that she'd made a friend, and suspected she'd never want to lose sight of this beautiful young woman. "Yes," said Minnie, "of course; I'm so glad that you've come to visit. Have you been on the prairie long?"

Callie smiled easily, looking even more beautiful. "I grew up east of Edmonton on another homestead. We're a family of girls, though, so my dad could only work one quarter section. But my sisters and I learned how to do just about everything on the farm that needs doing. When I met Tim, that didn't scandalize him like so many of the other men around. My sisters and I are all 'easy on the eyes,' as my dad would say, so we got lots of offers, but only Tim could see past the packaging and accept that I could really help him with our homestead. I could help you with things too, if you'd like," Callie laughed then, a little self-consciously. "You're going to think I'm right stuck up," she said, her cheeks faintly pink.

Minnie shook her head, "I think you're splendid," she said, and then stopped, rather aghast at her forwardness. Suddenly, Callie caught her eye and they both burst out laughing.

"That's settled then," Callie said, grinning broadly. "Friends it is—homestead friends. Now you must tell me all about yourself. How long have you been in Canada? How is it that your house looks like the Galician ones I've seen over near Edmonton?"

The two young women settled themselves down for a true heart-to-heart. They had a connection, a recognition of kindred spirit by kindred spirit. The words and the facts of their lives were almost extraneous, for the friendship had been there from the moment Callie and Minnie laughed together for the first time.

The Path to Kitty Islet

AUGUST 1909
OUR FARM

Dear Em,

I told you about Callie Lloyd last time I wrote, didn't I? If not, here's a bit of background. She's not much older than me and she and her husband, Tim, are our neighbours. She too is expecting, though she thinks her baby will come any day now. She is stunningly beautiful—and knows how to run a farm. She does almost as much work as Tim does on their homestead. She is kind and funny, and never tires of answering my unending questions nor does she make me feel foolish when she shows me how to do the simplest things. Needless to say, I am quite infatuated with her—she has a quick wit and an enthusiastic spirit. And she remains almost my only visitor.

No other women have seen fit to be neighbourly because of the talk roundabout. Apparently, we have been too friendly with the Chiruks and other "undesirables." There has even been a rumour that I am not British—that I have simply "put on" a British accent! Callie has tried to convince the others that of course I am British, but since they look somewhat askance at her as well, no one else seems willing to stop in. I admit that I was shocked and disappointed, especially after hearing all of Polly's stories. At least I now know where I stand, though, and why the women mostly regard me with suspicion. Harry has escaped some of the censure since it seems more ordinary for men to work with men of all kinds of backgrounds. But the fact that we—that I, a good Englishwoman—lived in one of "their houses" (that is how it is phrased) is apparently not easy to forgive or understand.

I am angry about all this, Emily. For I cannot think how we would have survived last winter without the Chiruks and their kindness. Indeed, we owe this house to their help as well. I will not renounce the Chiruks' friendship. But I do wish I could explain that the Chiruks are not dirty Russian peasants or filthy foreigners. I am not sure how people can say such things without knowing whereof they speak. It pains me to realize that the great sense of community Polly spoke so highly of seems to be predicated on nationality—and stupidity. I am extra grateful for Callie though. Without her I don't know how I would have managed over the last few months. She is a dear friend and an excellent teacher.

As for other news, I am waiting anxiously both for Callie's confinement and for my own. I pray that they do not overlap or coincide, as we hope to be of service to each other. She tires so easily now and her colour is high—surely the baby will come along soon. I still feel very well—though I think my stomach is big enough at present and am not sure if I can bear it if it grows much larger. I can no longer see my own feet! I am still able to do most of my work, and find that comforting, as it helps to pass the time—so that I only spend part of each day in breathless anticipation. I am still worried about the actual confinement—though, as I said, Callie should be able to help.

Our farm also continues to grow. Harry has cleared more land than either of us had thought possible our first year. He has also built fences along our drive up from the road and created a paddock near the barn. We have a few acres in seed—we are hoping that summer holds and it will be a warm fall, so we can harvest. Our barnyard has been busy and now we have quite a number of chickens, ducks, and pigs. It is hard to feel too lonely when there is such a racket of animal sounds so close to the house. One of the hens is a prolific layer—I don't think there have been many days when she hasn't produced a fine, large egg. She is good-tempered too.

The Path to Kitty Islet

Well, must off. Time to water both plant and animal. Hope you are well. Has that brother of mine put you out of your anticipation yet? I do hope that he has!

Love,
Minnie

SEPTEMBER 20, 1909
OUR FARM

Dearest Emily,

I am actually a mother! And he is a dear, sweet boy, who could hardly wait to arrive. No sooner had Harry returned with Callie and the local midwife, Mrs Clifford, than he greeted them with some very lusty screams. He was born on September ninth in the early evening, and we have named him John Harold Worthing.

Callie has a son too—he was born about two weeks before John. I thought she would never survive his birth, though—it was long and laborious. Even the midwife was beginning to worry. But it turns out that her son, Albert, was simply too healthy—he is one of the biggest babies I have ever laid eyes on. John is quite, quite different—he is much smaller (for which I am thankful) and much more alert. His little eyes are so quick—he follows movements and looks into everyone's face so searchingly. He is not unlike my brother Malcolm in looks, but I believe he will have Harry's chin.

And put your mind (and Mother's) at rest—I am well. I know Mother has been worrying, and that always brings on colds and the like. Dear Emily, do try to convince her that I am fine. Harry has been very proud and very helpful, and Callie and I are good company for each other. The midwife too has been back to visit several times. I am hopeful that she will help dispel some of those rumours now that she has gotten to know us. She has an excellent head on her shoulders, and never believed any of the stories herself. She knows we are good people, and I trust her. The circuit preacher will be by soon—and little John will be properly christened then. I know you and the family will hold us in your prayers.

Love,
Minnie

Minnie reread her letter to Emily. Though the words were truthful, they couldn't tell all of the truth. How to put what she'd seen and experienced during Callie's confinement, and her own, into words—when she had yet to find words for the pain, the joy, the fear, the separation? She had told the truth but had left out many things. Though she and John had come through the experience with their health, Callie had not. Callie's labour had lasted forty-eight hours. She had been unable to eat anything during that time. Even now, she was struggling to keep either food or drink down. And while the midwife had been back to visit and check on Minnie, she had also used these visits to give Minnie poultices and herbs to pass on to Callie.

The midwife could not visit Callie again because the very sight of the face Callie had seen for too long, from the abyss of her dark and searing pain, made her faint dead away. Tim was beside himself with worry, and the baby Albert—he had been the biggest, healthiest baby Minnie had ever seen. But with his mother unable to eat, Albert too became hungry. He had cried angrily at first, desperately shaking his head from side to side as he pulled at the breasts that in their youthful fullness mocked him. Then, as Callie withdrew, so too did Albert. He lay for hours in his makeshift cradle, a box, looking up, unblinking. The very

The Path to Kitty Islet

few times Callie had tried to feed him, he took the nipple in his mouth, but did not close his lips round it. He made no attempt to suckle.

Callie had managed to rouse herself long enough to help Minnie when John was born. She had even eaten a bit and kept it down. Tim had looked so relieved when he came to take his wife and baby home, for Callie seemed more like her former self—enthusiastic, smiling, alive. But when Minnie ventured out to visit Callie—her first trip as a new mother—she had been frightened by the change in her friend. Callie was listless; Albert was deathly still. Minnie had made tea and forced Callie to have some—loaded with lots of sugar and milk. Then, without even considering what she was doing, she had fed John and, when he was satisfied, had picked up baby Albert and given him her still-laden breast.

Callie made no comment; indeed, she seemed unaware of her surroundings. The only way Minnie could get her to respond was to put her face close to Callie's and speak softly and carefully.

Albert, seduced by his mother's apathy, at first made no move to feed from Minnie's breast. Minnie jiggled her nipple around his mouth until, all of a sudden, he seemed to realize that this breast, unlike his mother's, was functioning properly. He sucked gently at first, wonderingly, then in a frenzy, pulling ever harder, trying to get every last precious drop. Feeding Albert was a revelation for Minnie; she had had no idea, based on feeding her own child, John, how violent a ravenous boy-child could be. When there was no more milk, Minnie had to pry Albert's lips off her breast. And look into those eyes, so like Callie's, and see the hungry bewilderment.

After conferring with Tim, the midwife suggested that Minnie take Albert home with her, until Callie got her appetite back. Minnie wasn't against this plan; however, she desperately hoped that Callie would, suddenly, look up at them all and say with her trilling laugh, "You people can't look after my boy. Give him to me; I'm his mother."

But as Minnie and Tim packed up Albert's few small outfits and his baby blankets, Callie rocked wordlessly in the corner. She hadn't stopped rocking since her confinement, save for her time helping Minnie. Even when she was out of her rocker, she herself rocked gently, swaying to some internal rhythm. Minnie crossed the room and knelt before her young friend. "Callie. Callie dear. Albert and I will be with John and Harry. At our farm. Just up the road. You are to come and see us whenever you want. Albert will miss you if you don't come and visit him soon. You can rock him when you come, Callie; he'll like that."

Minnie's eyes searched Callie's face. Callie's eyes resembled an old house, long abandoned, with oddly blank windows. There was no sense that Callie had heard a word Minnie had spoken. Minnie picked up one of Callie's hands and touched it to her own cheek. Even Callie's hands felt abandoned. "You'll be back soon," Minnie said softly. "I know you will."

―

That fall was a kind one. Harry got his first crop, a small one, harvested. Both John and Albert grew by leaps and bounds. And Callie did come back. As the air cooled and the nights marched more seriously across the prairie, the small critters began to prepare for the long burden of winter. As they became less and less active, Callie began to stir. And as the nights brought the first hard frosts, she broke through the whiteness that had dimmed her world. Tim, afraid to believe in the improvement at first, kept it to himself. He dropped by daily to see his son, often coming more than once a day. Yet he was unable to tell Minnie that his wife seemed to be swimming toward the surface, that Callie was beginning to re-enter this world.

A week or so after Callie first left her rocking chair and began to do housework and speak to Tim, she asked him about her baby. "We buried him then, did we?" Her voice was flat, expressionless. She stood with her feet slightly apart, her hand on the back of her rocker. Tim took a quick step toward her, but when she flinched he stopped.

"Don't you remember?" he asked. "Minnie took Albert home with her. The midwife said he'd be better off with mother's milk and you—you weren't able to feed him, not being able to eat yourself. You've been sick, Callie, but Albert's not dead. He's well and growing strong." Tim paused. "But he misses his mother."

Callie's hand dropped from the rocking chair. "I really don't remember. I try, but—it's all just a white fog—I thought I couldn't remember because it was something bad—I was sure the baby was dead." The last words came out as a sob. But Callie took a deep breath and stood up straight, squaring her shoulders. "I'm all right now, Tim. I want to see Albert. And we should bring him home."

—

During that long winter, Minnie and Callie talked often of those weeks when Callie had disappeared. Callie wanted to hear all about her Albert: how he had looked, how much he had grown, what she had missed. Minnie was fascinated by the way Callie described her absence: an impenetrable whiteness, where people and objects were apparent only as sound barriers. Callie said she could sense people and things because the stream of music that was her own self bounced off these objects, had to swim around these obstructions, avoid them, or the singing would stop forever. And the singing was the only thing that mattered.

Despite her fascination with the music Callie described, Minnie deemed it best not to question Callie too much about her "sickness," as Harry and Tim called it. But that didn't stop Minnie from thinking about it. She felt Callie had been granted a glimpse of another kind of existence: a chance to experience a life independent of the body. It was a freedom of sorts and she wondered if she would ever experience it for herself. Sometimes though, she thought that perhaps it was another kind of cabin fever. She would shudder, remembering Harry's black moods and her fear of them, and then she'd fervently wish that neither she nor Callie would ever experience such "sickness" again.

She admitted these thoughts to no one. Not to Harry. Not even to baby John, whose ears she often whispered into. Though she knew John could not understand, and therefore not make fun of her feelings, she felt that putting her thoughts into spoken, breathed words would somehow give them actual power.

At night sometimes, while the two male Worthings slept, Minnie, a wide, patterned shawl across her shoulders, would make her way to one of the covered windows. She would move the covering aside and breathe on the glass, waiting for her breath to warm the pane, just enough so that she could make out the moonlit world beyond the fog of frost. She would imagine some kind of music—triumphant, joyous, an odd mix of strident church chords and an upbeat jigger's tempo. And she would pray. Silently, wordlessly. Just prayer. Not to the God she'd learned about at church. Just prayer. With no focus. No demands. No breath.

In the mornings, after one of these vigils, Minnie would sometimes feel foolish. She would open her mouth, ready to tell Harry about her silly night game in order to expiate it, when somehow the air would not rush into her lungs, or she would swallow wrong, or breathe in too deeply, and suddenly she'd be choking, tears streaming down her face, her breath now coming in great ragged gulps. When the crisis had passed and Harry had fetched her a cup of water, the urge to tell had subsided as quickly as her coughs. Instead, she would busy herself with tidying their room, playing with the baby, and sitting close to Harry, letting his presence alone convince her of her foolishness. There was no need to admit anything she thought then, for she had done nothing wrong.

It was on one of these mornings that Tim trudged up to the front door. He came in, bringing with him the nip of the wind and a swirl of snow. Stamping his feet in front of the stove, he removed several letters from his travelling pouch.

"I had to go in to see about some seed. Turns out you had some mail too. So I thought I'd bring it by." Tim handed Minnie the package. "I suspect most of them's for you, since I know he doesn't spend much time writing," he chuckled, jerking a finger in Harry's direction.

"Want some coffee before you head on your way?" asked Harry.

"Nah," said Tim. "It's so cold, it'd freeze up in my gullet before I made our house."

"Say hello to Callie for me," said Minnie. "Tell her I'll drop in when it gets a little warmer."

"Sure will." Tim tipped his hat and was gone.

Minnie sat down and examined her unexpected loot: three letters, all from home. She read through her mother's first. It was full of plans for the Christmas season and millions of questions about the baby. Minnie's heart contracted. She wished her mother could see him. She was sure her mother would notice his intelligence and see his likeness to Malcolm, his uncle. "Uncle," she thought. "Malcolm only five years older than John! What fun they'd have. And what mischief John would learn from Malcolm."

The second letter was from Ada, a school chum she hadn't seen in some time even when she'd been living in England. "I suppose Mother gave her my address," she thought. The letter was short and to the point. Ada was getting married and wanted to be sure all her school chums knew. Minnie couldn't help smiling. Ada hadn't changed one bit: she had always trumpeted any good news from the rooftops, or at the very least hoped the news would spread like wildfire.

Finally, Minnie tore open the thick letter from Emily. She was hopeful that this time the letter would tell of their dearly wished and plotted-for plan coming to fruition. If Edward were to marry Emily, she and Emily would be sisters. Harry had taken a seat and was studiously cleaning his good boots. He knew better than to ask Minnie questions until she'd read all the letters to herself. Then, and only then, she'd read each one aloud to him and baby John, carefully stroking every word as if it were a favourite cat.

As Minnie read through Emily's letter, a wounded sound escaped her lips. Concerned, Harry looked up. Minnie's face was stricken, her cheeks pale, her large brown eyes drowning in tears. Harry crossed the short distance between them in one large step. Minnie reached out for his arm, her fingers pressing to the warmth of his pulse. He cradled her head against his chest, softly stroking her forehead. She read and reread a single page as tears coursed down her cheeks.

Harry read the page over her shoulder.

In an uncharacteristically shaky hand, Emily had written that Minnie's mother had taken a turn. A cold had developed into something more serious. Minnie's father had sent Edward for the doctor, who arrived quickly and suggested that certain bitters be ingested. Lizzie was also sent for and came to tend to her mother. The cold had become pneumonia, and the pneumonia deepened. Two weeks before Christmas, and only a week after first feeling ill, Minnie's mother had died at home, missing her youngest daughter terribly.

Emily had been up to visit Minnie's mother and, between long quiet spells where she had barely seemed awake and shuddering coughing spells where it had seemed unlikely that her next breath would ever come, Minnie's mother had told her daughter's friend to make sure that Minnie knew she'd been thought of every day. "And," wrote Emily, "your mother wanted me to tell you that she loved you dearly and was glad to know that you had found a new life. She said to be sure to remind you to watch the bread when it bakes and try not to take it out too soon, as you sometimes were wont to do, and that she would watch over you if it came to that."

The letter dropped from Minnie's hand. There was more—Emily had written a long letter that covered both sides of many sheets of thin paper. But Minnie had read enough. Harry remained still, his eyes searching her face while she struggled within herself. She wanted to cry again, louder, deeper, with more feeling. She wanted to rage, to scream, to beat her fists upon the iron of the stove until they were burned and broken. She wanted to curl up and sleep, and wake to the rightful world, where her mother lived still. She was angry with herself, and with Harry. She should have been there. She would have noticed her mother's illness sooner. She would have kept the draughts out of the house. She would have sent for more doctors. She would have hung onto her mother so that the life inside her would not have found an open doorway through which to escape.

—

Real spring seemed to come late to Grande Prairie that year. Though there was a record early break-up of the ice on the rivers in 1910, Minnie didn't feel the arrival of spring. She had to force herself to keep breathing, and she often felt that the air had grown thinner over the past twelve months. John, fortunately, seemed oblivious to this atmosphere, and was active and happy. Through the delight he took in this new world—green and growing—Minnie was able to make new connections. Harry still had his black times, though since his mother-in-law's death he had been more conscious of his moodiness and made an effort not to burden Minnie with his silence.

The tender shoots of the swaying alder and swamp willow emerged soft and sweet to the touch. Minnie and Callie took their boys to the shore of the lake—allowing them to crawl about in the mud at the water's edge. They shaded their eyes and watched the graceful dips and swoops of the gulls. The boys watched for dragonflies—charmed by these monstrous, innocent bugs that always evaded their clumsy baby fingers. On rainy days, Minnie kept close to her home. She would bundle up despite the new spring warmth, and would hound Harry to do the same. John would whimper his frustration at being trussed in thick blankets, but even he sensed that in this his mother's will was unbreakable.

The geese flew over their small home. The V's of their spring migration were wide and freewheeling, unlike the tight, taut arrows formed in the fall. Sometimes they would land in their lake, their honking making even Minnie's face relax into a slow smile. For John and Albert, this first spring was a time of bliss and bravura. They revelled in the new sights and sounds and tried to outcry one another when the newness became overwhelming. And Harry and Minnie worked on their land. The clearing continued.

—

Minnie's letters to Emily grew shorter and more sporadic. It had taken her months to reply to Emily's letter detailing Minnie's mother's death, and when she did finally sit down to write, a certain coldness, born of distance, time, and grief, crept in. She could not feel the warmth of former days. She now wrote perfunctorily, each time telling herself that the next letter would be longer, that this one was simply the way it was because she was so busy, so tired, so very far away. But she knew, in her heart, that she wasn't fooling Emily and she wasn't fooling herself. She was a different person now. If she couldn't recognize the happy, enthusiastic girl she'd once been, how could Emily recognize the woman she'd become? It didn't bear thinking about. So Minnie didn't think. And she rarely wrote.

In January of 1911, Callie and Tim had their second child, another son. This time, the birth was relatively easy and the recovery uneventful. Albert's new brother, Edward, was another big, blonde boy with a hearty appetite and a lively cry. Callie remained on this side of the white curtain and seemed to have forgotten about her earlier experience. Neither Minnie nor Callie brought it up, and even Minnie's fascination with Callie's time out of mind had waned. Both Tim and Harry concerned themselves more and more with the operations of their farms; they sometimes shared the expense of renting farm implements, and they spent almost all their waking hours of the growing season out on the land.

Minnie had her second child, a girl, in August of 1911. Eliza Jane was named, in part, to appease her mother-in-law. The Worthings Sr. rarely wrote, but when they did their anger and hostility were clear. They had hoped that Minnie and the children would help convince Harry to come to his senses and return to civilization in Ontario—and since he hadn't, Minnie must be at fault. Jane's letters were full of admonitions—"Always boil the water. Out there, anything could be in it. Bugs, disease—What kind of schools will the children attend? Surely you don't want to raise savages?"—and little else.

That fall brought an abundant harvest. Harry had planted wheat and corn and a few acres in other crops. They got all of it in before it could be damaged by frost. If Harry hadn't been so tired he'd have strutted around like a resplendent rooster. Minnie spent much of her time in her extensive garden. She had weeded and fertilized with chicken manure so well that most of her plants produced mightily. She canned and canned—often into the wee hours of the morning. Eliza grew so used to spending most of her day in the sling Minnie had created by copying Mrs Chiruk's that she often refused to fall asleep anywhere but slung next to Minnie's body. John was growing into a wiry, sturdy little boy, and his two-year-old fingers were becoming adept at picking bugs off the potato plants and squishing them "to deaf."

One evening, as the darkness drew in, Minnie sat close to the lamp with her mending on her lap and looked across at Harry. It seemed years since they had arrived—even longer since they had stood on the ship crossing the Atlantic, going from her world to his. Sitting together but apart—as they always did now, it seemed—Minnie realized that Harry hadn't touched her since shortly after Eliza had been conceived. She hadn't thought about it until now, months and months later. She continued to sew—one of John's little shirts that he'd caught on a nail or something—but stole a few glances at Harry. He looked so much older; his dark hair was greying, and the long hours spent outdoors had made his face set and hard.

She remembered when his long silences had frightened her. They had seemed so at odds with his more usual joking manner. But now she couldn't even remember when she had last noticed one of his silences—weren't they both silent much of the time? She spoke to the children, of course, trying to teach John to speak in a more adult fashion, and crooning gently to Eliza. But as for speaking with Harry—their conversations had dwindled alarmingly, she realized. Usually, Harry mentioned where he'd be working that day and when he'd want supper. When he returned at the end of the day, she'd ask how it had gone and he would mumble something half-heartedly and dig into his waiting bowl. He would usually fall asleep before he finished undressing.

Minnie finished mending John's shirt and put her kit away. What of their silence? It was companionable, wasn't it? Really, what did she have to say that she hadn't already said before?

And, if he didn't want to touch her, perhaps that was simply a sign of his exhaustion and due to her nursing of Eliza. Minnie knew from what Callie had said that Tim didn't feel comfortable with Callie either when she was nursing. Minnie and Callie had felt that it was a man's way and even something for which to be grateful, since having two little ones was hard on mothers as well.

Did she still love Harry? The question gave Minnie pause. She hadn't realized until now that that was what bothered her. The silence, the separation, and the long hours of hard work, none of that mattered itself. But now she wondered. Did he still love her?

Though she was sitting down, she could feel the blood rush in her ears. Her heart pounded erratically, and her clenched palms became damp. Harry hadn't moved in all this time. He seemed unaware of her turmoil or of her eyes on him. There had been a time when he would have sensed her gaze at once, when he would have met her eyes and smiled that wide, slow grin just because he could. And everything would have been all right. Her doubts would have receded, washed out by the tide of his presence, the slow waves of their connection. Now, however, she realized she no longer knew the answer to either of her questions. She had deliberately avoided thinking about emotional connections since her mother had died. Perhaps it was her fault, that she and Harry no longer had meaningful exchanges.

She searched her memory trying to pinpoint a time, a day, or an occasion when she had avoided him or deliberately refused him. Her head ached as various pictures assaulted her mind's eye: Harry falling off the horse with his foot caught in the stirrup; John toddling, completely unaware, under the bull's belly; a prairie sunset with fiery purple clouds tracing the horizon; Callie's laughing face as she played hide and seek with Albert and John. She remembered reading Emily's letter. She clamped down, hard, on that memory, holding it at arm's length, looking at it as if it were some horrible species of bug, forcing herself to look at its markings, to recognize its shape, colour, and size, but refusing to acknowledge her fear in its presence. None of these memories held any sort of clue. She felt alone. And the questions repeated over and over again in her head: Did she love him? Did he love her?

The two questions continued to frame her musings. They were like bookends bracketing her daily activities. The snow and the whistling wind had come, and now Minnie and Harry spent most of the days together. She wondered that he couldn't sense the beating of those two questions in her brain; they sounded almost constantly for her. They had even become somewhat melodious, and she'd catch herself swaying in time to their rhythm as she rocked John and Eliza to sleep. Minnie now held herself carefully, for she felt brittle and fragile. Harry spoke to her a bit more often, but still there seemed to be a tremendous rift between them. Remembering Callie's disappearance into herself after Albert's birth, Minnie had begun wondering if she too had partially disappeared without realizing it.

But Minnie knew this wasn't true. It made her feel better—briefly—to think this until John or Eliza cried or John started prattling to her and she responded. Callie hadn't been able to react to anyone. Minnie began to play a game: she wanted Harry to notice her, to focus on her, to really see her again. In her mind, it was a test: a test of her love for him and his for her.

In the mornings, she would stretch in bed, purposefully lining her body along his. If John or Eliza were lying between them, she would gently move them to one side and take their place, snuggling close to her husband. Harry usually slept right through all these machinations. Once she had exhausted that approach, Minnie would get up, stoke the fire, and get dressed. She took more care with her appearance: brushed her hair until it shone like burnished wood and soaked her hands in buttermilk, rubbing them dry in a pan of cornmeal, trying to make their skin soft and smooth again. She also took care to stand close to Harry or to sit next to him, to brush him with her hand or skirts as if by accident. And, at night, when they readied themselves for bed, she undressed in the lamplight, pulling her nightdress on slowly and, she hoped, seductively. Though she hardly dared to admit it to herself—certainly not in daylight—as she lay beside her husband she acknowledged that she was trying to seduce him, to win him back. Quite who or what her opponent was she was not sure, but she felt certain there was one.

—

By mid-November Minnie had almost given up hope. Harry spoke to her more now—and, in fact, became downright animated when Tim and Callie visited—but the easy camaraderie that he and Minnie had had during their courtship did not return. She took turns blaming Harry, herself, even the harsh land around them. On one of the rare days when Callie and Tim had braved the cold to see them, when the women were alone inside with the children while the men prepared the sled for the trip back, Minnie tried to explain how she felt.

"Callie? Do you think—do you ever notice—I mean, I sometimes wonder—do you think Harry still cares about me?"

Callie looked quite thunderstruck. "Of course he cares about you. Why do you ask?"

"He hasn't, we haven't—well, not for ages—and he only really talks to me when you and Tim are here visiting."

"Oh, well, some men just aren't as forthcoming all the time as they are when they're courting. He works so hard. That's his way of showing how he feels."

"Is Tim different with you too? Has it been a long time?"

Callie blushed a little, then said, "Oh no, we're—well, anyway, every man is different, that's what my dad always says. I'm sure everything is going to be fine. Things always look worse in the winter. Don't worry, really. Harry's just so focused on making the farm work, but that's all for you. I'm sure he'll—the two of you'll—it will be better. It will."

Callie gave Minnie an extra hard hug before getting in the sled, but because Callie had not offered up any similar concerns of her own, for the first time in their friendship, Minnie felt that Callie simply could not or would not understand her. Her loneliness increased and Harry's small conversational gambits, at first so welcome, now seemed intended to taunt and wound. It was simply not enough. She continued to go through the motions of being visible, but her heart was no longer sure her plan would work.

She considered all of this again one stormy evening as she put extra wood in the stove and adjusted the dampers. Harry was out double-checking the animals and the barn. The wind had come up since nightfall and its intensity seemed to triple every hour. The gusts would make the house lean almost imperceptibly, but lean nonetheless, and then creak back to upright in the lull before the next arctic blast. Minnie felt she was at sea again, and her stomach lurched accordingly. John and Eliza were asleep, snuggled together on the sleeping platform atop the warmth from the stove. Deciding that it would be useless to undress in front of Harry again, Minnie quickly donned her nightshirt, choosing to keep her undergarments on as well as one of her petticoats—the room was so chill. She left the lamp burning but adjusted it so there was only a low flame, and clambered up onto the platform. She moved carefully so as not to disturb her little ones.

Later—an hour? A few minutes?—she woke with a start. Something had changed. The lamp was still burning, and her eyes flicked around the room. Close at hand, John and Eliza slept on, quiet and dreaming. The wood in the stove shifted and made small popping sounds. In the far corner of the room, over by one of the windows, stood Harry. He had taken off his thick outdoor coat and stood with one foot still in its rough leather boot. The other boot was in his hand. He was looking out the window and seemed frozen in time, regarding whatever was out there with intensity. Minnie, from her position in bed, could not see through the window at all. She propped herself up on one elbow, adjusting the thick wool blanket around her so as not to feel the cold.

"Harry?" she whispered. "Are you all right? What is it? Is something wrong? Harry?" The wind shrieked outside subsiding to a low groan before swelling to its highest pitch once more. Harry didn't move. Minnie wasn't even sure he'd heard her.

She had decided to get up and go to him when he turned slowly toward her. Even in the dim light cast by the lamp Minnie could see that the dark cloud had descended on Harry once more. But this time his face was not closed off from her; it was not cold and stern. He seemed to have frightened himself. His face was marked with the map of his tears, and because of the cold some of them had been frozen and glittered in his dark eyelashes. Minnie got up and walked toward him. She raised her hand and touched a gentle finger to his face, wondering at his sadness. It had been a lifetime, it seemed, since she'd seen him cry.

Harry made an effort to speak, but the cold and his tears forced him to clear his throat several times before his voice would work properly. "What have you done to me, woman?" His words sounded strained and harsh. He moved to touch her and perhaps put down the boot in his hand, but Minnie drew back instinctively. She had reached out to comfort him as she would John or Eliza, and she had expected Harry to react as they did. Why was he angry? How was she at fault? Her hands clenched and she started to turn away from him. "Let him find his own way out of this darkness," she thought.

His hand reached out and grasped her by the shoulder. His fingers dug into the flesh between her collarbone and shoulder blade. Minnie bit her lip to prevent herself from crying out. Harry seemed not to realize the pain he was inflicting.

"Why must you look at me with those infernal eyes of yours day and night?" he growled. "Don't you think I've noticed how you look at me? How you accuse me without saying a word? How you condemn everything I do? How you tally up my failures one by one with that look? I know you blame me for your mother's death; don't think that I don't feel that every day. I see you reading her letters over and over again. And the children, those tales you tell them of England and their relatives. Don't think that I don't know that you're turning them against me too." He paused, but only briefly.

"Well, I won't have it any longer. Do you hear me? If you live in my house and eat my food, then you'll be my wife. And you will support me. You will do as I say. You will do it when I say. And you will *stop* looking at me that way. I'd rather you didn't look at me at all than look at me like that. And don't think I haven't noticed the games you've been playing, prancing around like some sort of princess, showing everything off then letting me know by a look, a glance, that I can only watch, but not touch. That stops now."

Harry's stream of accusations ended as his fingers dug in ever deeper and his lips descended, punishing her, branding her. He had never spoken to her like that. And he had never treated her with such verbal and physical contempt. The kiss stopped. He raised his head. The frozen tears had melted now, leaving his face shiny and glistening. His eyes were unreadable. Minnie tried to wipe her mouth with her hand, tried to stop the phantom pressure that still pressed on it, but Harry caught her wrist in his other hand. She was horrified and her shock made it impossible for her to think. She had wanted the old Harry back, the one who had courted her, not this frightening man whom she hardly

The Path to Kitty Islet

recognized. She tried to speak, her voice barely a raspy whisper, "Harry, please, I . . ." but he shook her, hard, and interrupted.

"You will not make me feel like a thief or a trespasser in my own home." His mouth curved into a sneer. "Though I know how much you enjoy it when I take you, even if you never want to let on. Well, we'll see, won't we?"

With that, Harry pushed her over toward the sleeping platform. Before she could process what he was intending to do, he removed her nightshirt, ripped off her petticoat, and tore away her underclothes. Then he pushed her, forcing her to climb ahead of him up to the bed, and he was so close behind her, prodding her cruelly, that she had no option. In fact, by the time she had mounted the sleeping platform, his weight was completely on top of her, making it so she couldn't escape. He hadn't removed any of his clothes, he simply pushed aside the material, and then he was thrusting into her, riding her the same way dogs coupled, plunging into her from behind exactly as horses did.

There was no affection. There was no tenderness. Once he had entered her, Harry pulled her violently toward him, continually pushing and prodding her as if she were another type of livestock that he was directing. The friction and the pain increased with each thrust. She realized she was whimpering, but she deliberately didn't cry out. The children were still asleep on the platform nearby. It seemed to take him forever. Minnie could hear and feel his breathing at the back of her neck. Just when she thought she would never again be anything but a battered receptacle for his manhood, he finished and collapsed, his full weight once again pinning her underneath him.

Afterward, she could never be sure how long he had remained on top of and still almost inside her. Her face was buried in the quilt, partially covered by her dark hair. The quilt had been a wedding present. Minnie especially liked its intricate pattern of blues and whites, and always took great care with it. She lay there, her eyes focused on the tiny, intricate stitches that held every square in place. She kept trying to count the stitches, but was always forced to start again because she could not be sure that she had counted every one.

Harry lay now on her left side, so she could not see him. He kept muttering to himself in a low voice. Minnie probably could have made out what he was saying if she had wanted to. She chose to count stitches instead. Finally, when he had been quiet for some time, she shifted her position slightly. Harry said and did nothing. Minnie slowly eased herself out from under him. His sleeping weight slid completely to her left. She waited. Still nothing. She raised her head slowly and looked along the platform. John and Eliza were still asleep, their breathing deep and even. Her heart contracted at the sight of them, which surprised her—she had wondered, as she had counted the stitches, if she would be able to feel anything at all ever again.

Her head returned to the quilt. She was farther along now, and the pattern had changed. Even the tiny stitches looked different. She lay there, alternately counting them and watching the shadows flicker on the wall as the lamp continued to burn down. Harry slept on, his breathing regular and ordinary.

Her thoughts were muddled, disjointed. He'd noticed her after all. And he'd wanted her. But that—was that what she'd asked for? It had never been like that before. Maybe if she could've seen his face? Her stomach contracted. She hadn't wanted to; and it was clear that he hadn't wanted to see hers. Was this the way it would be now? What had she done? Was it her fault, as he said? Had she brought this on herself? Did she deserve this? So many questions swirled around in her head, swarming like irritated bees.

He'd been so angry and hurtful. Little John and little Eliza. Their creations so different. This wouldn't, couldn't—Minnie stopped herself. It was his darkness. The bitter wind. This prairie winter. But maybe all marriages became this way, prairie or no.

The Path to Kitty Islet

Her mother and father had fought. And they also had separate rooms—was this why? It was just a mood, wasn't it? It would pass. Tomorrow everything would be different; life would return to normal. It was just one of Harry's dark moods. No, said part of her mind, louder than all the rest—it was him.

That was her last thought before sleep claimed her for its own. When she woke up, Harry was gone. The children were still asleep, balled up together so that individual hands were hard to make out. Minnie started to push herself up, and as she did so she felt a searing pain. She paused, considering. It hadn't been a nightmare. It had really happened. The lamp was out, and the room was still and fairly dark. Minnie knew she needed to get up. To get the stove going. To wake the children. To face him.

As she dressed, she noticed the bruises. A large one on her shoulder, near her neck. One that encircled her arm like a bracelet. Bruises on her hips and buttocks where he'd held her. Bruises between her legs. There was chafing there too. And blood. That had surprised her. It didn't scare her, though. Rather, it was the proof she needed to vindicate this feeling of distance, this angry, red, passionate hate. She could use this hatred to keep her real self protected, and far away from him. Maybe she shouldn't have tried to connect with him, seduce him, but he never should have forced himself on her. The Harry she had thought she married would have flirted with her, not harmed her.

The children were up, scrubbed clean, dressed, and fed by the time Harry came in. Minnie had managed to eat a bit too. She had chewed the bread carefully and had taken a drink after every mouthful. She was sure this was the only reason she hadn't choked. Harry seemed much smaller this morning, especially once he'd taken off his overcoat. At first, he refused to meet her eyes. But she wanted to look at him. She wanted to see him and to look directly into his face. He tried to approach John. Minnie stepped between them. Harry had to look at her then. And when he couldn't look any longer, he looked away. And then, Minnie knew he'd seen what she wanted him to see. He too could see her swirling anger—the anger that he had brought into their home. She was not happy. But she was satisfied.

JULY 1912
GRANDE PRAIRIE

Emily,

I have continued to receive your letters. I always plan to reply, but find neither the time nor facts of interest with which to respond. You feel so very far away and I often wonder what we would say to each other in person. But then another of your letters arrives and I am again pricked by guilt. Maybe it doesn't matter what I say. Maybe I just need to say it.

This time I have news of another baby. Another boy, whom Harry called Frank, but I have overruled that and he has been christened Douglas Ephraim Worthing. I hope Father will be pleased. I was very tired during my time carrying him and have yet to regain my strength. Little John and sweet Eliza are curious about Douglas, but both remain standoffish.

Besides Harry, I see no one save Callie and Tim. I spend my days in the garden, the barn, the house. My chores are not too difficult mostly, but they are time-consuming. And I am always tired now. Harry has taken to sleeping outside under the stars— and mosquito netting—because of the heat, he says. I am glad for the separation. He needs his own place. It is enough that I have the children.

I should rest again. I feel another headache coming on. The children have come in from the yard, as a thunderstorm is about to break. Nature at its finest and fiercest.

Hope you are well. Forgive the shortness.

Minnie

MAY 1913
GRANDE PRAIRIE

Emily,

Forgiven? I do intend to write. But no matter. I write now. The family grows. John will be four this year. He has developed black moods like his father. A temper. I am doing all I can to fix that. But Harry undermines my attempts. Little "Liza" is all mine. You would see my former self in her, I'm sure. Her eyes look their own conversation. Harry is at once perplexed and attracted. She can do no wrong—one minute—and the next he is chastising her harshly. The baby, Douglas, crawls and wants to walk on tiptoe. I tie him to my apron strings on purpose. I do not want to fail him as I failed John. Perhaps, though, 'tis the name—John Harold—a lesson to learn, Emily. Choose a name you can live with.

Sorry to hear that your mother has been ill. Good that you are there. You will do all that is required and demanded of the best daughters. Warn Graham that your steel is of a better kind. I suppose Edward is of no use? He seems to have bowed down and out since Mother passed away. I had expected more, as had you I know. All our plans seem so long ago now. We were such cared-for Cinderellas. Of course Harry had only to act the prince. I was too busy seeing me to see him. Now I see too much of what I suspect is the real him. There are no princes on this prairie.

The farm gets bigger. Harry works always. My writing is now brief and awkward. Don't worry. Comes of being far away. Callie and I are both always too busy. I try to write to you, to the Emily I remember, in the old cheery way. But just a false storefront—and those are everywhere here. You should come when your mother improves. You could see for yourself. The sky—then you could tell me true. Is it the same one that arches over England? I have forgotten, you see. I am teaching the children their colours—sky blue and lake blue. Sometimes, though, they are the same. Then John and Eliza look at me accusingly. But neither have their father's eyes.

    The cows come home. Milking time for some. Again. The baby coos. Do come. No one else suits.

Minnie

EMILY

APRIL 1913
MCCRINDLE HALL, LONDON

The stars are bright tonight. Bright and very far away. If I were a poet I would say they were like diamonds or something. Sparkling with a cold, uncaring brilliance. I am here alone, with Mama. I sent Nurse away to bed, as I know she is exhausted. Mama has finally fallen asleep, heaven be praised. She has been coughing so much and it does tire her out. She can't seem to catch her breath. We have kept her room dark and damp with bowls of steaming water everywhere, just as Dr Patricks suggested. It is like a small dark cave, and Mama jokingly says she feels she will see Aladdin or his lamp at any moment. I cannot believe her good spirits through all this. That is what keeps me able to continue. And to believe that she will get better.

I'm also hopeful that her fever has broken. She seems much more peaceful and cooler to the touch. I have left her alone in her room, sleeping, and have come across to the upstairs sitting room. I'm sure she will appreciate some time to herself, even should she wake. All the sickroom bustle is hard for a patient to bear on top of the illness itself, I think.

How quiet the house is at night. Father is still at his office preparing some important case. He spends more and more time there or at his club. He seems unable to face mother in her weakened condition. But I know he is deeply worried about her.

I overheard him speaking to Dr Patricks the other day and was shocked at his desperate tone. He would never, I think, allow Graham or me to see how much he cares for her. He has always prided himself on his ability to remain detached and objective. But, as I've long suspected, his detachment is all a mere façade.

I don't know where Graham has gotten to—since Minnie married and moved to Canada he has been aloof and impossible to depend upon. Mama is always so chipper when he is near—I do wish he'd devote more time to her.

I'm hesitant to write what else I've been thinking. I meant this diary as a surrogate friend or a place to unburden myself so that I could be strong for Mother's sake, but perhaps some things are better left unspoken—and unacknowledged. And yet I can't stop thinking them. Perhaps the only "cure" is to write them out in order to dismiss them from my mind once and for all.

First and foremost, though I am hopeful that Mama will get well—her spirit seems so irrepressible—a part of me is frightened that I will lose her—despite everything. I was there when dear Mrs Sinclair died—and that was difficult enough. Like Mother, she got ill suddenly. And, like Mother, she was optimistic and sweet all throughout. I tried to help Minnie's sister, Elizabeth, all I could, and tried to stand in for Minnie. I know it broke both their hearts not to be together at the end—or at least not to say those last loving words.

And I'm now frightened on my own behalf. I can't imagine a life here without Mama. She is the heart of this house. She keeps Father and Graham going, and stops them from becoming bitter. And she has been my one true friend now that Minnie is so far away. Mama cannot leave us—she cannot leave me. I'm sure she is better. She will improve. This will all just be a memory of a bad time. And she will regain her health, I am sure of it.

She even had a bit to eat tonight before she slept. Surely, this is the tide turning and the sickness abating? Dr Patricks said we'd know in a fortnight. And it's been eleven days. I believe Mama managed to eat more than I did. Graham was supposed to be here for supper, or so I understood. Mary and I waited on him, but finally I dined alone so that Mary could clear up and get to bed at a decent hour. Nurse took a tray up to Mother and was just as pleased as I when Mama had a bit of biscuit and some tea. Mrs Sinclair had nothing from the moment she took ill. And Mama has always been able to accomplish whatever she has set her mind to—if she has determined to get well, I know she will.

I think I should check on her and try to get some sleep myself. Tomorrow is a new day. I pray God that he will help us in this struggle and will keep Mama in his care.

MAY 1913
MCCRINDLE HALL, LONDON

A fortnight has come and gone. Nurse, Mary, and I are taking turns with Mama. The fever has returned and the coughing spells have become even more of a burden. Mama seems to grow thinner before my very eyes. Father has taken a leave from work—he has never done such a thing—not even so they could have a honeymoon—and Graham has been more attentive. Mary has been after me to go outside and take a turn about the park, claiming that I'm pale as a ghost, but I simply don't have any desire to leave the house. Mama's high spirits have returned. She is full of plans for the summer and the garden and all the things she "must" do once the sickness has passed.

Dr Patricks comes more frequently now—and his face has become inscrutable. He confers with Father in a low voice for what seems hours on end, yet neither of them has spoken to me. My imagination has been just as fevered as Mama herself—I do wish they would trust me with their secret whisperings. It seems that Nurse has not been taken into Dr Patricks's confidence either. We both feel frustrated and slighted—as Mama's closest companions and those entrusted with her care, surely we should be told about all aspects of her condition? Perhaps I am in need of a brisk walk. As it is, I feel that Father and Dr Patricks are keeping Mama from improving—because of their secretive chats. It is as if their sombre conversations across the foot of Mama's bed or in the hall draw all the health and life out of her. She is always so much worse following one of these conferences. I have half a mind to bar the men from the room save for the fact that Mama herself often asks to see them.

I am finding it difficult to sleep now. I have had a small day bed moved into Mama's room so that I can remain close to her. When a coughing spell strikes, she often finds no relief unless Nurse or I can help prop her up and support her; otherwise, the spell goes on and on. I sleep better—when I sleep at all—in the day bed than in my own room, but it seems an age since I had a deep sleep. I no longer remember how to lose myself to oblivion. Dr Patricks has prescribed something for me to take, but I do not want to be reliant on some kind of medication. When Mama is better I know sleep will return. Until then, I will get rid of the medicine bit by bit so both Father and Dr Patricks will be happy.

I am very tired though. I admit that. Truly tired. I sit and dream sometimes as Mama sleeps. It is not exactly unpleasant. I can't say where my mind goes or what I see, but it is somewhat refreshing. Because of Mama's illness, Father is less demanding about meals and general housekeeping. In a way, I have more time to myself than ever before since school ended. I occasionally write letters to Minnie, and she—just as occasionally, it seems—responds. Of course, the distance makes letters slow to arrive as well. Mama enjoys hearing about Minnie's new life in the Dominion and often speaks of finding a way around Father so that I might go and visit Minnie—when Mama is well, of course.

In fact, Mama remains full of plans. She has even had me write a list of all the eligible young women we know, in the hopes that in inviting them to tea "in the future," one of them might perhaps catch Graham's fancy. Mama finds it both honourable and humorous that he has given his heart to no one since Minnie left. As Mama says, Graham had not exactly stated his case strongly—if at all, really—and Minnie could not simply marry him because Minnie and I had always planned that it should be so. It does me good to hear Mama's laughter as she chuckles at Graham's unfortunate love life—but then the cough strikes and that laughter exacts a heavy price.

But she is still fighting. And she is still strong. Despite Father's and Dr Patricks's looks of doom, I'm determined that we women shall win out in the end; we will help Mama get well.

JUNE 1913
MCCRINDLE HALL, LONDON

It is Saturday morning and the tide has turned once more.

Graham called for Dr Patricks, and he has been here for hours. I am waiting for Father. He should be back shortly. We'd expected him long before this. I don't know what could have kept him on this day. This day.

Dr Patricks offered to tell him, but I said I would. I'm frightened. I do not know how he will take it. I don't think I am myself. I cannot believe it has happened. She had seemed so much better. She was resting easier. Coughing less. Laughing and talking more. Indeed, she was her old self.

I came downstairs to the sitting room last night after making sure she was comfortable. Mary had the evening off, and Nurse was asleep in her room down the hall. As usual, I couldn't sleep. So I wrote, some trivial thing, a sort of story. I remember thinking that it might well entertain Mama, and now—I must have fallen asleep after all. When I awoke, the whole house was quiet, and shivering almost. The lights seemed dim. We were all underwater and I thought what a lovely image and a peaceful way to describe sleep. But it was more than that. I went upstairs to look in on Mama, tell her my idea if she were awake, and stretch out on the day bed if she were still sleeping.

And Mama was not herself any longer. Her skin was thick, solid looking, and her chest wasn't moving. I knew I must touch her to know for certain, but how could I? How could I not? My hands are shaking still. I stood there like a tree for lifetimes as thoughts ringed me round with fear. My own skin felt heavy, thick, old—like some sort of bark. It was she who made me young. How could I be young if she were to go?

I know only—only that I stretched out my hand—her hair loose on her pillow; she'd embroidered that pillow herself, tiny featherlike stitches, and all those stitches in time saving nine; she'd saved nine surely? Her hair looked the same, her cheeks smoother, even, and then I touched her cheek—and it was not cold, but golden warm still! How could it be? Except that I must have made a mistake; really, she breathed still. I knelt beside her, my arm cradling her head, watching, watching—with every pore of my body. I wanted to pour my spirit into hers, to cry out, make the sound that would make her eyes flutter open like butterfly wings—soft, soft, as the patterns she'd embroidered. No sound came, for my throat was dry and hot.

I just stayed there, one finger lightly on her cheek, in my very own, "once upon a time." I don't know when Graham found me and drew me back, but I do know that by then her warmth was no longer. He drew me back into the cold waters of this house. They closed over me and I was drowning soundlessly, though I could now speak and Graham answered me. He said she was gone. That it was all over. I cringed at that—what is "it"? Mama was there still. And I was cold—her coldness had come into our life, it had come into me.

The fire behind me is blazing, but I'm still cold. I will always be cold, I think. No fire can burn me. I'm a creature of the depths now, and water is my medium. And it is cold and dark and for always.

JULY 1913
MCCRINDLE HALL, LONDON

Ice-blood illuminates my veins, guides this pen. Crystalline, pure, mine.

Father accosted me after the funeral and said it was unseemly for a "dutiful daughter" not to cry at her mother's death. How very ironic, that comment from him, coming from a man who has shown no evidence of crying himself. I wept over Mama as Mary and I prepared her to be taken away from us. And I have not wept since. I will not, cannot, weep on command. My inner temperature continues to plummet—Father's anger and people's talk has no effect. It is a climate of extremes to which Mama's death has borne me. Only the hardy will survive. But survival itself means little to me now.

The Sinclairs were there. Not Minnie, of course. Elizabeth and Edward. Edward and I stood together silently. I could tell he was reaching out to me in some unspoken way. But I didn't know how I should respond. I said nothing, and he seemed disappointed. I felt that, but could feel no disappointment for myself. I'm encased in ice; it's blue and beautiful. And it protects me. I could identify how he felt as if his feelings were a species of bird or butterfly I used to observe—I knew what it must be like to feel that sadness, but the pain could not touch me. Mr Sinclair looked so very old. Only four years ago that he lost his wife. Father would not shake his hand. It all becomes so petty. Really, it always was.

The ice helps me to see. The feelings are gone, submerged I suppose, but my ability to see, to categorize, and to classify has never been better. I'm not exactly unhappy. I do feel her presence. Even away from me, she has given me a gift. And this sense of cold came through her; so, she is with me still.

And survival beckons, slowly. It means little, but at least it means. I watch the faces of the crowd, see their lips move, their tears decorate their pale faces, hear their mangled expressions of sadness—each and every one of them inept, sweating through the euphemistic phrases. But she has not passed on as they think. She lives through me. I must keep faith with her youth, her joy. These long faces, these lying eyes, hands, voices—I mustn't keep faith with them.

And Father is the worst offender. He expects me to keep house for him and Graham. He gave Nurse her marching papers and no references—loyalty means that much to him, it seems—and told Mary that she and I were to run things according to his instructions. Never a word to me, of course. I'm to stay until Graham finds himself a wife; then the house will be hers and I'm to be the spinster aunt lurking in the maid's quarters or some such. I cannot bear it. Won't. Graham finding a wife seems too far away even to contemplate.

I received another letter from Minnie yesterday. It had been written months ago, while it was still winter on those great plains they call the prairies. Odd how she was describing the bitter cold, the snow—and it was as if she were describing my inner soul. She said that we in England, the "Old Country," have never seen the likes of the snow they have there—it is all small darts, like tiny shards, aiming straight for one's eyes. Shards that multiply and aim also for the heart. I think I know exactly the type of world she describes. She also speaks of the sky: blue even in winter; a blue that goes on and on forever. A blue that aches with cold itself. I read the words over and over again. I can't hear Minnie in them. The words mean and form pictures, but she remains locked in their shadows. Sometimes her letters are different, open. But this one—it too is ice. Maybe. Maybe it is another way.

Goodness knows I feel trapped here. With Mama gone I'm virtually alone in this house all day. I went outside in an effort to see blue sky. It didn't exist. And this is summer. There is no one with whom to talk. Mary is rather sullen now that her duties have become more arbitrary and onerous. I try to explain to Father that his strict instructions and fierce demeanour are making her angry and unhappy. He pays me no mind. It is getting so that I have no way of dreaming even. At least with Mama, even on her worst days, I could dream. But I can't now, now that there is no one with whom to share them. Father grows more remote from me every day—which I have encouraged, I suppose—we are both practitioners of that icy art of separation now—was he ever near me? Mama could mellow him, but without her influence I fear that soon he will be completely unapproachable. Graham stays out until all hours of the night and I can't reach him either—were I to desire it. We're all grieving—in our ways—but we never speak of our sadness. Nor do we speak of her. Father will not allow her name to be mentioned. Her room is locked. Only he has the key.

I should not complain, I know. I must stay here and perform my duty. I am his daughter. If I cannot help him, help Graham, what kind of daughter, sister, am I? I should be thankful about the bounty and blessings of life. The protection of the cold. I shouldn't be bitter about life's trials or its lacks. But how hard it seems some days. How utterly hopeless. The ice has begun to crack, I think. And I have nowhere to hide.

AUGUST 1913
MCCRINDLE HALL, LONDON

I have neglected writing for weeks. There is nothing worthy of ink. Father has withdrawn further. I hadn't thought it possible. Graham is as a ghost—his laundry appears, food is consumed, but Father and I virtually never see him. There are footsteps. A door opening and shutting. And then nothing—again.

Mary has given her notice. I had warned Father about the possibility, based on his treatment of her and Nurse since that time. Nurse was let go immediately, and Mary has been sure her days were numbered. I didn't tell Father, but I helped her secure a new position. She has been a comfort, and I will be sorry to see her go. But go she must. Or the pall over this house, this family, will infect her too. It is a lethargy. A selfishness. An unthinking dismissal of all that is bright and good. A repudiation of what Mama stood for.

I'm still deathly cold. And the shivering sets in sometimes for an entire day. My sadness is never far from the surface, rippling under the scant British sun. The blinds are kept drawn in the house, though, despite the cloudy weather—Father's orders. I'm not permitted the park—again, Father's orders. But I begin to melt. And I am afraid of being alone when the frozen tears become water. Will I still feel her presence? Will she guide me through this time? I don't want to be alone. But where should I turn? Mama? I cannot be alone. Cannot do this by myself.

AUGUST 1913
MCCRINDLE HALL, LONDON

The ice has melted. And it has not drowned me. Mary has left and I am truly alone in the house, sometimes for days it seems. Father has been at work or at the club. Graham is as usual. Neither one thinks to speak to me. Or with me.

The flood of tears came. And I was alone. Yet, I felt her strength. Her spirit. She has not left me. But I am no longer frozen in time, in place. I've been dreaming again. Planning. And the bars of my cage may be set too widely apart. Of course, neither Father nor Graham cares to notice. But that then becomes my advantage. I have been walking in the park, sometimes for hours on end, in spite of Father—but what does he know of my doings when he's away?—and have remade an acquaintance—Mrs

Greenwood, who lives at the corner. They moved in not long before Mama's illness, so we did not really get to know them. But Mrs Greenwood did visit several times and did bring Mama some lovely delicate macaroons. Father thought that Mrs Greenwood was forward; Mama was delighted and thought she was kind.

I suspect it has done me good to speak to another woman. To speak at all. And Mrs Greenwood has been really most kind. I have had tea with her now on several occasions. Her house is so different from ours. Her children are scattered widely about the Empire. But the trinkets and letters they send back! And she has travelled everywhere to see them. To India. Australia. Even Canada.

My curiosity rattles at the bars of my cage. I have so many questions. Perhaps one day soon I will be able to ask her. Mr Greenwood is a sympathetic gentleman too, in his way. They seem a good match. Certainly a more amiable one than Mama and Father ever appeared.

I believe my chance for survival has improved.

SEPTEMBER 1913
MCCRINDLE HALL, LONDON

I have just returned from a long visit with dear Mrs Greenwood. And we have concocted a plan. It is an escape. A way out. And I feel real excitement. For the first time, I think—since Minnie left for Canada and I was part of her plans, her anticipation. But then the let-down of her departure, and, more recently, Mama's illness. It has been a long time. But there is one thing to consider carefully. Sometimes I feel it is a small thing and dismiss it easily. At other times I falter. For if I choose to go through with this I know that I could never come back. I need to be sure, very sure. Sure enough for always.

As for the plan itself—I think it will work. Mrs Greenwood will help me. And I know I can do it. But should I?

We had a lovely talk today and Mrs Greenwood showed me pictures of her daughter's home in Ontario. A lovely farm with a number of lovely buildings, and trees. Mrs Greenwood plans to visit her daughter next year and looks forward to seeing all of her grandchildren. She says the Dominion is really quite spectacular and that most of the people there are from what they call the "Old Country." Manners are different, especially out west, but she says she found everyone to be very kind-hearted and quite honest. She has been eager to hear of Minnie's new life too—and now at last I can share Minnie's letters with someone again. Mrs Greenwood has given me so much—I have rediscovered hope.

LATE SEPTEMBER 1913
LONDON

The die is cast; there is no turning back. I had worried that I would be unable to go through with my plan at the last, or that I would be overcome by guilt or some sort of daughterly sentiment. But I feel instead that Mama is somehow watching over me. We did, after all, plot together near the end of her illness for ways to get Father to agree to allow me to visit Minnie in Canada. I feel her near me, encouraging me and loving me.

So I have done it! I still cannot breathe calmly without the excitement of it all making my heart beat faster and my breath quicken again. The plan worked exactly as Mrs Greenwood and I had hoped. I did feel badly, at first, for taking money secretly from Graham, Father, and the housekeeping fund, but it was the only way for me to make my escape. Of course I have also used the money Mama left me, but much of that I need to save for later. Father had tried to take control of that money immediately after the funeral. It was simply dumb luck and plain stubbornness that helped me evade his machinations. For over a week now, I have been taking bits and pieces of my belongings to Mrs

Greenwood's, and together we have packed them into a trunk that she has been gracious enough to give to me.

And then this morning. At the last minute I thought I had been found out, for Graham stopped me and questioned me about where I was going—and my going was all the more curious as I was carrying our family photograph album. I could not risk Mrs Greenwood's reputation so fobbed Graham off with some story about the Spencers' niece being in town and being curious about him. I felt—and rightly so, it seems—that if I made his affections or the affections of those interested in him the reasoning behind my actions, then he would abandon any questions—which he promptly did. To cover my tracks, I did stop in at the Spencers' and did show young Evelyn Maguire all the pictures in the album. Circumstances may have forced me to become a thief, but I refuse to become a liar too. Evelyn is a sweet girl, and not at all young for her age. I am sure she will make someone happy one day.

But I digress. Had Graham been more aware of circumstances at home, he would have questioned me much more severely about the album. For it came from Mother's locked room. When helping myself to some money from Father's billfold, I chanced upon the key. Hardly believing my luck, I hastened upstairs and unlocked the door. I made sure it was closed tightly so it looked as if it were the way Father had left it and hurriedly replaced the key. But I now had access to the room. While Father and Graham were out the next day, I sat in there, quietly, looking at her things, feeling her gentle presence. I know she would want me to have some of her things, so I chose those that mean the most to me. Our family Bible. Some of her embroidery. Some of her clothes. A few trinkets. Some jewellery. And the photograph album. I will need these mementoes to sustain me, I'm sure. To keep me as I go toward a daring future—I hope. They will be my only ties to the past. Father will never speak to me again. He will see my leaving as the ultimate betrayal.

And that hard unyielding part of him, his inability to forgive others—that almost kept me here. But I know that this is not the life Mama would want me to lead. I am too young to be made into a useless spinster. I have a good mind, and I want to use it. I couldn't bear to stay here and be a faded replica of the woman I have always hoped to become. I feel that Mama is with me. It is because of her that I have done it. And I will continue to live, really live.

OCTOBER 1913
MID-ATLANTIC

It seems the gods and Mama are smiling down on me. According to many of the crewmen aboard this America-bound vessel, fall is not usually a comfortable time to be crossing the Atlantic. She usually shows her wrath via great storms followed by days of straight grey rain. But, so far, our voyage has been almost perfect. Though it has only been a short while since I left London—and everything I have ever known—I feel as if this has always been my life. I have always felt the buck and roll of the mighty currents. I have always followed my heart, my own destiny.

Being schooled in duty, however, has made my nights significantly less than perfect. At times like these, for it is night now and only a very few are awake, I feel the true weight of my decision. There is no going back. Father will have disowned me already. I only hope that Minnie will understand and will be able to help me determine my next step. Despite my leaving, and despite Mrs Greenwood's faith in me, there are times, in the dark of night, when despair and fear are my only companions. In vain I search my heart for evidence of Mama, but at such times I sense only Father's anger and displeasure. And then I write. I have quite a collection of thumbnail sketches and funny little essays—none of them are of any particular merit I feel sure, but perhaps they will entertain Minnie and the little ones when I arrive. And, after writing, I find that my fear subsides and my sense that Mama is near returns. No matter the worth of the actual writing; it has become a powerful restorative tool and I am grateful.

In part because our voyage has been so uneventful, I have had much time to consider my future—both immediate and distant. While I was staying with a kind friend of Mrs Greenwood's who happens to live very near Liverpool, I wired Minnie and her husband's family. No reply came back from Minnie, which I had completely expected since her letters are always full of the difficulties of communication with the rest of the world, but Harry's parents did respond. They seem eager to meet me and very happy to have me stay with them until I can arrange transportation out west. I have Minnie's letters with me and have been reading them through again, so they are becoming completely tattered and worn. She found staying with Harry's family difficult. Perhaps it will be less so for me, since I did not marry their son. But I am looking forward to meeting them with more than a little trepidation. But surely, surely, the most difficult actions are behind me? Naïveté and optimism can be great, if somewhat irrational, companions.

I must try to get some sleep. Perhaps my demons need rest too. Who knew when I started this diary what sorts of things I would need to record? That in itself is enough to think on.

OCTOBER 29, 1913
NEW YORK

My word, this America is a bustling, noisy adventure! Surely newcomers arriving in England do not feel such a sense of insignificance and unimportance? Our vessel unloaded with great haste so that she might return immediately to Liverpool, and all her passengers were left standing bemusedly on the docks surrounded by trunks and parcels—or so it seemed to me. A kindly fellow passenger advised me on a popular, but quiet, lodging house located not far from the train station. I managed to engage a taxicab and get myself out of the midst of humanity before the bustle made me cry due to sheer panic! I would have been horrified to cry over such a foolish thing.

This lodging house, or hotel I suppose, is on a quiet little byway. The proprietress, Mrs Burrows, is an older genteel-looking woman and made me feel rather less overwhelmed immediately. She asked about the way in which I dealt with the authorities as regards immigration, and though I didn't say so to her I realize that somehow I, completely without intent, evaded the usual routine. Looking back, I do remember a line forming, but I had already gathered up my belongings and I assumed that those people were waiting for their baggage. Absolutely no one stopped me or demanded to see any papers or information. Indeed, I am quite at a loss to explain how I failed to be queried. To the landlady's question I simply mumbled some sort of reply, though I know that I blushed for I do feel as if I am some sort of criminal. Perhaps when Mr Duddridge took me aside to give me the address of this lodging the authorities assumed I was one of his party and, he being a very well-to-do American it seems, I therefore got the same sort of preferential treatment. This is the only explanation that seems at all plausible. But I now have the distinctly unpleasant feeling that perhaps someone will discover I have "evaded" the authorities and seek me out. What an odd way to begin my life on a new continent.

However, I have told myself that really it is of no consequence since I am neither unwell nor intending to remain in America. I have made enquiries already and have booked passage on the train from New York to Buffalo, and then I will cross into the Dominion at the famed Niagara Falls. From there I can easily get to Toronto and make my way, via the Canadian railway, to

Kingston. As I have a few days until my train leaves (since securing passage immediately was impossible) I will use the time to explore this overwhelming metropolis.

Mrs Burrows assures me that she will find it no trouble to direct me to the many sights and, if I can just shake the sense that I am here illegitimately (as I'm sure Father would concur!), I know I will enjoy myself.

One final note: I have determined not to try to contact Minnie until I reach Kingston, as there seems little possibility of a return message arriving before my own departure. I am so eager to hear from her, though, that my common sense has to work hard to keep me from wasting money on another international telegram. I have also begun work on a plan, which may make it possible for me to be of real use to both Minnie and the children. I am quite embarrassed that I had not thought of it before, for it seems so obvious. "La Grande Prairie" is a new frontier community—growing every day, Minnie has said—so why couldn't I contribute by teaching the young children? I will need to find out about requirements, but I am fairly hopeful that they will not be too stringent. When I arrive in Kingston I will endeavour to find out—and collect some appropriate books.

It does seem as though I was meant to do this. Perhaps the calm voyage and the absence of immigration difficulties are simply small indications that my life is going according to some large design. I cannot see the whole of it—if one is ever allowed to have such knowledge—but I feel strongly that it is a bold and beautiful pattern. My dearest Mama would work hard to make that happen, I know.

NOVEMBER 1913
KINGSTON, ONTARIO, CANADA

Well, I am now in the Dominion of Canada. And I am ensconced, for better or for worse, in the Worthings' home. After my trip by train through pretty New England towns and through the town and past the waters of Niagara Falls—what a stunning sight they were, even at this time of year!—Canada came as no different and yet completely other. Here, as in America, people do not stand on ceremony with one another. Passengers strike up conversations all up and down the train, and appearances offer little or no clue to one's background. Father would be quite appalled; but so far, though I find it odd, I have also found this attitude charming and refreshing.

Canada is not so deeply settled or so populous as America, at least not in the areas I have seen. Toronto is large and busy, but still so much more refined and calm than the raging metropolis that is New York. Toronto's lakeside location seems well chosen, not just because of easy access, but because of the soothing effect such a large, inland body of water seems to have on every inhabitant.

Kingston seems old by Dominion standards. It is a well-established, quiet city that seems to expect and deserve a certain British type of loyalty. I do not feel out of place here, and could imagine staying and putting down roots. The churches are all quite beautiful—in a much simpler way than the grand cathedrals at home—and well attended. Though it may once have been an outpost, Kingston is certainly no longer an uncivilized or wild part of Canada. Things here are settled; life is measured. There is no daring. Knowing Harry only a little, I still find it completely understandable that his questing soul could not linger here.

And, coming to know his parents more each day, I find it commendable that he did not bend to their will. Mr Harold Worthing, Senior, Proprietor—for so he is designated on the brass plate both outside his store and his home—is much like Father. Things are to be done his way or not done at all. He has rather fierce grey moustaches, which make him seem even more forbidding and intimidating. He has made it very clear that I am

The Path to Kitty Islet

to go west, bring Harry and Minnie to their senses, and fetch them home. Because this is his decree, he is sure it will come to pass—and I, as his tool in this regard, am made very welcome in his home.

Jane Worthing is of a different sort entirely. Long years spent under Harold's control have made her very spineless and frightened. Perhaps she was always thus? Her only skills seem to be in hovering about one and in designing doomed matches. The young, insipid creature she had planned for Harry still comes almost daily for tea, accompanied by her overbearing, gossipy mother. The girl is obviously infatuated with Harry—and Harold Sr.'s position in Kingston—and seems almost oblivious to Minnie's existence. She constantly begs me to remember her to Harry and to be sure to bring him—not them!—back safe and sound. Harrumph!

So, for the moment, I am an anxious vessel beached beyond the high tide mark and unable to feel the water. It seems that travel to Grande Prairie is far easier in January, despite the bitter cold, so I must remain here through Christmas and then make my way west. I will go by train as far as Edmonton, and then I must enquire as to the best route to take. The train continues west to a small hamlet called Edson, from which a stagecoach goes north to Grande Prairie. As well, the Canadian Northern Railway goes north to Athabasca Landing, and this is the route that Harry and Minnie originally travelled. But I can find no one hereabouts who can advise me as to the best and quickest route. Mr Worthing simply shrugs his shoulders and suggests tossing a coin. Other people here merely shudder—"the last best west," as the area is romantically referred to, is also known for its hardships and deprivations. It seems I must wait to learn more in Edmonton.

And, worryingly, I have had no news from Minnie. I sent another telegram as soon as I arrived here in Kingston, but there has been no reply. Neither Harry nor Minnie has written to the senior Worthings in months. I cannot help but be concerned. I must trust that no news is good news and hold on to my approaching departure date. It seems far away, but I must hope that the time left will pass quickly!

I am still attacked by doubt, especially at night. I broke down and wrote to Father, but he has not replied. I fear he never will. I did not anticipate just how lonely it would be to feel that I'm without any family anywhere. I am also sure that this interminable waiting is in large part responsible for my occasional weakened spirits. At other times, I feel a sense of euphoria—until I remember that Father has most likely disowned me. Fear of his censure and disapproval can still affect me all these many miles away. I vacillate between fear and hope—fear that I will not survive, that I will be unable to live a daring new life on my own—and hope that by living away from Father's influence I will never become a woman of Mrs Worthing's diminished character. But no matter my mood—black and worried or buoyant and gay—I am lonely. I miss Mama's kindly presence and the easy camaraderie Minnie and I once shared. It seems all my kindred spirits have fled—will I ever locate another? Will Minnie be the friend I need now? Will I be the friend she needs?

Meanwhile, I fill this diary with anxious, jostling thoughts. I spend hours reading the photographs, in Mama's album, wondering what those familiar and unfamiliar faces can tell me. I plot and dream. I know I am on a threshold. But a threshold to where?

FEBRUARY 1914
EDMONTON

My trip from Kingston to Edmonton is accomplished. The trip, was uneventful. I travelled the whole way in a day coach and thanked my lucky stars that I had amenable seatmates, for the most part, and that I have always been able to sleep easily, save during Mama's illness. This land called Canada is truly immense and the varied terrain is awe-inspiring, even when mostly covered by a thick blanket of white.

We travelled alongside Lake Superior for about two hundred miles, with glimpses of memorable landscapes almost every minute so that soon one became almost immune. We saw so many lakes in Northern Ontario that I have no clear recollection of any of them. They just blurred together as one. Winnipeg was windswept and cold, and very dull and grey. I was glad that it was not to be my destination. The white of the bulk of the prairies seemed, and I should say is, endless. The train went on and on. And the white endured.

Again, I was blessed with good travelling weather, as our train was nowhere held up by snow or cold. Apparently, when it is too cold the air enters the firebox of the engine and cracks the water pipes from the boiler. This then leads to the water pouring down and dousing the fire, which effectively stops the engine. The train comes to a halt, dead in its tracks, and can only be restarted after being reignited at a roundhouse. Or so I learned from a knowledgeable and talkative fellow passenger. Fortunately, I did not have to experience such a cold weather calamity.

But here I am in Edmonton, unsure of my next destination. I have visited many of Edmonton's sights, such as they are, including the imposing Hudson's Bay Company store, made of brick—very many of the new buildings are still only wooden structures, though many of the banks are already solid stone or brick affairs. It is quite a large city and has grown up fast, as everything still seems raw and new. I have also visited several stagecoach lines and the railway station, but am in quite a quandary as I have received such conflicting reports.

It seems that the Edson trail is much shorter, but quite, quite difficult. Going by Athabasca Landing is easier, but takes much longer. So, here I sit with a choice to make and no clear idea of what it is I am deciding between. Perhaps if I could meet up with a congenial group also travelling to Grande Prairie, then that would make it easier for me: I will simply take whichever route they decide upon!

APRIL 1914
GRANDE PRAIRIE

It seems decisions can be made for you at times after all, and things happen which no one can easily predict. I arrived here almost a fortnight ago now, with a group of new homesteaders, but I was not prepared for the reality with which I would be faced. It's not that the prairie is so empty, or that conditions are so primitive, or even that the neighbours are distant. No, it is that both Minnie and Harry are completely foreign to me.

I barely know how to begin to explain—

They both look work-roughened, as is to be expected. But their spirits have also been changed. And Minnie's, I fear, is quite broken. I cannot write of it all now. Suffice it to say that Minnie had been in Montrose—the hospital here—for almost two weeks a while before I arrived. She had been slipping in and out of consciousness and often woke in hysterics, and she came home in not much better shape.

But she recognized me when I arrived—and how she clung!—however, since then she has continued to go in and out of conscious understanding. She clearly hadn't bathed since she'd been sent home from the hospital. When I got water boiled for Minnie and washed her, I found that she was covered with bruises, old and new, bruises that look as if they were made by a man's hand, bruises in places that—that I cannot bear to mention.

The whole house still smells of death, decay, and animal dung, no matter how much I scour it. The small barn is attached, so that explains it in part. But, since Minnie's illness, Harry has not done what needs doing, and, I am certain, he has also mistreated Minnie terribly.

But he doesn't seem to really understand that I am actually here, the heavens be praised, for I have never seen a man in so black and scowling a mood. And he is in it at all times. He has said almost nothing to me save grunting or the odd, lone word. He spends most of his time in the barn or in a shack he has constructed a fair distance away. He mostly ignores Minnie now and seems to barely tolerate me if he does chance to notice me. I am definitely frightened, but I hope that together Minnie and I would prove to be too much for him, should he ever try to approach either of us inappropriately. I do not trust him one jot.

I cannot tell if he suffers from what is called the prairie madness—brought on by the relative isolation and the never-ending work—or if it is some inherent defect, which has only now become apparent. If I could determine the cause I might be able to ascertain a course of action—if it were the prairie madness, perhaps his parents' wishes might be the best thing for all concerned—perhaps leaving the prairie would return mental stability. But if it were the other, I do not believe that the Worthings Sr could or would want to cope with a mentally unhinged son, his delicate wife, and their three young children.

Callie has had her hands full up until now keeping all the children at her place. She says Tim has been a rock, so she feels it is not too great a burden. She is a wonderful help, just as Minnie wrote. I have told her that as soon as I get a bit more accustomed to the amenities, or lack thereof here, and help Minnie recover somewhat, I will have the children brought home. I can only hope that their childish prattle and energy will bring the old Minnie back permanently.

Once more though, I fear I am at a loss. I simply do not know where to turn if Minnie doesn't get better. Or what I should do.

Callie and Tim cannot keep the children indefinitely, and, despite my brave words, without some support from Harry at least, I do not think I can look after everyone here myself. And I certainly cannot be the perfect farm "wife"—I don't know the first thing about managing a homestead, garden, livestock, or quarter section on the prairie. Nor can I possibly ask Callie to teach me the way she guided Minnie. She has her own children to raise now. She doesn't need to be burdened any longer with Minnie's children or with my lack of knowledge.

This may be the "last best west," but will I last? And Minnie? I just hope that my presence here is a comfort to her. Sometimes she knows me and sometimes she knows no one.

I cannot write more.

MAY 1914
GRANDE PRAIRIE

I have the children at home now. Harry has chosen to ignore us all, though he continues to do his farm chores and work. Tim assures me that Harry is doing all that needs to be done—and at the appropriate time. Harry and I now never speak. He lives out in his field shack and seems to have more in common with the mute beasts of the barn than with any of us.

I have been somewhat heartened by Minnie's progress, though it continues slow. Callie has regaled me with the stories of her first confinement and assures me ever that Minnie will become her old self in time. I pray Callie is right.

The children provide the only joy here. Little John is a sturdy four-year-old, nearly five, with noticeable dark moods. They are improving, though, as he learns to trust me. He is very like his father, and I cannot but fear the similarities. Little Eliza is a sweet, quiet, almost three-year-old with her mother's eager spirit and busy hands. She latched onto me immediately that Callie brought them back. She practically never leaves my side. Unlike

John, she is afraid of Minnie most times. And baby Douglas is almost two. He toddles everywhere at speed and gives love to everyone. He has a special affinity for the old mare and for a certain creaky board in the barnyard fence. He loves animate and inanimate alike. He mimics the cry of the noisy magpies, though he talks with real words not at all. And he has given me the beauty of the prairie.

Without Douglas's steady stream of musical but unintelligible murmurings, I would never have looked up to see the arched sky embroidered with silk knots of the purest white. I wouldn't have seen the sod roof over the house as anything other than a nuisance; I would have ignored the riot of spring colours blooming all at once in a chorus of careless grace. He can infect me with his enthusiasm and, for his part, he seems not to notice anything ugly in his world. His chubby fingers tuck stray flowers into Minnie's clenched palms; his reedy voice hums in time to her rocking. And he can smile little John out of his angry moods.

It seems hard to believe that a boy of not even two can do so much for us all. Perhaps it is the very existence of his innocence that changes us. Perhaps.

The days are lengthening now—out of all proportion to days in the Old Country. The children find it hard to be sent to bed when evening seems never to begin. I have spent long hours cleaning and mending, cooking and chasing livestock. My back aches and my eyes droop closed the moment I sit still. I have neglected this diary. But my heart is too full for words.

Minnie knows me most times now, but sometimes she speaks to me as if we were still girls in London. She plays with the children, but then asks when they are due back at their mother's. She rocks silently for hours. With the weather fine most days, I have put her rocker outside in the hope that the sunshine and fresh air will revive her completely.

But then Minnie cries. Oh, how she weeps at times. The tears course down her cheeks, her arms wrap protectively around herself, and I cannot console her. The recovery Callie and I had hoped for is not yet fully upon her, but sometimes it appears very close. With a heavy heart, I keep wondering—and I wait.

Part Two: Fire

MINNIE

JULY 1914
VANCOUVER

A new province. A new start. So it is an appropriate time for a diary. It seemed to give Emily comfort whenever she was able to write in hers. Besides, there is no one for me to write letters to now. Emily is—gone. My dearest friend, dear Emily. The fire destroyed her and took the person I was—before meeting Harry, before leaving England, and before the fire aged and anointed me. The person I used to be does not exist any longer. I have forgiven her her childish ways, and I have had to let her go.

The children amaze me: their energy, their joy in a million small things, their ability to live their very best life each day with no regrets, and very few second thoughts. They have pulled me back from the edge of despair. What my friend began, they will finish. I can only hope to record a deserving life on these pages, after all the great losses we have suffered. I feel as if it were I who is learning from the children more often than they learn from me.

We took the train in stages to arrive here. An older gentleman sitting near us was very helpful and would watch one of the children whilst I took the other to wash up. We were in the day car, as I felt the sleepers were too expensive. I have only the money from selling Lady to Callie and Tim, and the savings that Emily brought with her. The other livestock was given over to pay the debts we owed in Grande Prairie. I know Emily would not begrudge me the use of her money, as her father and Graham have no real need. Not the need that I fear. I sent a carefully printed letter to my family, telling them that I was alive and that I would be moving on, but I did not say where.

I asked Callie to send telegrams to Harry's parents and to Emily's father—I just could not bring myself to write either message. I can well imagine that both fathers will be beside themselves with grief and anger. I briefly considered taking the children to Ontario, to Harry's family. But my memories of his parents, especially of his father's cold, hard implacability, made me realize that I could never let these children experience that. Besides, Harry's black moods had to come from somewhere. I can't risk exposing the children to his parents if they had anything to do with them. And his parents' grief would colour all of us. Better to be alone with the children and my own sadness than to burden the children with their grandparents' smothering emotions. I'm going to at least attempt to make a life for us myself, a fresh start, before I ask Harry's family or my own for any support. I am determined to erase any shadow of how Harry treated the children or me from their minds and that is best done far away from his family in Ontario.

Only now does it occur to me that I have not wired my own family to tell them the news. My letter will take weeks or months compared to the telegrams Callie is sending. It will be a double shock when my family hears the news from Graham or Mr McCrindle. I did not intend to be so thoughtless.

It seems the fire has disturbed me more than I realized. I have lost so much; I've lost my boy, John—and Harry. It's odd, but I can't really remember Harry as he was on the prairie. Now I can only picture him in London; perhaps it is best that way. Perhaps I can forget the bruises he made too—perhaps.

And the other great loss—the loss of dear Emily—I do so miss my bosom friend, my Emily. I still can't believe that the fire took her from me. I wish I didn't have to leave her behind, leave what is left of her there on the prairie.

But I must focus on the here and now. I must go forward. I will go forward.

This hotel is noisy, and near the poorer section of town. There are a number of Orientals here too. I am afraid I do not find their faces inscrutable, as so many have said, but I do find them round moons of deep sadness. And a chord is struck. This is not the world they expected, or the lives they led or hoped to lead. Nevertheless even as they shuffle by, most stop to admire my children with their bright button faces. Douglas speaks his language to them, smiling, and they regard him with dignity and respect—they cannot be as evil, as some say— perhaps my moral compass has had its wings singed, I don't know. But I feel more comfortable around the very old, the young, and those who speak in other tongues. They do not try to draw me out, yet the smiles we exchange seem richer than correct English chatter. I fear I am not myself. At least not the self I am used to.

We will go across to Vancouver Island on one of the CPR ferries. I have been told that we can travel from Vancouver's harbour to Victoria's, arriving in Victoria proper with very little trouble. Vancouver Island is the westernmost part of Canada, but yet they say Victoria is a very British city. I feel drawn to it, perhaps because of the British influence, perhaps because of the mild climate. Or perhaps because Victoria is as far away from Kingston as I can get. I needed to get away from the endless prairie skies. The heat. The cold. Its fire and ice have burned me and branded me. I hope that the bracing salt air heals some of the scars.

Only yesterday, as I was washing, did I notice the marks on my right hand—small white lines, deeply etched into my skin. I know their cause, but I cannot think why it took me so long to notice. I felt no pain earlier and saw no blistering. But I know I will be marked for life.

JULY 1914
FERRY BETWEEN VANCOUVER AND VICTORIA

Another ocean voyage, and another forgetting.

The children are nothing but big eyes and breathless wonder. All is new to them. The waves and immense stretches of rippling water are inconceivable to eyes used to the wind waves in prairie grass and men as tall as houses. Eliza's hand never leaves mine. Douglas engages all in his conversation, though no one understands his murmurings. Once on board, his language quickened and seemed to broaden as if by magic. I finally recognized one of his words—"water."

I believe I was right to bring them to this miracle. Waiting for magic to appear seems much less trustworthy. I think we must make our own.

They are asleep now; their senses were overwhelmed, their eyelids drooped, and sleep stole in despite their best efforts. I can hardly believe in the sturdy reality of these children, especially when my clothes and hair still give off that heart-rending smell of burnt grass, burnt home. The scars on my hand now throb too, as if in sympathy. My throat aches with unshed tears for those I have lost: my poor, poor boy, my damaged man, and my dearest friend.

Looking out on this briny ocean, placid today, does little to erase the picture engraved in my mind's eye. Perhaps in time, wave will work its magic upon sooty stone.

I am reminded of what Emily and I used to chant as children:

Sing a song of sixpence
Send your troubles to the sea
Sing a song of sixpence
Send sorrow far from me.

This rhyme has been in my head since we boarded. An omen? The hands of loved ones in the unseen world giving me hope? Hope for today, or hope for a lifetime?

JULY 1914
VICTORIA

It's a funny little town—certainly a large metropolis compared to Grande Prairie, but really it is very provincial—and very gracious. I was almost entirely at a loss when the ferry docked in the harbour. After all our travels, and all that westward movement with Victoria as our only aim, to be cast ashore with no fixed plans made my heart sink. I almost sat down and wept. However, the children have become the catalysts in my new life. Eliza tugged so diligently at my hand and pranced ever so excitedly on the tips of her toes that her excitement became contagious.

Then, in the flurry of collecting our one small trunk, she scampered away from me. For one agonizing moment, as Douglas was balanced on my hip and panic had control of my heart, I stood transfixed, unable to see her or hear her. And then—the patter of her busy feet and her trusting hand in the hand of a complete stranger, but both heading rapidly toward me. Turns out that, even though she is not yet three, Eliza is already adept at meeting people and arranging her world. The man she found, a Mr Simpson, had come down to the ferry to collect a parcel. More importantly for us, he works for a man who has numerous properties, some of which he rents out. Mr Simpson assured me that his employer was extremely honest and completely above board. Trusting my instincts, and Eliza's, as well as Mr Simpson's kindly face, soon we were ensconced in the automobile Mr Simpson was driving making our way past the stately Empress Hotel and out of James Bay into Victoria proper.

The office of Mr Simpson's employer was neat and well furnished. Nothing in the room was either too ostentatious or too shoddy. When Mr Simpson came back in with Mr Westby and introduced us, I was pleasantly surprised by Mr Westby's appearance. He was much younger than I had anticipated, and his eyes twinkled with warmth and good humour. After we exchanged a few polite remarks and established that I did indeed have some hard cash, he opened a drawer and drew out a well-used map of the area. Determined to take hold of this new life with both hands, I threw caution to the winds, admitting to Mr Westby that I had no idea what constituted an appropriate neighbourhood in which a widow with two small children should live, and requested his help. It was a liberating moment to be able to be that blunt.

Mr Westby pointed out several features of Victoria and noted some of the most important business districts and local communities. He then cleared his throat, placed his elbows on his desk, thoughtfully matched each fingertip of his left hand to those on his right, and regarded me directly.

"There is no Mr Worthing, then?" he asked.

"There was, but he is now—well, gone—he was killed in a dreadful accident," I replied, never allowing my gaze to drop from his.

"Right, then." He cleared his throat again. "I'll take you home to the Mrs before we make any other decisions."

With that, Eliza, Douglas, and I hurriedly said our good-byes to Mr Simpson and we were ushered out of the office and back into Mr Westby's car—turned out Mr Simpson had merely borrowed it for his errands. We were soon driving up Fort Street and over to the village of Oak Bay.

The Path to Kitty Islet

I must stop here for now. I am feeling quite fatigued and yet blessedly safe. For the time being, the children and I are staying with the Westbys. I could not be more relieved. That girl of mine has found us our first Victorian home.

JULY 1914
OAK BAY

Where to begin? We stayed with the Westbys for just over a week. They have a lovely house very near Oak Bay itself, on a quaint street called St. George. Thanks very much to Mr Westby's kindness, and Mrs Westby's determination, we have now become the proud—and grateful—renters of a home on the same street, though ours is much nearer the newly built elementary school. It seems that the last several years have been a busy building period for this area, but sadly for the builders and happily for us, the boom now seems to have gone bust.

Never mind that—we have a lovely wee bungalow just right for the three of us. I have determined that the children will sleep in the same room for the time being at least, and that frees up the third bedroom so that we can take in a boarder. I am relatively uncertain of the viability of such a notion here in Victoria, but Mrs Westby does agree with me—it would be a way to earn additional income, and another woman in the house will provide some much needed adult companionship. However, I am also feeling very wary of getting too comfortable too quickly with anyone. I know that I am in an extremely vulnerable position and must do my best on my own to make my way. It is imperative that I provide for the children and myself without making any commitments or fostering any friendships that feel too close. I cannot bear to lose people close to me right now. Better to be thought solitary and standoffish than to learn to rely too heavily or to trust too deeply. There is too much at stake, and all is very new.

I have just reread today's entry. What has become of me? I sound like Emily's father, the barrister, pontificating and preaching away. While what I have said is true—I must be wary and careful—I do not also have to become less than human; surely I can strike a balance?

But balance is perhaps the one thing it may take me years to find. After the fire, in my immediate grief and fear, I merely existed. Then there was my decision to come west, a decision that provided a direction and a goal, though in reality I don't know how well I actually thought it through. Now, a month later, I am still struggling to understand how to move past the tragedy that took so many constants out of my life and added such vulnerability. I know that women have raised children on their own for as long as there have been children—and I know they have done it well. What I need to figure out for myself is how I will do the same.

Eliza and Douglas have so much love and faith and trust; surely it is not wrong of me to bask in their steadfast emotions and use their belief in me to give me courage? They like the Westbys—and the Westbys have given us so much already. It cannot be wrong to rely on them, trust in them, be friends with them, can it? Could I not make friends with a tenant as well? Some reserve should be allowed, of course, and perhaps even be expected. But I do not have to be completely isolated, do I?

When I am beset by thoughts such as these, I look out at the front of our new home. There, on either side of the walkway, are the beginnings of a beautiful garden. The previous tenants were seemingly amateur rock wall builders and created a low wall at the front of the house for a bed there as well. Mr Westby has kindly loaned me a few of his own tools so that I might continue landscaping and adding plants. I have been honest with him and have explained that neither my time in Grande Prairie nor my girlhood in London has fitted me to become a terribly effective or productive gardener. He simply "pshawed" my deprecatory remarks and told me that once I'd gotten my "feet wet and boots dirty," he'd send over Mr Sing and all would be well. It strikes me now that the process of building a garden for this house mirrors the process of planting the children and myself in our new life. Each day our roots will grow deeper and no one will know the final shape until the garden is done.

So we have our house, and it is already more than just a roof over our heads. If we get a female boarder, that extra income will feed us. As for the monthly rent, once my nest egg is depleted I will need to think of something. Teaching may be an option, or giving music lessons of some sort. I've spent years taking them myself; perhaps with a little practice I could remember what I learned so long ago in another life.

'Tis time for me to lay down my head, though. Eliza and Douglas have been asleep for hours. And it has grown very late, for even the streetlights have gone off—and they are not turned off by the constable until well after midnight.

AUGUST 10, 1914
OAK BAY

The world has become alarmingly small. A few short days ago, Germany declared war on France. The day after, England issued a severe warning, then England, in turn, declared war on Germany. Canada, ever faithful to the mother country, will support Britain. The mood here in Victoria, and indeed around this vast empire, has been almost one of jubilation. Though the older statesmen seem to speak in more careful and measured terms, the young men are all anxious to begin—to venture forth for King and kin, to see foreign parts of the world, to win glory for themselves and their country.

I do not know what to think. That Britain may be in real danger of attack frightens me. What of my family there? What of my brothers? Will they go off to fight? Are they, too, jubilant at the prospect? Albert is twenty-five and Edward twenty-four, and there is Emily's brother too; Graham and Edward are of an age—will they go to war? Thank heavens that Malcolm is still much too young.

I cannot conceive of what the word "war" actually means. It strikes fear in my heart and my throat tastes of burnt grass again. These boys do not know the look of death. Or the sounds that go with it.

I have not been sleeping since we heard the news.

Mrs Westby is deeply affected as well. Her two boys, Duncan and Samuel, are promising young men in perfect health. Samuel has already made enquiries about joining up, and it seems certain that he will go immediately. I call them boys, though they are my age; sometimes I just feel so old in comparison to them, as if I have lived several lifetimes already. Samuel believes the newspapers, which continue to speak of the war being all over by Christmas, and so he is desperately keen to get there before everything is finished. Duncan has not said much one way or the other. He can be more sensitive and withdrawn, and perhaps he is more aware of his mother's fears. Both of them remind me of my brothers. I can well imagine that Albert and Edward have already enlisted. So too must have Graham if that is the case.

I feel that I should write to all of them, but each time I put pen to paper my throat closes up and I have no words with which to write. I haven't written to anyone since I left Grande Prairie. Would a letter from me seem like the insane ramblings of some colonial ghost?

AUGUST 10, 1914, CONTINUED

Lily Westby interrupted me as I was writing earlier. She came in haste to collect me—and perforce the children as well—as her mother was in need of help.

The Path to Kitty Islet

All is well now, at least for the time being. Mrs Westby had been feeling faint—very unlike her—and had sent Lily to fetch me. Turns out, Samuel had come home with his official papers, for he has volunteered for overseas duty, and ships out almost immediately. It was no wonder Mrs Westby was not herself.

Although Lily has a good head on her shoulders, she too is rather swept away by the romance of it all—men in uniform, fighting to protect Britain and her empire, travels to faraway places, and the overarching taste for excitement. All of that rhetoric numbs me. War is not something I have any knowledge of, but death has come to be an intimate comrade of mine; in fact, it has but lately left my immediate field of vision. The scars on my right hand still throb with a cold and bitter heat.

Once I arrived at Mrs Westby's, I made sure she was lying safely on her bed. Duncan had wisely escorted her to her room when her dizziness increased. I asked Lily to watch Eliza and Douglas while I made some strong tea. Samuel was concerned for his mother's well-being, but he was obviously pleased as punch with the fact that he was off on such a "nifty" adventure. To distract him from himself I asked him to fetch me a bottle of spirits from the sideboard. Once the tea was made, I added plenty of sugar and a dash of liquor. I told Samuel to keep quiet and stay out of the way for the time being, while I went upstairs.

Mrs Westby had mostly stopped shaking and she was no longer crying. As I approached, she looked at me somewhat ashamedly and managed a weak and watery smile.

"I'm sorry for the trouble," she said. "I'm afraid I don't have any real excuse. I just wish I could hold Samuel close on my lap as I did when he was little and never let him go."

I placed the tea on the bedside table and helped her sit up. I murmured some sort of comforting platitude, but was hardly aware of what I said. The words themselves matter little anyway, I have found; it is the tone and sense of company that prove of use.

We sat together, she and I, for quite a long time. Then Mrs Westby began speaking. She told me of her courtship, of the birth of her two boys, and the arrival of Lily. She told me all those mother facts and precious stored memories about Samuel and how he always worked so hard to catch up with—and then better—Duncan. How many times Samuel had injured himself in order to prove his physical prowess and agility took up much of Mrs Westby's recital, but, in the end, she finished with a sweet story of how he used to pick flowers for her on his way home from most of his crazy and daring exploits.

By this time, she had finished her tea and was clearly spent. I suggested that she have a rest, and then she would be ready to face the world and her son. She was so tired that she acquiesced immediately. I pulled the drapes and left her.

Downstairs, Lily was reading to Eliza in the front parlour. Douglas was fast asleep at their feet, his arms akimbo and fair hair dishevelled. My memories of him seem so sparse and insubstantial compared to Mrs Westby's of her sons. Yet I could not, and cannot, entertain the thought of dear little Douglas ever leaving me to become a soldier, especially not after already losing my John.

I left the two children in Lily's capable hands. I felt I needed air and a brisk walk. I'd walked for some time before I even knew where I was or was able to take in my surroundings. I'd gone south, then angled east through the forest just past the school, and had finally come out on McNeill Bay. On that side of the bay, there is a wee little half-island, still attached by a slim isthmus. I walked over to the islet, looking for a quiet niche in which to shelter. The sun was warm, but there was a cool breeze coming off the water as it often does. I found a comfortable rock and, not caring about my skirt, sat and looked to those mountains across the strait.

The Path to Kitty Islet

Why should solid masses of rock, inanimate and uncaring, provide such solace to the soul? Is it their very insensate obliviousness that makes them comforting? I feel as tiny as a pebble on the beach behind me. I will disappear, and all my fears and doubts will go with me long before those mountains change or erode. Instead of making me feel as if I am too small to matter, or that all is lost, or that nothing in my life or in the world is of any value, my mountains seem to give me permission to move beyond this moment. I don't know how else to put it. I do matter. But not so much that if my world looks dark, all is lost. There are other peaks to come. Different perspectives for me to see, and a new life for me to lead: a life I cannot wholly author, a life that will reflect both my choices and the implacable stillness of those timeless peaks.

AUGUST 1914
VICTORIA HARBOUR

I had very mixed feelings about today. However, I felt I should be there for Mrs Westby's sake. Perhaps things will go well and the war end before Christmas, as the papers all say.

Samuel never did let on how he arranged to be on the first ship out. He has a golden tongue, and he must have done some quick talking to get himself outfitted and through all the hoops in time. It really doesn't matter how he did it, though. It simply matters that he's gone.

Today we all, and much of Victoria, watched as the *Princess Sophia*, a CPR steamer, full to the brim with our young men, cast off and made her way to Europe. The crush of people on shore was tremendous. Flags were flying, women were crying, and children were at risk of being trampled. I kept Douglas in my arms and Duncan had Eliza on his shoulders, so she was safely out of harm's way.

Since that day when Samuel told his mother he had enlisted, Mrs Westby has never shown her fear or tears publicly again. Today was no different. She was composed and almost joyously proud. I have no idea how she managed to be so courageous. The papers continue to applaud the war and to trumpet the praises of our newly enlisted men, and Mr Westby takes it all to heart. He is proud of his son and would probably enlist himself, were he younger.

Duncan has been quiet. He has borne all Samuel's jibes and taunts with good grace, generally shrugging his shoulders or laughing lightly. Of course, Duncan's unflappability has only served to provoke Samuel, so his most recent comments have been quite mean and cutting. I will never be able to understand the rivalry that seems to exist among brothers. I do recall how Albert and Edward often aggravated each other, but I also remember how each rose to defend the other from any outside attack or slight.

We waved and shouted and sang ourselves hoarse as the *Sophia* cast off and rounded one of the points, moving out of sight. A number of people then made a mad dash to abandon their posts in front of the Empress Hotel and to make their way over to Beacon Hill or Ogden Point, and from there watch her steam away. I was thankful that the Westbys had determined not to attempt such a feat; my heart was already overwrought. We made our way quietly home.

When Duncan passed Eliza to me, once we reached Monterey Avenue, as St. George Street has now been named, he was quietly humming. I recognized the tune and felt as if someone were walking over my grave. Neither he nor I said a word, but, as I write this, the words continue to echo in my head:

> It's time to lay the sword and gun away
> There'd be no war today,

The Path to Kitty Islet

If fathers all would say,
I didn't raise my son to be a soldier.

APRIL 6, 1917
OAK BAY

War has wreaked havoc with our lives. We, who live so far away from all the horrors and realities, are still affected in ways none of us can fully comprehend yet. I have been unable to write in this diary; in part, because the litany of loss and deprivation for those in the Old Country is at times overwhelming, but primarily due to my own fatigue. When it is night and my duties complete—or at least complete enough—I sleep. We have all taken on more. There is work, the children, and all of the volunteer war efforts. It is likely though that our physical exhaustion is something for which to be grateful.

Today, America has declared war on Germany. The Allies have been waiting for so long to hear those words. The war has not gone well for our side, and the losses have been immeasurable.

Here, in this small corner of the Empire, we have been lucky. Though there are rations and hardships and talk of conscription, we continue to live a life forgotten by our soldiers in France. Many families have suffered great personal tragedies, however. The dreaded telegrams offer no comfort when they are received, no matter how many times one reads the terse words. Death far away, death right in front of one—both are impossible to accept.

As far as we know, Samuel Westby continues to be lucky, if lucky means that he is still alive and floundering in the mud of Ypres in northern France. His letters are sporadic at best, and, reading between the lines, one can sense his utter despair.

At my hearth and in my heart, I am fortunate. Eliza will be six this August and dear Douglas will be five in early June. They know of the war, for it is all around us—in the airwaves from the radios, plastered on posters, on the minds of us all—but their innocence and enthusiasm for life counteract its insidious presence in our lives. Eliza has been at school this year and she has made many friends at Monterey Elementary. She can read most simple words and is becoming quite adept at printing. It touches me more than I can express to see her dear ringlets pouring over her left shoulder as she laboriously composes a letter to send to "Uncle" Samuel. Douglas is most often my shadow. As soon as I come back from work, he accosts me with a ferocious leg hug and a barrage of stories about his day.

I should also introduce Agatha. She has taken up residence with us. The extra bedroom and small sitting room have become hers, as has part of Douglas's heart. She is an interesting woman who, as I do now, expected to face the rest of her life alone. However, in 1915, she met and fell in love with Thomas. She tells me that even old "schoolmarm spinsters" can blush like teenagers and see fireworks when they meet the man they know they'll marry. They were married in early 1916, and, in consequence, Agatha was made to give up her teaching position.

Thomas though, after living a Spartan bachelor existence for years, has a tidy nest egg put aside. He has promised her that they will build their very own home when he returns from the Front. In the meantime, he didn't want her to live alone, so, as his family knows the Westbys, Agatha was quickly ensconced with us. She has become a godsend and we, in our turn, especially Douglas, have ensured that she has very little time to fret about her husband's safety—at least not during the daylight hours.

Although she is older than me, she is more important to me as a friend than she will ever know. She is quietly capable and never really asks me any searching questions about my past. The irony, of course, is that her not asking often leads me to disclose more than I am even aware. I believe I could trust her and feel certain that she would always honour our friendship and any confidences

The Path to Kitty Islet

I made. But trust is a shy thing with me now. My trust is as bold and skittish as the deer I see sometimes near Anderson Hill—full of natural bravery, but one wrong move makes them melt away into the underbrush as though they had never been standing in front of one. It has been years since I trusted my whole self to anyone, and it is a burden carrying it alone. But if I make a mistake, or if the one I trust even unintentionally betrays me, all will be lost.

I believe my original resolution must stand. I cannot risk losing all that I staked my life on. I must soldier on, as bravely as possible, on my own. I can trust Agatha with much, and I am grateful for that.

With the advent of Agatha as a boarder, permanent helper, and friend, I have been able to increase my hours at Spencer's department store. David Spencer is a strict but fair employer, and I have surprisingly enjoyed the work. I have worked in several areas of the store and find that I am a quick study. It has been an eye-opening experience, earning a paycheque and realizing that I am capable of much more than I ever dreamt. It sounds almost presumptuous or arrogant to say, but I am proud of myself—and slightly amazed too. Long days on my feet do leave me feeling quite tired—though never as exhausted as our boys at the front.

When I am all ready for work with my hat on and coat bundled up, I look in the hall mirror and wonder at myself. I appear so grown up and knowledgeable. Of course, I know how very lost and vulnerable I actually feel at times. Some mornings, a tiny, niggling voice pipes up inside me. It says that everyone, at all ages, feels just as lost and confused and afraid. It goes further and points to those boys in Europe, "on a darkling plain / Swept with confused alarms of struggle and flight / Where ignorant armies clash by night." I think that's how Arnold's "Dover Beach" goes. Agatha has been a teacher to me too, not just to Eliza and Douglas. When neither she nor I can sleep, she pulls out one of her favourite anthologies and we puzzle through poems together. She is, of course, better at it than I am, but I do enjoy it—and I am learning! Perhaps all adulthood is a façade. At worst, it may even be some perverse kind of farce.

My job at Spencer's, though, allows me to keep up my end of appearing adult better than anything else I have done, except raising the children, which is still an ongoing process. I earn enough, with Agatha's contributions, that I can support our household and even save a little by and by. In an odd way, rations make it easier to economize, and my mediocre cooking repertoire is easily blamed on what one could not buy at the store for love nor money.

There too, Agatha has proven to be worth her weight in golden butter; she is able to shop and stretch our budget in ways that amaze me. She is also helping me learn how to run the house more efficiently. I believe that, at first, she was afraid of hurting my feelings or belittling me somehow, but she is such a gracious person that I have never felt pushed aside. On the contrary, I feel that we are almost like siblings, and I have been relieved to be the youngest. Agatha has become my anchor. In the midst of all the turmoil in the world and in my past, I have found a safe harbour and a firm friend.

JUNE 1917
OAK BAY

Thad has just left. It is evening and the children are both at the Westby home, no doubt tormenting Lily. Agatha was here when her brother arrived, but she departed, not so very discreetly, almost as soon as he had arrived. Thus, Thad and I were alone.

I was certain that he could hear my blood singing in my veins. It was so loud in my ears that I almost could not hear his dear, melodic voice. He has become so precious and I have been such a fool.

The Path to Kitty Islet

I must explain. Thad, Thaddeus Cosgrove, is Agatha's younger brother. He's eight, no seven, years my senior. He's a local doctor and has become a regular visitor to our home. At first, I convinced myself that he came solely to see his sister, and perhaps the children, but soon even I could see he spent as much time talking to me as speaking with Agatha or the young ones. And it made my heart fly—with fear and hope. He is so kind, so like Agatha, and yet he is so much more to me. He has this way of speaking to one, in a low, intense manner, while his head is tilted to one side and his shock of blonde, almost white, hair tumbles over his right eye. So often I have wanted to reach out and gently brush it back, stroking my fingertip along his temple. So often.

And then this evening. He and Agatha had obviously been plotting. It warms my heart to realize that she must have approved, but what will she think of me now? Once she'd left, Thad suggested we sit out on the porch and watch the last of the sun. My nerves were jangling as if I were the Victoria telegraph office. I could almost taste the moment in the warmth of the evening breeze.

Thad sat closer to me than usual. Soon he had taken my hand in his. I did not, could not, resist. Those slender and strong fingers caressed my skin. He held my hand so gently in his right hand and touched me so softly with his left. It was almost unbearable. And it was not enough. I wanted—oh, I don't even know how to express what it is I wanted. More.

He began speaking, head tilted as usual. He loves me. He was asking permission to court me. He was asking me since, of course, my father is nowhere to be seen. He loves my stubbornness; he loves my independence. He loves me. I hung onto that fiercely, but the world was spinning so quickly and my blood was singing so loudly, so sweetly, that I could not speak. Like a dolt, I sat there, tears in my eyes, unable to move a single muscle. His eyes never left my face and I do not know what it was that he saw there or what it was that he thought he saw.

Suddenly, he sprang up, pacing, speaking quickly, saying he'd been a fool. Saying no woman would ever want to marry a man who had refused to go to war, who had refused to defend King and country. He blathered on at some length and still, idiot that I am I said nothing. I wanted to laugh, to shout for joy, to accept, to tell him to be quiet and to stop being ridiculous, but I couldn't.

Finally, I managed to choke out that I couldn't court him—that of course I cared for him deeply—more deeply than he'd ever know, but I was afraid that I just couldn't. He looked at me wordlessly. I don't know whether he really understood any of what I said, but before I could add anything else, he was gone. And I? Well, I was the fool on the porch with dread in her heart, weights on her lips, and a lock on her voice. I did not call him back. I did not run after him. Have I ruined everything?

I need to think. Firstly, Thad is completely wrong about me. I do not care at all that he is such an ardent pacifist, except for the fact that it means he will not voluntarily leave us to go and fight in those terrible trenches. But his pacifism has obviously cost him and pained him more than I think even Agatha suspected. But what of my own reaction—my inability to let him woo me? I believe I love him. My heart lifts up when he is near; my spirit sings when he is in my thoughts. But my scars are throbbing.

I am such a bundle of contradictions. My whole heart wants to hold him close and never let go. My whole head is afraid. Can love exist in my life? Love between a man and a woman, after all the other choices that I have made? And what of the children? Thad loves them too, I know, and he would be a truly wonderful father—but they are mine. Is it possible for me to let them go, even that much?

Perhaps it is all moot now, anyway. The foolish widow on her front porch, frozen in time, yet burning with a desire she can't express or let loose. I am a fool. A cold and lonely fool.

JULY 1917
OAK BAY

Thad and I seem to have developed an unspoken understanding. We're both being careful with each other, and things are not as they were. However, nor are things so terrible; time may eventually enable us to move closer again. Agatha and I had a very forthright conversation in which I implored her to tell Thad that his pacifism in no way distresses me. Of course, then she begged to know the reason behind my unwillingness to agree to be courted by Thad, and I could not explain.

How could I, when I can barely understand my fears myself? I am not the woman either think me; I am also so full of doubts and fears and downright foolishness, how could I be loved by such a wonderful and open man as Thad? And yet I cannot deny my feelings for him, and I know that Agatha perceives them in my manner and in my face. I believe this is why she finds the whole situation so odd. On the one hand, her brother is angered and hurt because of my rejection of him, and, on the other, her friend is quiet and downcast because of her refusal to tell Thad about her feelings. It is no wonder Agatha shrugs her shoulders so often and so bewilderedly.

But Thad and I have developed a careful truce. He still visits fairly often, and I welcome him as warmly as ever. Eliza adores him and always prattles on about some "new" discovery she has made—a snapping beetle, a double-headed foxglove, a nest of kittens. It was foolish of me to even wonder for a moment about the children's response: they would be overjoyed.

But it is impossible for Thad to know me, not the real heart of me. And I do not know if his love for what he can see and what he thinks he knows is enough. I don't know if it would be fair to him, given the aspects of myself tucked so carefully away inside me that even I have forgotten where I have hidden them. Clearly, others have their own secrets too; witness Thad's reaction when he thought I'd refused him because he refuses to enlist! And yet I do know I have more hidden than my fair sex ought. Can two people come together, become married, and yet be the keepers of deep secrets? Is it possible?

SEPTEMBER 1917
OAK BAY

Today my wee man trod bravely, and defiantly, off to school, refusing to hold Eliza's hand and refusing to allow either Agatha or me to accompany them. I can't believe how old he is now; he's grown so much in the years we've been here. As far as I can determine, he has absolutely no memory of Grande Prairie. Eliza tells me she only vaguely remembers the sea of grass and flowers growing on the roof. Memories can be gifts, but I am glad that time has wiped the horror of the fire from their minds; that memory is not one they need to keep.

I was home when Douglas returned from school. His eyes were big as saucers, and his tongue kept tripping over itself in its haste to tell me everything, all at once, and emphatically. He thoroughly enjoyed being a "real student" and can't believe he's had to wait so long to go! Eliza's report too was happy and positive; she's met a new friend and adores her teacher already.

And so both have set sail on a new adventure. I am proud of them, but also feel a sense of loss. They will need me less and less as time goes on, yet I suspect I will need them more and more—one of the ironies of life that is supposed to make us smile wryly, I presume. I wonder how many parents feel this?

DECEMBER 1918
OAK BAY

It is almost Christmas. I have neglected this diary terribly for over a year. Life needs time for living, and I haven't made time for recording what's happened.

The Great War is over. The Allies defeated the Germans, and peace was declared on November 11th of this year. I think the world has forgotten what peace means, and so we are all stumbling about in this dream world where the violence has stopped, but its imprint and shadow reign supreme.

Samuel Westby is still alive. He is in England, at a hospital near London, recuperating from injuries he suffered when the tunnel he was working in collapsed. He is not sure when he will be able to get transport home, but he is alive. Duncan, his brother, was finally conscripted in late 1917. Fortunately, he never made it off Canadian soil, so he has been home for weeks.

Samuel spends much of his time in hospital writing letters. He writes to his parents, and, rather surprisingly when I think of what he was like before he left, he also writes to me. Today, after having read his most recent letter, I dropped it on my lap as I sat lost in a reverie. I feel such a sense of guilt; I should have been there in England during the war too. I should have been there with my father, my brothers and my sister, yet I was not. My home in this faraway land is intact, and my quiet neighbourhood sleepily prepares itself for a peaceful Christmastime. I cannot begin to imagine the losses Samuel describes; yet I can feel some of the pain only too well.

Once again I feel torn. Part of me yearns to go back. Perhaps I could help rebuild my birth country's peace. Perhaps I could comfort the wounded—and find both my brothers and Emily's amongst all those other young men. I wonder about Edward and—I pull my thoughts back. I cannot go to that dark place of loss again.

In the midst of this reverie Eliza tugged on my hand. She had carefully read the pages that had dropped to my lap, and I had been so blindly caught up in my imaginings that I hadn't felt her presence. When she touched me I startled and let out a slight yelp. The poor thing thought she had somehow hurt me physically and was immediately contrite. However, she still had questions and, Eliza being Eliza, nothing would deter her from asking.

She demanded to know why I was crying, especially since Samuel had spent much of the letter repeating, "Everyone is doing quite well under the circumstances." I admit I hadn't even realized that I had been weeping. Soon enough, though, my Eliza had me giggling, for she was also determined to discover if one could get "over" the circumstances. Such a funny egg she can be! A bright, inquisitive seven-year-old whom I love more than I ever thought possible.

It was foolish of me to even contemplate returning to London; my life doesn't exist there any longer, and never could again. Someone would realize how different I was and that realization could change everything, destroy everything. But the heart is such a contrary thing; it so often wants the exact thing that the head knows is impossible. Part of me yearns for England, but the voices of Eliza and Douglas are louder, more present, and that is really what recalls me to my own self.

They need me and they need to stay here in this safe, new country with all its wonders and wide-open spaces and hearts. I think the Old Country would stifle something in all of us. Something intangible, but important.

The Path to Kitty Islet

DECEMBER 25, 1918
OAK BAY

Christmas truly is a season of joy—and miracles. The world has been given peace, at long last and at an incredibly high price, and I have been given my own second chance.

This past year has been one of many awkward moments between Thad and me. Agatha continued to be my stalwart supporter even as she did not understand my inability to let Thad court me. After a while, Thad ceased his fairly regular visits, preferring to meet Agatha in the village or downtown. And then one day, Lily let slip that Thad had started courting another woman, the daughter of a doctor with whom he worked. I called myself a thousand kinds of fool for letting it get so far, for refusing his love, and for minding so deeply now that he'd found someone else to receive his attentions.

The children still saw Thad occasionally through Agatha, but they too seemed to be pining for him in their own way. Douglas spent many an afternoon at a friend's house, desperately drawn to a house full of four boys—his friend being the youngest—despite the tormenting he and his friend endured at the hands of the older boys. Some days, he would return home covered in mud and bramble cuts from head to toe. When questioned sternly, he would own that he and his little friend had been made to pretend to be Germans and had been forced to crawl across the "trenches" on their stomachs and surrender to the Allies. Eliza began to create elaborate imaginary games; her entire half of the room has become a new country, where she is alternately the Princess of Evil or Queen Peace. These games worried and intrigued me; clearly, both the children were working through elements of the times in which we live, and yet I sometimes felt a frisson of fear as I heard them describe their play. It was so full of darkness. Do they remember other dark times?

It was at moments like that that I missed Thad the most, not just for myself, but also for the children.

May arrived. And Thad returned. Lily had no real information to pass on, other than the fact that the doctor's daughter had plans to go to nursing school in Vancouver, or perhaps even back east, the school here being "too confining." Did I even care what the gossip was? Yes, I admit that I did want to know. I also didn't want to jinx my renewed luck.

As I mentioned earlier, there were many awkward moments between us. One or the other would catch the other staring a little too directly or focused in a lingering way on lip, hand, or brow. The attraction we had first felt so many moons ago had not altered, nor even really diminished. I, however, remained wary. Physical, even intellectual, attraction is one thing; emotional honesty is quite another. And I had not figured out a way to both appease my conscience and follow my desire.

Agatha, however, had clearly decided that she would break our stalemate. Her dear Thomas Arundel was wounded in April 1918 and began a long period of convalescence in an English hospital. All the energy she would have so loved to devote to his nursing and care, but could not because of all the distance between them, was directed to "nursing" my feelings for Thad, and Thad's for me. She is a very determined woman is Agatha, and I do not think either Thad or I could have escaped her ministrations, even had we wanted to. And, truth be told, I no longer wanted to.

Our matchmaker made sure that we two were thrown together at every opportunity, even on the odd occasion when no real opportunity existed! In fact, one bright August day, Thad came in his automobile to take the children and me out to Cordova Bay for a change of scenery and to visit some local farms. Agatha, however, had other plans: she managed to have both children invited to separate birthday parties "at the last minute." So there we were, Thad and I, with a huge picnic lunch packed and no children to take! We both asked Agatha to come with us, but she too had a mysterious last-minute invitation (ha!). There was nothing for it but to go on our way ourselves.

It was a bit awkward at times, but it was also a very lovely day. Thad is such an easy conversationalist; one can speak to him about any subject. He is also just as happy to be silent and, as the day went on, our silences became more and more natural. We found a lovely spot to picnic, and waded about in the water after eating our fill. The water was shockingly cold and Thad took my hand. We were wading, and footing was treacherous, so it seemed the most natural thing in the world for him to do.

I believe that was our new beginning. While Thad had been coming over again much more often to spend time with Agatha and the children, he also started spending time just with me. I encouraged him to; I won't deny it. The ache in my heart, which had never gone away after I had refused him, was finally beginning to dull and slowly disappear with his renewed attentions. I still didn't know how to reconcile what my heart wanted with the life my head knew I must lead. It has taken me all these many months and uncountable chats with Agatha to find a compromise.

I finally admitted to Agatha that Harry had been terribly unpredictable, with dark, black moods and that sometimes—sometimes, he was improperly violent toward me. I admitted that I was afraid to contact my family, or Harry's family, or even Emily's family, for fear that the truth would come out. Above all else, of course, I don't want the children to know about this facet of their father.

Once I'd managed to say that, I found it much easier to tell Agatha of my concern that there are parts of me, aspects of my past, that I have chosen not to dwell on or think about. Yet I know that they colour the woman I have become. How could I enter into a marriage—with a man as sensitive and perceptive as Thad—and know that I could not be open in the way that I might wish, and in the way that he so deserves?

Thus, the story of my truth came out at last. Though Agatha will never know all—indeed, I suspect none of us ever knows all, even of our own stories—Agatha has heard enough now to understand my silence of 1917 and to understand my careful enthusiasm toward her brother this year.

I do not know what Agatha told Thad. I only know that, after our summer picnic and our other times alone, we seemed to reach a new kind of agreement, albeit an unspoken one. Our hands seemed to touch each other of their own accord, and, often, our eyes met and twinkled more and more frequently. And finally, today dawned.

It was Christmas morning and the children were up early, elation in their voices as they saw the presents placed carefully beneath our tree. Agatha and I could not have slept any longer even had we wanted to, but to ensure our wakefulness the children visited each of us, treating us to several excited bounces on our beds and precise details of the sizes and shapes of the presents they had seen, spoken of in awe-filled tones. Of course, we were also both eager ourselves to watch the children open their gifts.

They opened up their stockings, delighted to find nuts, a special orange, and a few candy sticks waiting inside. We had a quick breakfast and then retired to the front sitting room, where the children could hardly contain their excitement. One by one I doled out the presents, and we all opened ours carefully being sure to save the brown wrapping paper and string to be used again. My job at Spencer's has given me the means to provide a few extras at times like these. Both of the children received books—two each—new clothes—they do continue to grow like weeds!—and one toy. Eliza has long had her eye on a wooden penguin with "walking" feet, while Douglas was desperate for a spinning top. The children were ecstatic to receive them.

Dear Agatha gave me a lovely bound volume of poems, and the Westbys had found an absolutely lovely shirtwaist dress that looked to be a perfect fit. I was feeling positively spoiled. Then Eliza found one more small package. "Open it! Open it!" chanted the children. The box was quite small, about the size of my fist, yet there was nothing inside except a folded piece of paper. With a growing sense of wonder, I opened it up. It simply said, "Open your door." Now my heart was knocking, somewhere down at the level of my knees! The children clamoured for me to "Hurry! Hurry!" and seemed to have some knowledge of what was to come. They leapt up, we all trooped down our short hall, and I opened the front door. As I did, a chill rush of air came in, followed by the sound of a small soft, "meow."

There on the porch, in a covered basket with the lid slightly ajar, was a lovely kitten. It was not tiny, but rather seemed to be more of an adolescent. And, leaning up against the rail, was Thad. He definitely looked like the cat that'd swallowed the canary, with his smug grin and self-satisfied air. Was I glad to receive such a gift from Thad? Of course! Honestly, I was as excited as the children and, more importantly, I knew I had been forgiven at last for my earlier stupidity.

We still have not settled on a name for our new cat, but I am sure something will come. Meanwhile, the children, Agatha, Thad, and the Westbys have spent the day suggesting all manner of weird and wonderful names. I do hope something strikes a chord soon, or we will all go mad!

We spent the afternoon and evening at the Westbys—Agatha and Thad too—and had a splendid Christmas meal. The children were full of high spirits and cajoled us into playing numerous parlour games, ending with an uproarious round of charades. It was truly a miraculous day.

I feel very blessed. And for the first time in forever, it seems, I have a real sense of hope for what may await me in the new year.

JUNE 1919
OAK BAY

Since the war ended, it seems as if time has sped up. Days fly by, and slowly the darkness and grief of all the losses of war become memories instead of living and breathing wraiths dogging our every step. The children do not play at war so often now—it has been a relief to watch them invent new games, to read with enthusiasm, and to become innocent anew.

Samuel Westby has come home. He will still need time to convalesce, both physically and mentally. Nevertheless, his mother, Colleen, is so thankful that he was returned to her relatively unscathed. Ironically, there is guilt too—so many other mothers lost their precious sons and will never hold their dear boys again.

I often go and sit with Samuel in the long evenings. He is not the same young man who was so eager to be part of the "grand adventure." He is, however, the Samuel he shared with me in his letters from London. He has seen a darkness and experienced a terror of which I only have the barest understanding, and it makes him look at us with such sad and haunted eyes. He will not speak of much. Every so often he will mention a French town or a soldier he knew, but of the fighting and his injury he says nothing.

This evening, he turned suddenly to me and asked why the darkness touches me too, yet I don't seem to be afraid of it. I could not be evasive; it was one of those rare moments when only the truth would serve. It was so hard though, to know how best to answer, to know what he really wanted from me. I hesitated a bit and then said that I had lived in darkness, feared darkness, but had finally chosen light—light that was offered to me. So the darkness is always present, as it is my past and the foil for my new life. But it does not fill me, nor does it guide me any longer.

A very abstract and oblique answer, I know. Yet Samuel nodded slowly, and thanked me for being honest. I had been, even though I too had stayed miles away from details. Perhaps one day I will have the freedom and the strength to be specific. Perhaps Samuel will be someone whom I can wholly trust—for he too knows the reach and strength of the darkness—and the choices one makes in its shade.

SEPTEMBER 1920
OAK BAY

More than a year has passed since my last entry. Isn't it strange how, as one's life improves and becomes happier, one is much less inclined to find the time to record the whys and wherefores of one's contentment? I have become so lucky and so happy, I think I am almost afraid to describe my life for fear that speaking of it will make it all disappear. But this diary has also been a gift—of solace and comfort—and I feel I need to write down at least some of the joys too.

The children have started back to school once more. Eliza is now a winsome nine-year-old, by turns diligent and mature and then full of shrieking laughter and mischievous fun. How her big brown eyes light up when she's teasing any one of us or telling us a "fantastic" story that has "just come" to her. She has also begun to jot down some of her stories and "poetic thoughts"—all her words and phrases there. Thad feels that she takes after me. I do hope that her writings will give her as much pleasure and comfort as they have provided me over the years.

Perhaps because of her desire to write and her wonderful ability to imagine, Eliza came to me a few days ago and asked about the "sad lady." As she put it, "Remember when we lived in the sea of grass? Remember the sad lady who couldn't see any of us but looked through us as if we weren't even there?" Of course I remember. I felt a tingle of electricity run through me. I had believed, and hoped, that Eliza remembered nothing of those days. Her final question for me was: "If she didn't see us, Mama, what did she see?"

I have never intended to have to lie to the children, nor do I want to dwell on the tragedy of the fire. They deserve to know as much of the truth as they are ready to understand, so I answered her questions as honestly as I thought I could. I told her about Callie, our neighbour who had had such a difficult time after her pregnancy and had retreated into herself and her sadness. Eliza listened carefully, thoughtfully, and then told me that she wanted to write a story about where people go when we think they are daydreaming or deeply sad—"like Uncle Samuel," said my ever-empathetic girl. Eliza believes that the world they see is the world that is meant to be, and when they do come back, they will be ready to help us all find it here, in this world.

I can't even begin to express my amazement. Eliza is only nine. Yet she has developed her own philosophy about withdrawal and despair. Some children are not only given great gifts, they themselves are gifts to us.

Eight-year-old Douglas has not become a philosopher, at least not yet! He has, however, grown a tremendous amount over the past year and continues to love all the things of nature—animals, plants, and mud! His grey eyes are so suggestive too—they reflect his moods just as the ocean changes colour and texture, depending on the wind and the sky.

Sometimes he can be pensive and quiet, but he soon talks himself back into happiness and gets busy with a new project or game. He loves making things, and our yard is littered with driftwood, shells, fir cones, and other treasures he has collected. He is also firm friends with Martha, the cat that Thad gave us. Douglas and Martha have grand old conversations on our front porch as they contemplate the neighbourhood.

As for me, I am engaged to Thad. He is a very patient—and ever persistent—man. He has such a good heart, and the children love him. It is not fair, though, for me to put it as if my heart were not involved. I love him. I sincerely do. I think I have ever since I first met him. It is not the earthquake of feelings I once would have expected, maybe even preferred; rather it is a quiet depth of emotion and intense joy in his presence. I have wrestled for so long with the shadows of my past, wanting to be fair to Thad yet needing also to be true to myself and my profoundest dreams, and so I finally accepted his proposal.

Agatha no longer lives with us, now that her "dear Thomas" is back from the war. He built his bride her very own home, just as he'd promised, and I am thankful that it is within walking distance of our bungalow. Agatha and I have spent hours in conversation, always drinking tea, speaking of the honesty owed to one's spouse. As she has pointed out so many times, most of the soldiers who have returned, even if more or less physically unscathed, do not tell their wives about their experiences. It is a dark period of their existence, one that shattered their innocence and haunts their dreams, but they have the ability, by keeping silent, to ensure that it infects no one else. Agatha feels quite strongly that I can, in good faith, tell Thad next to nothing about my life on the prairie. She feels that he loves the woman I am now and needs not necessarily know who or what I was before we first met.

I believe her. Though there is some part of me that wishes I could unburden myself completely, I have become too independent to feel that way for long. And perhaps one of the secrets to a good marriage is to keep some of yourself to yourself. That way, your husband will never feel as if there is nothing left to discover—and you will still be yourself and not only Mrs So-and-So.

We will be married in November of next year, in part because Thad has a study leave coming and wants to go back east to Toronto, to work with some of the doctors there. They have new methodologies and ideas, and Thad feels it is time for him to improve his skills. I think his pacifism during the war, though very sincere, still plastered over a very real desire on his part to join in the adventure—to see more of the world, to meet new people, to learn new things. War was not his theatre, however. This study leave will be just the thing. I am sure we will all be the better for it, especially his patients.

I am selfishly glad about the prolonged engagement. Much though I love him, it will be an adjustment for me—and for the children. But it is their love and trust, in part, that has given me the strength to do what I had believed impossible.

I imagine that once we are married, memory will shift once again, and I won't be able to recall, precisely, how it was when we were just three. I think that is one of the gifts of memory—how it shimmers and changes once your circumstances change. However, it is also one of the saddest things about us, for we lose the taste and tangibleness of what was good in our past all too easily; yet what was bad too often lingers on, casting a spell on our future.

The children are very pleased with our plans. Eliza has a strong wish for a very large wedding, something more fit for a princess, I'm afraid. Douglas is pleased that Thad will soon be able to sleep over just as his small friends do. Thad seems to want whatever kind of wedding I want, but I'm really not sure. I believe we are both too old—and too miserly—to have a wedding with all the frills and finery. Yet it will also be an important day for all of us, and I do want to mark it as ours—and create a memory that will not fade quickly into the merest whisper all too soon.

The wedding is still over a year away and already I'm fussing about the day itself. I suppose my worry shows my true feelings, no matter what I think I should feel or do. I love Thad and am very proud and pleased that he has asked me to be his wife, especially because I thought I had lost him. And I want society to know that we are married. I do not want any of the local mothers or their daughters to miss the news: there I have said it! Dr Thaddeus Cosgrove will no longer be an eligible and handsome bachelor. He will be mine and I his.

NOVEMBER 1921
OAK BAY

Thad and I are married! It is hard to fathom, both because it is so wonderful and because there were times when I thought it would never happen.

In the end, Thad asked the minister to come to the Westbys. We had only a few guests, and chose not to have too much of a fuss made. Thad's parents were there, and Agatha and Thomas, of course, and the Westbys, and the children. I asked a few of the women from Spencer's and one or two of the neighbours. Thad had a couple of childhood friends come, and a few of the local doctors. Ourselves included, we had a party of thirty or so. The wedding was in the late afternoon, after the day had drawn in. We were married in their large drawing room, in front of a twinkling fire and surrounded by boughs of fir. I did wear white, though I agonized over the decision. I decided to wear white for Thad.

It was a beautiful and very simple ceremony. Thad is handsome, but he is not the "knight" of whom I used to dream; he is ever so much more. And, best of all, he is real. Eliza and Douglas are both very pleased. Eliza was my flower girl of course, and Douglas was the "keeper of the ring" for Thad. They both looked so solemn, so enthusiastic, and so focused on making sure the wedding took place "as it should"—as the Westbys and Agatha kept commenting.

Thad had another trick up his sleeve to add to my happiness. We had determined to spend our first night in the bungalow—the children were to stay at the Westbys'—and take a few days for a honeymoon in the spring or summer, when the weather is better and more predictable. I had no idea that Thad had added to the plan—but he had—he bought the bungalow! He and the Westbys had been scheming, and now our home is truly his too.

I owe a debt of gratitude to someone. I have been given much more than I once thought I would ever experience in life. I am thankful, deeply thankful, and say my prayers more honestly than I have for years. I know I sound maudlin, but I'm almost scared by the depth of my happiness.

And nothing marred it, not even our actual wedding night. The last time I was with a man was another lifetime ago and so I was very jittery about it. Thad is a wonderfully kind and patient man, but still, he and I both had our own expectations. I was concerned that my body would betray me, but I needn't have worried at all. The body knows how to respond to true gentleness, all by itself. Thad was kind and generous. He appreciated my shyness, even if he didn't fully understand it. He didn't mind that we kept the lights off or that I kept some of my clothes on. He even didn't mind that I left much of that first time up to him; I felt so paralyzed by my past that I could hardly respond in any coherent way. Really, we both seemed to be complete novices, despite his medical training and my first marriage.

And then—and then—it was like a starburst above me. I was free. My body was free, my mind was joyful, and I could love Thad in a way I have never loved anyone else. It was scary because it was different, and so much more than I had ever dared to imagine, even after all that had gone before.

DECEMBER 1921
OAK BAY

It's Christmas Eve. The entire household sleeps behind me. I'm sitting here, writing, and looking out the window, waiting for Father Christmas to arrive. I am tired so won't write long, but I'm also filled with excitement. Our first Christmas together, all as one family, is one to be savoured, written about, and remembered.

The Path to Kitty Islet

Martha, Thad's gift to me already three Christmases ago, is curled up on my lap, purring softly. She adores having Thad here always, and she loves to become his scarf when he sits in his very favourite high-backed armchair. She's a good companion to us all.

I struggled mightily trying to find a gift for Thad this year. I suppose I want so desperately to find just the right gift because I'm so wonderfully happy. I want to thank him, as he has done so much for me, for the children, and for our family. I finally settled on a beautiful, proper doorknocker. Not very romantic I know, but it is very ornate and richly symbolic. I chose one with intertwined leaves and animals lovingly carved. And I wrote on the card, "So that others may easily knock at our house, filled with love." I feel certain he will like it.

Merry Christmas, world. God bless.

SPRING 1922
OAK BAY

The crocuses have long been up and the early flowering trees are already pink. What an enchanted isle we inhabit! Thad is bound and determined to make our garden a true showplace—he has been busy drawing up plans, planting bulbs, and reading as much as he can about horticulture.

No matter how exhausted he is when he comes home from his medical duties, he always makes time to listen to the children and to me. Only then does he make time for himself—and the garden. He literally uncoils as he does this, and I can see his cares and concerns lessen as he putters about or learns about plant propagation by way of cuttings or by seed. Agatha and I always did our best to keep the garden as tidy as possible, though we weren't exactly helped by Douglas's penchant for collecting driftwood, sea stones, and whatever else caught his fancy, but I think Thad is going to give it new life. He too has put down roots in this house and we are all growing together.

Now when I go to sleep, I'm no longer alone. I drift off listening to the deep resonance of Thad's heartbeat and smelling the faint scent of spring coming in through our slightly open bedroom window.

MAY 1922
OAK BAY

One of the Westbys' cousins used to work with the legendary Jennie Butchart. He and his father even lived out at the location of the cement factory at one point. His father is a well-known landscape architect back east, and William Westby is making a name for himself in the same field. Thad has been itching to get out to see Mrs Butchart's spectacular gardens and has been hoping to go with William, since he's one of her key gardeners. William has finally found a day that both he and Thad are free, and he has promised Thad a visit with Jennie as well. Thad is very pleased. He has asked me to accompany them, and though I know very little about gardening there's no one in our fair city who has not heard of Robert and Jennie Butchart and their beautiful gardens. I am very curious to meet Mrs Butchart and to see the way she has sculptured the landscape to make the old, ugly quarry so incredibly beautiful.

MAY 1922
OAK BAY

Thad and I have just returned from "Benvenuto," the Butcharts' beautiful property. It is truly a showplace estate now. William accompanied us as planned, and Thad was so happy all the afternoon. He has been working too hard lately and he needed a distraction. This trip up the Saanich Peninsula was just the thing. William Westby knows Mrs Butchart well, of course, the two of them conferring together—along with his father—over

The Path to Kitty Islet

the plans for the garden in the old quarry and then making them come to life. He had rung her in advance, so she knew to expect us. William knew just where to find her when we arrived, and she came with us as we toured the grounds.

Listening to Mrs Butchart describe how she used a bosun's chair to hang over the cliff walls of the quarry made me truly dizzy; however, the results are spectacular. In less than two decades she has managed to make what used to be a tremendous scar on the land into a fantastic garden. She feels happy with the results now and has no other plans for her "Sunken Garden." An apt name, for after looking out over the deep quarry, one descends a shallow stepped staircase and walks along inside the sunken part. There is one large "island" of hard rock, which provides another lookout and also provides a focal point as one descends from above. There are beds and beds of brightly coloured spring flowers—"brightness rampant," as Thad kept repeating.

He was just like an eager boy, asking all kinds of questions about frost, companion planting, and fertilization. I didn't listen to half of what they said, preferring instead to hang back and walk at my own pace, and watch. I caught my first real glimpse of Thad, the child, today. I'll have to ask Agatha about my impressions and see if they match up with her memories.

William was a kind companion too, alternately keeping me company and joining in with their horticultural excitement. Though I have met him a few times over at the Westbys, I had never really spent any amount of time with him, and was delighted to discover yet another kindred spirit.

Mrs Butchart made us tea, another Benvenuto tradition. She served us herself, as she has so many others, strangers and acquaintances alike. I wouldn't have believed it had I not seen it with my own eyes, but there were well over a hundred other people there with us. The day was fine and lots of people had made the pilgrimage from Victoria, many with their own picnic lunches. Some spoke other languages, and had clearly come from regions abroad. We saw Mr Butchart accompanying small groups on little tours. I felt even luckier that we had Mrs Butchart to ourselves.

After our tea at the main house, she escorted us down through the Japanese garden, her "first garden," as she says. From her house and its garden, one looks out over a small cove and then out to the waters of Brentwood Bay itself—just lovely. There is a teahouse there too, but we had been so lucky as to have been Mrs Butchart's especial guests in her actual home. She had also showed us pictures of the quarry before she began her work. It seems almost incomprehensible that the gardens we visited started as such a stark, gaping pit. Mrs Butchart told us she is actually a chemist by trade, and I believe she has indeed practised some kind of alchemy here, magically transforming a base material into a new kind of gold. Amazing. Her determination forced beauty out of ugliness; her will made the difference.

Thad was very quiet this evening. Though I knew our afternoon adventure had pleased him and done him a world of good, I was surprised by his unusual silence. Thad has been extraordinarily busy in his practice and, as I mulled things over, I realized that there is likely something he isn't telling me. Once the children were settled in their room, I decided to approach him. He was sitting quietly in his favourite chair with Martha on his lap when I cleared my throat. I tried to ask him what was the matter, but at the last moment my courage failed me. Am I not keeping things from him too? It seems so unfair to demand to know all that is in his heart and mind when I am not willing to do the same. Although he waited for me to speak, I shook my head and quickly left the room.

The Path to Kitty Islet

JUNE 1922
OAK BAY

I am more positive than ever that Thad is hiding something from me. He comes home even later than usual, almost every night now, and is evasive about where he has been. He is more exhausted, and preoccupied. Though he clearly still tries to connect to the children, he spends very little time with them—they are often about to go to bed when he arrives home. I have noticed no real difference in his attitude toward me, though, leastways when he is here—he still tries to be sweet, attentive, and loving—but he seems to be here less and less. I am trying not to worry, not to imagine the worst, though frankly, I am not even sure what that might be. I cannot believe that Thad would ever betray our family, betray me, yet something is affecting him and keeping him from his home and his family.

I feel so caught. My natural desire is to speak to him, to ask questions, to demand answers, to put whatever it is out in the open, so that it no longer comes between us, as I am more and more afraid it is doing. But how on earth can I be so hypocritical? This is my own dear Thad, who has accepted me secrets and all. Is it not right that he has his own secrets, and that I grant him the same leeway he has given me?

Paradoxical or not, I do not want him to keep anything back. I feel that this preoccupation is like a noxious weed. It grows taller every day, and more of its tendrils wrap around us all. I know I have no right to complain. I know that. But I am sore beset by fear. Trusting Thad has been so difficult for me. It has taken years for me to be able to do so, and now, so soon after our marriage, I find that I am filled with doubts. I am angry at myself for having them, and equally angry at myself for feeling that I cannot act. I do not know what to do.

EARLY JULY 1922
OAK BAY

I woke up in the small hours of the morning and could not go back to sleep. I lay still for what seemed like forever, but one glance at the clock informed me I had been lying still for only twenty minutes. Those pre-dawn hours lend themselves to worrying and fretting, and I had given in to both of these useless activities too easily for sleep to return. I must have been fidgeting more than I realized, for suddenly Thad's hand reached for mine, and he squeezed it. With that, I burst into tears. He let me cry, stroking my back and holding me close. When I was done, he turned on the bedside lamp. It cast a lovely pool of pale pink light on his dear face, and he cupped my chin in his hands.

Before he could say anything, and before I lost my nerve again, I told him how much I love him; I told him that I love him unreservedly, for always, and that I am so grateful to him because he has never once pushed me to confide in him more than I am able, and he has always respected my reticence. I told him that I want him to know how much I value that, but also that I am willing to listen to anything, anything at all, that he wants to share with me. I mentioned that I do want to tell him more about my past, one day. I hadn't planned on saying that last part, but when I said it, I knew that it was true.

"Turns out, my dear Minnie, that there is something I need to tell you," he said. And then, at last, it all came tumbling out.

He told me that he has been called upon by Dr Sheret, a respected medical man here in the city, to participate in a secret and possibly very dangerous activity. Dr Sheret found out that a small group of mostly Oriental lepers have been quarantined away from all other Victorians by secret order of the government. These poor wretches have been virtually abandoned on a small island, which the government owns. Most residents of Victoria

The Path to Kitty Islet

aren't even aware of the lazaretto's existence, let alone its location—just off the Saanich Peninsula—or the number of lepers there. For years, these men have been left almost completely on their own as they wait to die. A supply ship drops off a few provisions—some food, clothing, gardening tools, and coffins—every three months, and there is some sort of resident caretaker. But really, these poor men are not being helped.

And that, of course, is where Dr Sheret and Thad came in.

Leprosy. It is a word we have all been taught to fear—even doctors. There is that Biblical story of the leper, and the disease remains mysterious in many ways. Though it has been proven not to be hereditary or a curse—as it was believed to be for centuries— its transmission is still complicated. It has been proven to be caused by bacteria, Thad tells me, but why some people fall prey and others do not is not understood. There is also no cure, though some doctors around the world are trying a variety of substances with varying success. Nothing seems to have provided any long-term hope for those who suffer so desperately from leprosy.

Thad is an excellent teacher. He explained all about the disease, methodically and carefully. For several months, he has been reading all that he can about leprosy and the theories of its origin and contagion. He said that Dr Sheret is not only a local expert on the subject, but it seems he is becoming a bit of a worldwide authority. Though he was not asked to do so by way of any official government request, Dr Sheret had been made to understand that if he were to take it upon himself to make his way to the D'Arcy Island leprosarium, no one would interfere with him or any of the treatments he saw fit to deliver. And Thad has been going with him.

I am so grateful that Thad has finally told me what has been filling his time and his mind for the last few months. On the other hand, leprosy is such a terribly frightening thing for him to be exposed to. Could the bacteria come home to the children, and to me too? It is a sobering thought. No wonder Thad has taken his time telling me. But I am reminded, also, of those Orientals we met with in Vancouver, and dear Mr Sing, who used to help me with my garden. They are a kind and gentle people, I believe. They deserve doctors and care. I cannot think how anyone could abandon them to a lonely death on a deserted island.

LATE JULY 1922
OAK BAY

The weather has been quite fine so far this summer and Eliza and Douglas are revelling in the freedom of long sunny days with no school. I have been busy as well, trying to improve my dressmaking skills in order to keep up with their growth spurts. Now that they're older, Eliza especially, they are getting a bit more discerning and the sewing is becoming more complicated. Dear Colleen Westby continues to be my able and amenable tutor; I like to think that I am a conscientious if not particularly brilliant pupil.

Thad and Dr Sheret continue with their "fishing" out near D'Arcy Island. The two of them regularly go out on the sea, where they spend hours attempting feats no other men or doctors have been able to accomplish. Both Thad and I feel some trepidation about his newfound hobby—how could we not?—yet I can see a new light in his eyes too, especially now that he has told me where he goes. I so appreciate and respect what he and Dr Sheret are doing, and am glad that Thad feels he has found a real outlet for his talents. Though I remain fearful of the implications, I can only support him in this endeavour. It was so very difficult for him during the war, since so many people did not understand or even condone his pacifism. But he is such an empathetic healer; he could not have served his king and country as a purveyor of death. He simply could not. But this he can do, and the light in his eyes is the same light a peaceable knight in shining armour would have had in his.

In order to assuage my fears, and his own, both doctors are being very careful. Before they come home they clean themselves very assiduously on board the boat and again at Dr Sheret's home. He has an outdoor shower of some sort—his house is on the waterfront at Ten Mile Point, so they use that first—and then Thad changes his clothes completely and comes home to us.

When he does return, he is so very present, and loving. Helping those poor souls on D'Arcy Island has done wonders for him. He has a renewed sense of purpose and says that he feels again the joy he found in research that he hasn't had an opportunity for since he qualified as a doctor. He is learning a lot from Dr Sheret, and his respect for the doctor seems to grow each time he returns from another "fishing" expedition.

Thad doesn't tell me too many details. He has found the lack of medical care given to these men quite disheartening and also finds it difficult to converse with them, as they only have a smattering of English. However, they are growing to trust both Dr Sheret and Thad and are finding ways to express their needs and fears. It is a slow process, and time is needed to help all parties—but time is what is lacking for some of the sufferers. Thad says a few of them are nearing the end of the disease cycle and will probably need the coffins that were dropped off last time by the supply ship.

I cannot imagine what it would be like to become less and less able to use my limbs; to watch as the disease not only disfigures, but also incapacitates me; all in the shadow of a coffin placed just outside the row house where I lived.

AUGUST 1922
OAK BAY

I am almost afraid to write down what I know to be true. I do not want to speak too soon, but I am so very happy that it is hard to contain myself. I must record it here, so that I do not shout it from the rooftops in a most unladylike manner. I am with child! Thad's child. I do not think Thad has realized it yet, but if he does not notice soon, I will tell him with great happiness. I know he will be extremely pleased. We have been hoping, ever since our marriage almost two years ago now, that this would come to pass. I am just so very happy. I have also been feeling absolutely wretched every afternoon. That is how I first realized, for the nausea and torpor come rising every day at teatime like clockwork, so I knew. As long as I have some well-sugared tea, a very plain biscuit, and then at least an hour's rest, I do not actually get sick—at least so far. Thad is usually at work at that time, so he hasn't seen the most obvious of my symptoms. I believe that Colleen has guessed, so I will speak to her soon. But I will tell Thad first!

—

Thad returned early today and came upon me napping. He was very concerned, his mind leaping to a very different source of my malady, until I was able to assure him that I have had other signs as well. He is so proud! His face is glowing, and he actually threw up his arms and bellowed with delight! My reserved Thad! I knew he would be pleased.

His first thought, though, did give me pause as well. Although he and Dr Sheret have taken every precaution it is very worrisome still, especially now that I am pregnant. Thad has assured me that my feeling so very sick this time is actually a good sign, and most likely means that I will have a very healthy baby. But I do wonder.

I suppose that one always does, whether it is an unnamed fear or a feeling that one can easily point to and identify. I simply must trust. I must give myself over to Thad's care and God's grace, and believe that the icy finger of fear will recede into nothingness as time goes by.

OCTOBER 1922
OAK BAY

As my father used to say, Douglas "has come a cropper." The poor boy was with friends and off on the streetcars for a bit of a Saturday adventure. I suppose they thought they were being daring and swashbuckling rather than heedless and foolhardy, but nonetheless Douglas fell off the back of the car and tumbled onto the tracks. Right in the heart of Oak Bay Avenue, in front of lots of spectators, including Thad! So there was no way around admitting his foolishness and accepting responsibility for breaking the rules. The conductor noticed immediately and stopped the car, but once he realized Douglas was really hurt and that his father had seen the whole episode, the conductor gave him only a brief talking to before going on his way.

Thad took Douglas to the Royal Jubilee Hospital, as he was pretty certain our boy had broken his arm. Sure enough it was broken in two places. Douglas is home now, tired and feeling rather sorry for himself; more so, I think, because he well knows he has no one else to blame for his predicament. At least it is his left arm; but still and all, it will be very awkward for a long time and he will not be able to play any more fall sports this year.

Other than that, we are all well. My pregnancy continues to be somewhat difficult. I have lots of fatigue and nausea. Thad assures me that every pregnancy is different, and even though I have never felt like this before it in no way means that anything is wrong. I must admit that though I feel a faint, far-off fog of concern, in the deepest part of myself I feel that all is well, and that this baby will be healthy.

Eliza has settled into another year of school quite handily. She gives me such help now, especially in the afternoons, when my fatigue and nausea are at their height. As soon as she returns from school, she checks in on me and makes certain I have had my tea and biscuit and am resting. Thad jokingly calls her the "little mother," and her chest swells with pride every time he does so.

I am blessed. We all are, even if Douglas is feeling a little less blessed than usual.

APRIL 5, 1923
OAK BAY

My baby daughter is fast asleep. Nurse has put her feet up and is having a catnap too. I am taking advantage of her closed eyes to write. She is an excellent nurse, friendly and capable, and absolutely certain that writing is too tiring for a new mother. But I must write about my baby, for she is here and healthy. She has taken her place in our home and our hearts as if she had been with us always.

She was born four days ago, on April 1st. She is a dream child so far. The birth wasn't too bad, though I think Thad found it more difficult than I. The attending doctor wouldn't let Thad help much, which was probably just as well. It is a different experience when it is your own wife and child than when it is simply another patient. I was very tired at the end and needed some help to actually deliver her to this world. Once she arrived, though, she let everyone know. She has very strong lungs and a lusty yell. She is also quite slender, but very long. I think she will be tall. She has whorls of reddish-gold hair all over her head and deep ocean-blue eyes. She has long, slim fingers and moves them almost unconsciously, as if she is trying to catch butterflies. She is beautiful. And I am her mother. Thad is so very relieved—and happy. All is well. And soon, we will choose a name, I hope. I need to know her better first, though. My girl; I feel so lucky.

SEPTEMBER 1923
OAK BAY

Our family seems so complete now. Another school year has started and we were able to enrol both Eliza and Douglas as Eliza and Douglas Cosgrove. Thad has officially adopted them, not just relying on our marriage to make them his. The children were in absolute accord and seem very pleased—especially since it means they have moved up the alphabet for roll call and team selection too; as Douglas put it, "It is so very nice to be a high C rather than a lowly W!"

Georgina Anne Cosgrove—for that is what we finally settled on, as a name for our wee girl—remains an utter delight. She is five months old now, and mostly sleeps through the night. She loves to be naked, so I am afraid of what the colder weather will mean—until now, she has spent so much of her young life lying on a blanket in the dappled shade of our backyard, alternately being entertained by her siblings or cooing at the birds in the trees above.

Thad and Dr Sheret have continued their work on D'Arcy Island. It is much easier to get out there regularly during the summer, when the weather is better and storms are fewer. They had to curtail their visits last winter, and Thad felt the lepers really suffered for it. The caretaker there keeps himself to himself and, as Dr Sheret was promised, all the authorities have turned a blind eye to his and Thad's visits. There have been several deaths in the sixteen months since Thad and Dr Sheret began their activity, but at least they have been able to ease some of the pain and suffering while also providing some companionship too.

What has cheered us all, especially the lepers, is the government's decision to construct a new leper colony over on Bentinck

Island near Albert Head. There, the government will see to it that they will get better care, instead of the isolation of D'Arcy Island and the-cloak-and dagger subterfuge Thad and Dr Sheret have had to engage in. They are very pleased with the changes. They have been speaking behind closed doors with anyone who will listen and have been told, in confidence of course, that it is in part due to their research and advocacy for these people that the change has been put in place.

Despite all our trepidation, my own wee daughter is completely healthy. Thad's work with the lepers was not passed on to her. Georgie—for that is what Thad, Eliza, and Douglas all call her—she may be unhappy with that moniker when she gets older, only time will tell!—seems likely to have her father's green eyes. The baby blue is changing and her eyes most often look blue green now.

She makes all kinds of sounds, especially when her brother is making funny faces for her benefit, and she is always trying to reach for things and to roll and rock her way to where she wants to be. I believe she will be an early walker. She seems to love being in motion next best to being naked. We have each spent countless hours pushing her in her pram all over the neighbourhood.

Only just yesterday she and I were out for a leisurely promenade when we came upon a young raccoon, in broad daylight, leaning back on a neighbour's lawn, cleaning his back toes, just as our cat Martha does every evening after her supper. It was remarkable—and it became even more notable, for when the raccoon noticed me watching, it got up on its feet and ambled off, almost entirely unconcerned by my observation or by the fact that it had no tail. The things one sees when one is out with Georgie!

CHRISTMAS 1929
OAK BAY

Hello, Diary.

The Path to Kitty Islet

I have neglected my writing shamefully for years now, but I no longer feel the need to write myself out, as I used to. I feel so much more solid and am so busy living that I never seem to find the time to write.

However, I was searching for the angel chimes today, as we're hosting Christmas dinner this year, and when I pulled them out I realized they were on top of this diary. I've always kept it fairly close at hand—top drawer of my bedroom dresser—though I haven't needed it lately. I glanced back over some of what I'd written and thought I should add a new entry.

We had a blessed family Christmas today. Eliza is now eighteen and a beautiful young lady. She has started her nurse's training and seems to really like it. Her brother, Douglas, is seventeen—already!—and bound and determined to have some sort of adventure before going to Victoria College, or perhaps to a school back east. He is so bright he could do anything he puts his mind to, but he is not yet ready to focus on one profession. Perhaps an adventure, a safe one, would be the best thing to help him settle down to one course of study or career. Finishing his schooling early has been both a blessing and a curse: a blessing for him—and his high school teachers—and a curse for us to try to keep him occupied. He has a truly good heart, though, and I love him and Eliza more than ever.

Georgie started school this fall. She was aching to have her chance in the big brick schoolhouse and has been pleased every moment, I think—except the day her curiosity led her down to the boiler room and got her locked in there for a while by accident! Such a hue and cry there was with everyone looking for her, one teacher even coming up here to see if she'd made her way home early!

We are certainly always busy. Thad and I are so very happy with our children and our lives. He continues to be a good, caring doctor, well liked and respected. He spends hours out in our garden, sometimes with the children and sometimes with me. It is our own bit of Benvenuto here in Oak Bay. I love him dearly for his gentle way and solid determination. We do seem to bring out the best in each other. I have been so very glad that I allowed myself to override both my pride and my fear and to marry a true friend.

And here is old Martha, nose twitching, reminding me I'd best get back to the kitchen and check on the turkey once more, before the Westbys and Agatha and Thomas arrive. She is still a spry old cat and will soon be demanding her piece of the bird, loudly and repeatedly.

We are all healthy and well, and I am filled with a true sense of the joy and peace and hope of the Christmas season. God bless us as we begin a new decade. May it be as happy as the one we are leaving behind, full of sweet memories and treasured days.

Part Three: Stone

ROSALIND

1991
VICTORIA, B.C.

I never thought too much about the way my mother—Georgie—and Grandmama—Minnie—were always such a package deal, even when my mom lived in her own condo. In fact, the two of them were often together, especially as Mom's faculties really started to fail.

When I was young, we all lived together in the bungalow on Monterey. Many multigenerational families lived together, especially during the war. I only have a few memories of us living there when Grandpapa was alive—I was, after all, only three when he died—but I have hundreds of memories of Grandmama, Mom, and me all in that house. And almost all of them are happy memories. It may seem strange to say that, since by the time I was three I'd lost my father and my grandfather, but I swear it's true. I know many of my friends feel that I must be lying or repressing the bad times, but I'm not. I had a happy childhood; I truly did.

Yes, I was no stranger to tragedy, but regardless of that Mom, Grandmama, Aunt Eliza, Uncle Douglas, and the Westbys all made me feel that I was part of one big, joyful family. And if

Mom was more than a little forgetful? Well, then I was there or Grandmama was there to help her remember.

In talking to Mom's doctors later, I asked about the fact that she had always had a terrible memory. Some of *my* earliest memories, in fact, are of her forgetting important things—like my birthday, or where her keys were, or what she had done the day before. Later, she even forgot the names of my children, her grandchildren, whom she saw almost daily. I wondered if losing my dad, so soon after I was born, affected her mind somehow, and maybe even contributed to her developing Alzheimer's when she was older. Like all good doctors asked to explain the patient's past, hers were noncommittal. There was no way of knowing, they said.

For all that she was so forgetful, I'd like to think that she was mostly happy. She seemed to be, up until almost the very end. Since she and Grandmama took such care to make sure that I was a happy, contented child, I really hope that Mom was happy too.

GEORGIE

MARCH 3, 1962

Keys—they're always getting away from me. Not on the hall table. Not in my purse. Bathroom? No. Foolish of me. Stop. Think. Slowly. Need milk, eggs—yes, yes, but keys first. Two different shoes on. Need a match. Ah, here are the keys, in the other black shoe. Silly. Door locked. I shall walk up Newport Hill to the village.

I should really call on Mother. I'll do that last and then we'll have a cup of tea together. She'll have milk, of course, as she still has her milkman. Perhaps—no, no, too much trouble remembering to be home on Tuesdays—or is Wednesday the delivery day? What is today, anyway? Cool weather, no matter the day, a bit foggy out on the water.

I'm almost at the village. List in my pocket. No, here are my keys. But where is the list? Ah, here. Milk, eggs, biscuits, fruit, more jam; prefer homemade, but I've eaten it all up. Needs must, I suppose. All paid, but all in a fluster. New cashier, I think. I didn't recognize her, and she talked so quickly. Done though. Now, where to next? Ah yes, Mother's.

She likes that I knock or ring, even though I have a key. Is it with mine? Ah yes. Here she is and she is always the same. That same sure step. She must be how old now? Must be in her seventies. She ages well and is still busy.

"How is Rosalind, Georgie?"

"Well now, I have heard, but what did she say?"

"She told me she likes the big campus, but misses home. At least UBC isn't too far away; we'll see her on weekends occasionally."

"Of course, of course. All those books to bring back on the ferry; they'll be very heavy."

"She has your car, though. Remember?"

"Yes, yes, but she still needs to get them into the car."

Lovely tea and scones and jam—apricot and something else. It's like eating bottled sunshine or liquid amber—smooth and sweet. Put my coat down somewhere. Must be going. Where is my coat? Mother is agitated, rushing. Oh, she has my coat. It is very warm, too warm, on the sleeve, it's almost burnt. Where could she have kept it, or did I? No, no, of course not—surely not.

Greyer outside now. Just a few blocks. Could go across, but a bit foggy, it will be easier to walk back up to the Avenue and then down, yes, quite; a nice stretch for the legs after tea. This building here, this is the one; harder to know it's mine with the new paint job. Looks like the neighbouring building now. Confusing. But home. Keys work. Bring in all the packages and put them away. Now.

Wasn't I going to have tea? And bread and jam. Yes, that's it. Coat and scarf off. Kettle on and teapot warmed. Toast in and almost ready. Need a bit of milk. Let's put it in a jug. Where's the jug? Or just pour, since there's no one else here but me. Hungry, though. I wish I had bought scones. I feel like eating scones with jam, not just plain toast. Ah, lovely. A good cuppa. A nice afternoon; I should have stopped in to see Mother. Perhaps I will tomorrow.

APRIL 14, 1962

Weddings are always so complicated. All the people and the food. I do like this dress I'm wearing; it's a beautiful blue. Stuart's favourite colour. Sea blue, sky blue. Of course, he's not here. He's been gone so very long. He loved flying up into the blue. It creases, though. Perhaps I can find an iron? No, someone is coming to help me to my seat now; I can't dash back and look for an iron in the church hall. A long aisle, with so many people. Where am I to sit? Oh yes, at the front. And there's Mother. I'll sit with her. She will remind me what comes next. It's important; today is very, very important, but I'm wearing blue and Stuart is not here. The minister is young, too. I don't remember him.

"Hello, Mother."

"Hello, Georgie. Have a seat and wait for Rosalind. Douglas will walk her up the aisle to Brian. He doesn't look too nervous, does he?"

Of course, of course, Brian. He's here too. He looks different today. I can't quite place him. Oh, the music is swelling up, carrying us all to our feet. I turn and see Douglas behind us now, down the aisle; he's such a nice big brother. And he is walking with someone. She has a veil, but I'm sure it's not Eliza. She's older than me, Eliza is, and this is a young thing. She's beautiful and she has Stuart's eyes and smile. *Rosalind*. It is. This is a wedding for Rosalind. How splendid. I'm glad I'm here. I could've been out walking, but they got me here. If only they'd let me know sooner.

But I did know. Yes. The wedding. My Rosalind and her Brian. The minister is asking all the questions. I'm sure they do. Rosalind has always known exactly what to do. She's always been so certain. Mother passes me a hankie. I guess I was snuffling. I don't want to drip on the dress I'm wearing. It's sky blue—Stuart's favourite.

FEBRUARY 11, 1963

This is not my baby. This is a boy! I have a girl, but I can't remember where I put her. I won't put this one down though, because he is small and crinkled and perhaps I'll need to trade with his mother to get my girl back.

There's Mother. She'll help me.

"This isn't my baby. It's a boy."

"He's your grandson—he's Rosalind's baby and Rosalind is just fine. Brian brought the baby right out to meet us. The nurse was quite angry. Remember? We're at the hospital and Rosalind just had her first baby."

He's small. And my hands are more wrinkled than I remember. Can he be Rosalind's? Mother is not one to tell falsehoods. His wee fist closes around my finger. He's strong. Oh, I wish Stuart were here. He misses everything. All to be up in that great blue yonder of his. No wonder blue is his favourite colour.

Someone takes a picture. There's a flash and it's hard to see. Mother takes the baby. Another flash. My arms are empty now. I'm cold. I don't like it here. I'll get my baby and go home. Mother will look after us, and she'll write to Stuart. I'm too cold and too tired. But I need my baby. Where did I put her?

MAY 17, 1964

A lovely day. Lovely day for a drive. I've got my keys and have a snack in the basket. I'll take the car out. Down the stairs, out of the lobby, and over to the parking area. Where is my car? Not here. Someone else is in my spot. Number 11 is mine, isn't it? But the car—could call the police or Mother or Rosalind. But then all the fuss. Perhaps I can take the bus and call later. Yes, yes, much the easiest.

Up to the Village and then onto the bus. Downtown. Perhaps a walk over to Beacon Hill Park? Yes, just the thing. Such a pretty day. Warm and fresh, and lots of flowers out. Where's the park? I've been walking for blocks. Oh, and here's the Bay. This is the other end of town. How odd. I'm sure I got off near the park.

The Path to Kitty Islet

Perhaps a cup of tea here first and then a walk. No, I'll go to Eaton's and have my tea there. Halfway, and all that.

Busy street. Lots of people. They don't notice the sun. Ah, Eaton's at last. Down below for a drink; no upstairs here. Up, yes. A nice cup of tea. Quieter in here. Not lunch yet. I have my basket. It must be filled with shopping, as it's so very heavy. I'll get the bus home and walk a bit along the Avenue; it's so sunny and warm. What day is it today? So very warm. Wish we could go swimming again.

But Stuart's not here. He's always away.

I remember our first swim. We were out at Thetis Lake. I was with friends, and he was too. Such a hot summer day. I loved to swim. Mother always encouraged me, and Douglas made sure I was almost as good as he was. So many of my girlfriends simply splashed and paddled about in the shallows. I always swam as far and as fast as I could. I wanted to be better than Douglas one day.

The light was dappled. I'd swum a long way. The beach was far away behind me. The trees and the cliffs shadowed the water. A tremendous splash and then a swimmer almost right next to me. Stuart. I didn't know his name then. He smiled and shook his head like a dog; water droplets everywhere. He was so handsome. He seemed to just appear out of the water, up from the depths, despite that big splash. We treaded water for a bit, then clambered out onto some rocks and talked. We both interrupted each other and laughed and talked over each other some more.

Smoke. I could smell it. It had been such a hot, dry day and now smoke. Stuart took my hand and we started out trying to get back to the main beach. So many rocks on bare feet. All at once he pulled and we both splashed into the lake again. We swam together. Looking up, we could see smoke and some sparks. The forest was on fire. We swam as fast as we could and we did get to the beach. People were everywhere. Some were running to their cars. Some had buckets—ridiculous small toy ones—and were

159

trying to get closer. I couldn't see my friends. Stuart held my hand tightly in his own.

Too warm, it was. It is now too. I'll get off the bus at the next stop. It's too hot to be on a bus. Too many people. I'll walk home.

Ah, yes. Much cooler. I'll walk the rest of the way. Surely I have had lunch. But I'm hungry. Perhaps I bought something I could eat. I should look in my basket. I see it's all food—sandwiches, crackers, cheese, fruit. Was I meeting someone? I'll walk to Mother's.

The door's open. She must be here. "Mother?"

"In the kitchen."

"It's me, Georgie."

"Come in. Do you want lunch?"

Should I offer up my basket? I suppose so. I can't remember why I packed it.

MAY 8, 1965

This baby is like mine. She's loud and squirmy like Rosalind. But the eyes are different.

Mother takes her from me and croons a lullaby. A young man looks on. He is holding a very small boy, not much bigger than a baby himself. The boy looks familiar. Perhaps I have met them all before here at Mother's. They might go to our church. The boy struggles to be put down. He manages to toddle over to me without falling. He holds my fingers and laughs. The man seems so pleased that the boy is holding onto me. The boy giggles and sits down all at once. He cries. I pat his head. The man swoops him up and puts him on his shoulders. The boy stops crying, but the baby's crying now. Mother takes her out. She returns quickly and sits beside me.

The man speaks as he jostles the boy on his shoulders. The words cascade over me like cold water. They are surprising and hard.

The Path to Kitty Islet

"We'll stay here for a few days, if that's all right, until Rosalind can get back on her feet. The baby's not feeding well yet. And we're both so tired. Perhaps Georgie could watch Michael?" Mother shakes her head no, and sees that I am watching. I don't know a Michael, so how could I watch him? I am grateful for Mother's good sense and quick response.

"Michael will have to stay here with me, Brian—with us," says Mother firmly.

This Brian seems chagrined by her decision, but he recognizes Mother's organizing voice too.

"I'm going now." I realize I must have said so out loud, as they are all staring at me.

Brian shifts the boy's weight in his arms and looks at me questioningly. "Don't you want to see Rosalind first?" he asks softly.

I shake my head no. "I'm going home. She can come and see me one day."

I start to leave, but Mother comes forward. She puts her hands on my shoulders, just like always, and looks into my eyes. "Rosalind wants to see you before you go. I'll come with you."

I'm ready to go out to see her, since Mother put it like that. I can't quite remember where she's staying, now that she is at UBC. Mother will know. Mother takes my hand and draws me into the second bedroom. Rosalind's there, on the bed. My Rosalind. She looks pale and tired. The baby is beside her. The baby—Rosalind's baby.

"Oh," I say, eagerly and quickly. "Is it a boy?"

"No, Mommy, we have our boy, Michael. Remember? The new baby is his sister. Michael has a sister. You have a granddaughter."

I sit on the bed gingerly. Another baby for Rosalind? How will she cope? She's at UBC and now she has two babies. "But what about your courses?"

Mother nudges me and says, "Rosalind graduated from UBC. She's finished. She and Brian are having their family now."

Rosalind moves the baby down the bed, closer to me. The baby looks familiar. She looks a little like Rosalind did, I think. Does she also look like her brother? I don't know. I decide not to ask.

NIGHT, JUNE 7, 1966

My feet feel heavy, like lead. I know I am not supposed to be down here. It's an important day, and I'm wearing a new dress. It's not to get dirty. I can hardly see anything, but I know I'm alone. I can smell burning and something hot. I'm cold though. I was sweating and nervous, but now the air in this corner, away from the heat, is making me shiver. My new dress is stuck to my back and it feels itchy. I want to go home.

It's dark and smelly. I'm scared of the noises. I came down here for a special reason, to show that I could be brave and more daring than all my new classmates, but now I just want to go upstairs again. I cannot move the door. The handle turns but the door stays shut. I think I can hear my name. I open my mouth to shout "I'm here!" but I cannot make a sound. My legs won't move, my feet are heavy, and I'm scared.

I—my heart is beating fast and it's very dark. I cannot smell anything. I put my hand out. I feel my bed, my sheets, and my blankets. It's still dark. It's night. I'm in my bed. But where? How?

It's quiet. I strain my ears and eyes. I can't really hear or see anything. I must have been dreaming. An old nightmare really. That was the boiler room—at Monterey School. I was . . . six. They found me after a long search.

I'm safe. My breathing slows. It's dark, but I am safe. I sleep.

MAY 21, 1967

Rosalind is here. Two children too. Hers. The boy's very quick. He's not interested in his toys. He likes my things. The girl is sleepy. She'll have a nap soon. Maybe the boy will too. Rosalind is asking questions. She wants us to look at pictures together. There are so many—I don't want the boy to touch them. He's a sticky, busy boy.

So many old pictures, but not many of Stuart. He was a fine man, and so very tall and kind. He talked as much as I did. Rosalind wants all the old stories again. I do remember those, sometimes even better than I used to. Always was so busy after Stuart went away. Never had time to think. Mother helped. Always she helped, but the baby—Baby Rosalind. Mother took pictures right away and sent them along to Stuart. He had the pictures with him in England. He wrote about them in his letters. He must have had them always with him. They never came back. Rosalind was a happy baby. Always smiling. Making noise. For a while, she was the only one who was happy. Mother tried her best, but it unnerved her. She faltered. Missed steps.

I remember the telegram. It was very direct, but had no real information.

Father was a tower of strength. Mother and I both took to our beds. Father told me later that she kept going on about "the fire," always asking if it had been put out. Completely put out. She'd twist her wedding ring and ask about the fire. Sometimes she'd stop and ask if it had been damped down properly, but it was summer and there was no fire. But she'd ask. Father would bring me Rosalind, and take her away again when she was done. I slept. I could hear Mother's voice when I fell asleep, and even in my dreams.

One day, Mother got up. She brought me Rosalind. She combed out my hair. She sent Father out to cut fresh flowers for my room. She made me get up. She willed me to get up. There are no pictures of any of that to show Rosalind.

Rosalind has found the telegram. I'd forgotten I'd put it in with her baby pictures. I cannot remember her children's names, but I know what the telegram says. I only had to read it once.

He was so young. He never saw our Rosalind. Never even held her.

Father died after that, a few years after. He was a fine man too. He was always so careful of Mother, and a good father to all three of us. Eliza and Douglas were as much his as I was. He had a gentle soul and hated war. Doctors take war personally, that's what Mother always said. He lived to see the end of another war, but that was all.

Rosalind has found the headstone pictures. My father's, and Stuart's—her father's. There is no body there, though. He's up in the blue forever; there's only a stone marker to hold a bit of him down here for us.

The boy is back. He had been quiet. Rosalind puts him on her lap. He does not care to be contained. Perhaps tea and cookies. Put the past back now. The girl will wake up soon and we will all sit together. No more pictures, though; I have too many for such sticky fingers.

OCTOBER 14, 1950

He is a friend of Stuart's from the air force, but I don' t recall hearing his name before. He was stationed at the same base when Stuart was killed. Stuart was flying his plane, flying over England, testing something—a new piece of equipment or strategy. The plane began to plummet, but it was over England, not over the water, and there were lots of villages, people, houses everywhere. He could have bailed out, used his parachute. Stuart chose not to. The plane crashed in a field, at the edge of a large village. No one on the ground was hurt. A huge bang. A fireball. He helped keep the plane away from the village. He perished—my Stuart, a hero.

My Stuart, still gone. My Stuart. A ball of smoke and flames like a great plume of a peacock's feather arching into the air. Into the blue. Never to touch the ground again. My Stuart and Rosalind's father. The man stops speaking.

Rosalind is weeping. Mother too. My hand is at my throat. Stuart gave me the necklace I wear. I never take it off. My cheeks are wet. He has a nice voice, this man. He came all the way from the Maritimes to tell us the story. He flew with Stuart sometimes and always wanted us to know the truth. I should be grateful.

I get tea. Rosalind helps. Mother is talking to the man, asking him questions about his family. I don't care. I don't want to hear his answers or his nice voice. I don't want his presence in our house. My house. Where Stuart came courting. Where we were married. Where Father opened the door and the telegram—he shouldn't be here. I make Rosalind take in the tea. I go out the back door and walk quickly down to McNeill Bay, and clamber over to Kitty Islet. I'll wait here; I will not go back until I'm sure he's gone.

These rocks are cold. It is spitting and my hair is already wet. I'm cold inside and out. I look across the water, but all I can see is that giant plume of smoke he described. My hands hold some sea stones, all polished. No ragged edges, nothing rough or grating. Some are almost silky. They are different colours, too; some are grey, some black, some green. No real blue ones, though. None.

MEMORY

I'm little—four? Five? Mother and I are home by ourselves. The others are at work and school. It's a funny day. Something is not quite as it should be. Mother is distracted, different. I play quietly. I know it's not the right day to ask her to play with me or to go for a walk. I wonder about asking to go visit the Westbys. That is almost always agreed to. I don't think Mother notices me. It is cold today, damp and wet, unseasonable weather. I pull on

Mother's sleeve as she stands looking out the window. She finally reacts. I tell her I'm cold and ask, "Can't we light the fire?"

Her head snaps round and she looks at me in such a way that I'm frightened. I let go of her sleeve and take a step back. She's muttering, to herself I think, but she says, "Never another fire today. Never." I don't understand, but I decide to leave her alone.

Later—that day? The next day?—she finds me and cuddles me the way she usually does. The air is normal again, and the damp is gone. Everything is as usual.

SEPTEMBER 23, 1970

Don't get a lot of sewing to do now. Rosalind gets things for herself and the children. Mother has me alter a few things. I miss sewing quickly and hurriedly, always pinning things, patterns everywhere, with every surface covered. I still have stacks of material. Got lots of it at Woolworth's and Woodward's, especially on their $1.49 days. Lots of pretty patterns, and good quality material too.

Perhaps Rosalind is right. Perhaps a newspaper advertisement. A small note in the lobby of my building. I need to keep busy. Walking two or three times a day is enough. I need to busy my fingers too. I know Rosalind worries about me, because I do forget. I never remember her children's names—my own grandchildren! I have to stop and really think about her and them, and then immediately think of something else. If I do that, I can usually remember. Michael. Michael and Amelia.

Amelia is an old-fashioned name. I'm still a bit surprised that Rosalind chose it. I don't think it's very common, and it's certainly not romantic like her own name. Unusual. But names aren't always what they seem. We give them power, and sometimes we give them too much. Or so it seems to me. Mother was funny about Rosalind's name. She hardly commented on it, except to say that Rosalind Anne sounded well together. I've always remembered that. I wonder what she said to Rosalind about her children's names? I should remember to ask. I'll write a note and ask when I visit. I have been better at writing notes and reading them. Perhaps Rosalind won't have to worry so much.

—

Now I need to do something. Go for a walk? Not again so soon. Perhaps I could sew. I could make something simple. Rosalind had an idea for sewing; I must ask her what it was.

FEBRUARY 27, 1975

Rosalind is rushing about. Mother's had a fall. The ambulance has been, and is taking Mother to the hospital. Rosalind's husband (Bradley? Benjamin? Brian!) is away on some sort of business trip. Her two children need to be with me while she goes to the hospital to see about Mother. There's no sense in flapping.

"Rosalind, we'll be fine. Mother will be fine. You go, and the children and I will busy ourselves."

"Mom, you'll be all right? You don't mind waiting to see Grandmama?"

"I'll wait. The children and I will look after each other."

"Yes, yes. I suppose. I'll phone you when I know something." Rosalind is gone.

The children and I are alone. We are never left alone. The boy is older. He must be twelve now or thereabouts. The girl is shy—of me, it seems. She must be ten or eleven. We're usually together at Mother's house or with Rosalind here. What does one do with children this age? We regard each other warily. They know I can't remember their names. Sometimes I simply call them Douglas and Eliza. It's easier. They must think I really am dotty.

How odd for them today is too. Their great-grandmother knows them better than I do. Odd for me as well, but Rosalind always worries so—and then takes them to Mother's. Easier all round, I suppose.

"Walk?" I ask.

They nod, silently.

We dress and I begin the hunt for keys. Where might they be this time? I check pockets, tables, and other shoes. I open drawers. Ah yes. There they are, in the bathroom. The children are still standing by the door, looking hot and worried.

"Shouldn't we wait here until Mom phones with news?" The boy speaks firmly, but quietly.

"She'll call twice if need be."

I lock the door, and drop the keys into my pocket. Outside we hunker down into our coats away from the chill wind. We head over to the park along the waterfront and choose to walk along the water. Lots of boats in the marina. The wind zings along their masts and rigging, making an odd, metallic sort of ethereal music. The children are dead quiet and sunk into themselves.

"Let's go visit Mother," I suggest.

They both look at me slightly askance, but make no comment.

"We'll walk. It's not far."

We arrive at Mother's. The door is locked, which is very unexpected. The children shift from foot to foot. The girl opens her mouth to speak, then closes it again without uttering a sound. I search my pockets for the key. Try two keys before I set on the right one. The door opens. The house is warm, but it feels empty. The hall furniture seems a little askew.

"Mother?" I call. "Mother?" I call again a little more loudly.

"She's gone," says the boy.

The wind gets knocked out of me. "Gone?" I query. "Dead?"

"No." The boy shuffles his feet. "She's in the hospital because she fell. That's why we're with you. Mom's with Grandmama." He looks everywhere, but at his sister or me, as he says his piece. He's embarrassed.

The Path to Kitty Islet

Rosalind must have told me about Mother. I simply do not recall.

"Perhaps we should go for a walk then?" I suggest. The children exchange glances. I cannot interpret them, but feel I am missing something. I lock the door. We three walk down Windsor Avenue toward the water. The children remain quiet. It's not a comfortable silence.

MARCH 2, 1975

I'm hungry. I've woken up I'm so hungry. I can't quite tell where I am. It's darker than usual. My eyes slowly adjust to the quality of the blackness. I realize I'm in my old room, at Mother's. I really have no idea why. But I am hungry.

I get up carefully, feel about with my feet for slippers, turn on the bedside lamp, find a sweater, and then make my way to the door. The hall is quite dark, but the kitchen light is on. I make my way toward the light, trying to move quietly. The boy is here, rubbing his eyes, blinking at me like an owl.

"Hello," he says. He is clearly uncomfortable.

"Hello," I reply. "Are you hungry?"

He nods. I go to the cupboard and get down some bowls, the big old ceramic mixing bowls in bright primary colours.

"Do you like ice cream?"

The boy nods again, and his eyes widen a bit.

I go to the freezer and get out two kinds of ice cream. Next I get chocolate chips, coloured sprinkles, and glazed cherries from the baking cupboard. I fill the two largest mixing bowls with as much ice cream as I can, putting several scoops of vanilla and several scoops of chocolate in each. I pass him the red bowl, carefully. I also push the chocolate chips and so on along the counter closer to him. I actually remember to put the ice cream back in the freezer, and turn in time to see his wide grin as he pours chocolate chips into his bowl.

I do the same, we add sprinkles, and then we both dig in. I must be very hungry.

"What's it like?" he asks.

"What's what like?"

"What's it like not remembering things?" he says.

I pause. Sometimes I convince myself that only I know that I forget, but deep down I know they know. Even the children know. But he asks me curiously, politely, not with malice or condescension. It's almost as if he'd said, "What's it like wearing glasses?" It just is.

"What's your name? Douglas?" I ask, knowing it's not.

"I'm Michael. I'm your gr—."

"My grandson, I know. I just can't remember your name very easily. It's like—it's like hearing a piece of music in your head, but not being able to sing it or hum it out loud. I know where things are in my head. I have an impression of names or words or memories and know they used to be over here somewhere, but when I go back to find them, they're gone. Like a sweater you thought you put down in your bedroom, only to find it a few days or a few hours later in the front room."

"Oh," he replies, gently. Sucking on a huge spoonful of ice cream, he looks at me with consideration. "Do you always remember your own name?"

"So far," I say.

"Are you scared?"

"Sometimes."

"Are you scared it will get worse?"

"Yes." I have never said that out loud before. I am scared. But some days I remember everything, even where I put my keys.

I change the subject. "Why are you and I at your great-grandmother's?"

"We're all having a sleepover to celebrate her first night back from the hospital. She fell and twisted her ankle really bad. She had to stay in hospital for a bit, and Grandmama was really mad. You were too, because you would come over here to visit and find her out, and I guess you thought she was trying to avoid seeing you, because you would phone my mom and be very upset."

I can picture myself in the hallway, calling Mother. Yes, I'd missed her.

"Is your sister here too then?"

Michael nods.

"Does she like ice cream?"

"Yes, but she hates being woken up."

"Okay, just us then."

We finish our snack and lick our lips carefully. I put away the baking supplies and rinse the bowls. Michael tries to stifle a yawn but isn't very successful.

"Time to go back to bed—for both of us."

He nods, gets off the chair, pauses, then rushes over to me and gives me a quick, fierce hug.

"Goodnight."

"Goodnight."

JULY 12, 1975

Mother limps a little as she carries the teapot out to the back yard. It is warm today, so we are sitting in the shade. I love Mother's garden. She and Father worked so hard on it. She still does some of the work, but also has a boy in. I can never remember his name. I suppose he's a man really, but she always calls him a boy, so I do too.

Though the sky is a bit hazy and the air is thick, I feel very clear today. Rosalind will be here soon too, with the children and possibly Brian. Maybe we could look at pictures today, outside, under the shade of the apple trees. I think Mother and I could both remember things today—not that Mother ever forgets!

Perhaps I'll go get some photos. I could get started, to make up for the days when I don't want to look at the past. I bring out a few boxes, then settle back into my spot.

I must've dozed off in the warm air. Mother is knitting.

"Hello, dear; nice that you've woken up. Rosalind and Brian and Michael and Amelia will be here soon."

I stretch and nod. I don't think Mother has ever forgotten anyone or anything. I hear doors closing and opening, and then the children burst into the dappled shade.

"Hello!" they shout, almost in unison.

Rosalind and Brian follow. They both look hot and a little wilted. Mother offers them tea or iced tea, which is ready in the fridge. They both opt for iced tea, and Brian gets it. Rosalind turns to me and is clearly surprised to see the picture boxes out. She sits down on the old lawn chair rather gingerly, then rifles through the nearest box.

The first picture she extracts is of Father, with Eliza and Douglas, ankle deep in water at Willows Beach. "Mommy, where are you?"

"I don't think I was born yet." I take the picture from her and look at my father. He looks much younger than I ever remember seeing him. Of course, there is no date on the back. Mother holds out her hand, puts her glasses firmly on her nose, and takes a look.

"That was before we were married. It was likely taken in 1918 or 1919, I think. Eliza and Douglas look so young still, and Thad was such a good friend to us all for years."

Her words make me think of another day at the beach. Eliza and Douglas had been there too, but both were much older than me, of course. I—I was maybe three or perhaps four. They would've been teenagers, and probably not very happy about having to watch out for their little sister.

The Path to Kitty Islet

Mother and Father were much farther ahead of us, walking slowly, obviously talking about something adult, something important. They were so good together and so clearly respected each other. I think I always knew that, even as a toddler. Eliza and Douglas had been holding my hands, one on each side, helping me to skip over the waves. I loved doing that, but always wanted to do it forever. They had let go, and I was disgruntled. I remember I wanted to make them hold my hands again, but I didn't know how to do it. I started lagging behind. They were walking and talking, of what I do not know. At the time, I probably didn't fully understand anyway. Suddenly, I remember darting up the beach to the high tide line and finding a big log to duck behind.

I lay down on the warm sand, and squeezed my body as close to the log as I could get. I remember lying still, very still, and feeling the warmth of the sun caress my shoulders, legs, and back. I must have fallen asleep, for the next thing I remember is being pulled up, a little roughly, and lifted into Father's arms.

Mother was saying, "You gave us all such a fright, darling! You mustn't run away and hide, Georgie. You're too little to be by yourself."

Father stroked my hair, and nuzzled my cheek with his slightly scratchy chin. "You scared us," he said.

Eliza really did look scared, and she was holding one of my hands in hers. But Douglas was away from us, sitting on another log, looking out to sea. He looked—hurt. Father carried me over to him and said, "It's all right, son, we found her. All is well."

At first Douglas didn't say anything, but then he said, "She's what matters," in an odd, half-strangled tone. I didn't understand what he meant, not until years later, but Father did.

He squeezed Douglas's shoulder and said, in a low, but absolutely certain, voice, "You all three matter. All three."

I don't remember anything else about that day. I don't even know if I can remember anything else about being that age. But

173

Father knew. He knew that Douglas and Eliza were his too. And that sometimes they would wonder if they belonged to him in the same way I did. And I believe they did. I hope they believed it too. I wonder, though.

Rosalind is watching me. Should I tell her the story? I wonder if Mother remembers? Probably—she seems to remember all our stories, and to remember them much better than I do. Before I can make up my mind, the children are back, moving here and there, looking for drinks and cookies. Rosalind goes inside to find some more goodies. I turn to Mother. "Do you remember the day I got lost at Willows Beach?"

"Yes, of course. Why?"

"The picture made me think of it. Who found me that day, anyway? I can just remember Father lifting me up."

"Douglas found you. He was very upset when you disappeared, and took some time to come and tell us you'd gotten lost. I think he thought we'd blame him, but you always were a bit of a will o' the wisp and could disappear in an instant."

Just so. Some of my memories are exactly where and how I expect them to be.

APRIL 19, 1976

The phone is ringing—ringing. It makes no sense. I am swimming, in the middle of the lake, drifting, watching the few clouds pass gently overhead, but the ringing continues.

I become more fully awake. Yes, the phone is ringing. I get up and answer it. "Hello?"

"Georgie, it's me, Mother. You need to get dressed. You need to walk over here and meet me. You need to come quickly. I'm fine, but you need to come. Now. Do you understand?"

"Yes, Mother." It's easy to say yes even though I don't understand. Mother is that sort of person. It's just better to say yes and hope for understanding later.

The Path to Kitty Islet

I dress quickly and even put on a watch. It is only 3 a.m. My keys are actually by the door. Unusual, but helpful. I walk to Mother's. Only a matter of a few minutes, as it's no more than five or six blocks. It's odd to be out so late, well, so early. No one else is about and it's very quiet.

Mother opens the door as soon as I arrive. She is dressed too, wearing her sensible clothes and shoes. No fancy things needed for 3 a.m. She is quite pale, though. Once I get in, she calls for a taxi. We wait. I still don't know what we're doing, but I don't ask. I could simply drift back off to sleep—Mother is shaking me awake, and bundling me into the taxi. She really is an extraordinary woman. I can't recall her exact age, but she must be over eighty, and she's still made of steel. And she never misses a thing.

Bright lights now, a waiting room. The children are here. Are they hurt? No, they look to be all in one piece, but they've both been crying. Mother holds them close. Now, I could ask, but I don't want to. I want to forget all of this. I know that for certain. And I probably will.

We sit and wait. The girl comes and sits by me, puts her head on my shoulder. Soon, her breathing is slow and even. I don't want to move, I don't want to wake her. Mother and the boy are holding hands. He is sitting up ramrod straight, watching every person come and go through the emergency ward.

A long time later, a man in a white coat comes in, goes over to speak to the admitting nurse, then comes to us. He takes us all in in one encompassing glance, then addresses himself to the boy. He's very clearly the doctor in charge, and he very clearly has bad news. Douglas (the name comes to me though I know it's the wrong one) sits up even straighter.

The doctor states, slowly and calmly, "Your father has died. Your mother is still with him. He had a massive heart attack, and there was nothing more we could do. I'm very sorry for your loss.

You can all come back to the room with me, if you'd like, or you can stay here. It's up to you."

The girl has woken up. I know she heard all that he said. Mother and I look at each other; we stand up as one, and the children follow suit. I had heard the words, and I knew what they meant, but I couldn't call to mind the children's father. I could neither think of his name nor see his face. All I could see was my Stuart.

The pain and sorrow come at me in waves again, even after all these years. Father had opened the door, took and read the telegram from the deliveryman. I saw the envelope and knew. Mother came from the back of the house. She started toward Father, then changed course and came and took my hand. It was a moment where time really came to a standstill. Father did not want to give me the telegram; we could all see that, but it had to be done. Once it was, it could never be any other way.

Poor Father. How he hated war and all that it entailed. He was a doctor, a pacifist, and this was the second war he'd had to endure. But he never enlisted. My Stuart did; he wanted to and he was excited; he saw the adventure, the romance; he wanted the glory. Glory everlasting. Father crossed over to me and Mother. I held out my hand and took the very flimsy piece of paper. I only read it once. Mother and I could no longer hold each other up. We sank to the floor together and cried.

For a little while, Father had two invalids on his hands as well as a baby. He was a rock. Mother was very upset, which was so unlike her, really. And one day, she did put aside her own emotions. And she made me get up. One does what Mother says, even if one doesn't want to.

Our feet sound a bit in the hall; it's a long walk. The boy is still ramrod straight. He looks like he has Mother's steel. The girl's hand tightens its grip on mine. We follow the doctor into a small curtained-off room. Rosalind is there, as the doctor said she would be, and she's holding the hand of the person in the bed. She turns her tear-stained face toward us and we all stop at the edge of the curtain. And then I—I go forward and clasp my girl to my breast. She sobs then and lets go of his hand. It's time for her to let go. I stroke her hair, her back, and feel her shuddering sobs echo in me.

Mother and the children inch closer. The finality of seeing is its own pain, I see that now. Never seeing leaves the memories pristine, but the imagination tries to paint in the missing pieces. A plane going down in flames—but seeing makes a mockery of one's images of the deceased. The waxen form left behind is too real and too unlike the person to be of true comfort. The girl cries again and the boy's eyes fill with tears before he turns away. Mother takes them out. The doctor has already disappeared, silently. Rosalind and I are left. We must leave too; this isn't a picture she needs to hold in her heart. I turn her around in my arms and make her walk with me. I don't think that she's aware we are leaving her husband behind.

OCTOBER 27, 1945

The memorial service is over. Hundreds of people attended. Mother is still sitting in the front pew. When the hymns were over, she simply didn't move. The plan had been for the family to exit first and then for us to accompany the casket out to the cemetery. But Mother refused to get up. The minister took stock of the situation and smoothly changed gears, helping the mourners leave quietly and quickly. I've been hesitating here, hovering, unsure. Rosalind is only three and has been very good, but she will need to run soon, the day of her grandfather's memorial service or no.

I look around. We are the only ones left in the church. Rosalind tugs hard at my hand and then pulls her fingers from my grasp. She runs down the long aisle, takes a deep gulp of air, and runs back, this time letting out a "whoop" as she returns. I start to shush her and then realize that Mother is whooping too; she's taking in great deep breaths and letting them out with the same force as Rosalind. Rosalind changes course and heads straight for her grandmother. She offers her a hand, and Mother takes it and gets up. The two of them careen haphazardly down the carpeted aisle, whooping together. It's unseemly; it's crazy; it's release.

Mother never went to the cemetery that day. Neither did I nor did Rosalind. We stayed behind at the church, and then walked slowly back home, all the way from downtown. Mother and I took turns carrying Rosalind when she got tired of walking. Mother never heard from any well-wishers that day. She shook no hands and saw no tears in the eyes of the people of Victoria who would miss the good doctor, her husband, so. She allowed his memorial service to be large and public, but she didn't allow her grief to be.

Rosalind is in bed. Mother and I have eaten a little. The house is quiet. There are masses of flowers in most rooms, despite the season. Some of the people from Chinatown have sent fruits and vegetables. At least they're edible; people don't know what else to offer. I check on Rosalind again. She is fine, sleeping with that sense of abandon and deep purpose only the young have.

I stop and lean on the doorframe of the front room. Mother is kneeling on Father's favourite chair, with her head in her hands, leaning where his head used to rest, sobbing. I am indecisive. I don't want to intrude but, as I turn, she feels my presence, or perhaps hears a creak. She puts one hand out behind her; I take it in mine.

Our men have died three years apart. We have lost them both. Father, husband, son-in-law. Even breathing seems hard today.

Mother turns around and sinks back in Father's chair. I have collapsed in a bit of a heap on the floor. She gently rubs my fingers, smoothing out the knuckles, careful of both our wedding bands.

She starts to talk. I lean forward, so that my head is resting against her knee. I'm not really listening to what she says. It's too hard to hold each word and figure out its meaning. Instead, I let them trickle over me like a soft rain. Her voice has always been so beautiful. Melodious. Douglas and Eliza had wanted to stay with us, but there isn't really room here. I know they wanted to be with us tonight, but Mother was adamant. She sent them both home. I remain somewhat surprised. I think Eliza and Douglas were too.

Her words eddy around me. "A good man, such a gentle soul. He always was. Careful, thoughtful. So completely understanding, yet I never once told him all of it—never was able to fully trust that he wouldn't—and now he's gone, and I will go too, because he was the only who should know, who deserved to know, the only one." She says more, mostly all on the same theme. I find it easy to understand her sense of loss and regret, but don't understand her meaning.

I stir a little, and finally say, "Mother, he knows you love him. You told him so yourself. Every day. You showed him. He knew it. He knew we all loved him. He understood. He did."

She looks at me, searchingly. Her eyes are very red and puffy and swollen, but there's something else, something behind her grief. I don't know what else to say, or to offer. "Should I call Agatha?" I ask. She had been at the service, and she had gone with Eliza and Douglas out to the cemetery, and then had briefly come back to our house with them, to make sure Mother had made it home. "I could call her. I'm sure she'd come," I say, knowing full well Agatha and Mother should mourn together.

Mother looks at me one last time. "No, now is not the time."

"Mother, I'm sure Agatha would—"

"Yes, yes. Call her. That's not what I meant when I said no. Call her. Please."

Agatha comes very quickly. I suspect she's been waiting and hoping Mother would want her. The two have been such friends, always, and after all, Father was Agatha's brother. They've both lost so much. I have too of course, but they knew all of him. Children know portions of their parents, and know them differently. I would never have expected Mother not to go to the cemetery, for instance. I leave Mother and Agatha together. I make tea and check on Rosalind again. We're now a household of women. No men will be returning here. It's not a completely cheerless thought, despite all the grief we have had to bear. How odd.

APRIL 15, 1979

Mother wanted to go to a movie in order to give Rosalind a quiet night at home, so she asked me to come with her and the children. The taxi came for all of us and took us downtown. The children are teenagers now, and both look quite embarrassed to be with their grandmother and great-grandmother at a theatre. Luckily, Mother chose an early showing, so I think neither the boy nor the girl has seen anyone they know.

We're in the theatre now. I do still love the smell and taste of movie popcorn. So very yummy! I've already asked about the title of the movie, more than once I think, so I dare not ask again, but I still don't know what we'll be seeing. I'll endeavour to enjoy the surprise. Mother wanted to pick something the children would like, which is hard to do, when they're at this age.

The lights go down and the trailers start. Then the movie. Its title sounds familiar, but of course I've heard its name because I asked before. There's a lot of violence, warring young men all trying to impress each other and a pretty girl. A very old story really.

Suddenly I'm on my feet shouting "Fire! Fire!" Mother's pulling me down, and the people around us seem angry. But there are flames, right there in front of me: the building is about to collapse. The usher comes and confers with Mother. She's white-lipped and shaking herself. She'll make him do something, surely. I cannot smell smoke yet. The boy is on my other side. He's holding my hand. He keeps telling me that it's over and, it's true, the flames are gone now. There are faces instead. One boy is burned. If only everyone had listened to me.

We stumble out into the street. I feel I have run a mile. The girl walks beside Mother. The boy has hailed a taxi already. Mother has decided I should spend the night. I don't argue. We all get out at the house on Monterey. Rosalind opens the door for us and seems to recognize something has happened. I can't recall what, but when I look over at Mother I see she looks very pale and drawn and old—really old. It's one of the first times I remember thinking so. Rosalind gets both Mother and me sitting down in the front room. Mother says not a word; she just keeps twisting her wedding band. I feel I've disgraced her somehow.

The boy calls his mother from the hall and Rosalind goes out. Mother and I are left alone. She's silent and I don't know what to say. My hands are greasy as I hold them together in my lap. I wonder what from? Perhaps we've been out to dinner? I know we weren't here or at my apartment, but that's really all I'm sure of. I think it's time I went home. I get up, rather unsteadily, and move toward the door.

"Not tonight, Georgie," Mother says softly. "You must stay here tonight. You can sleep in the extra bed in Rosalind's old room. I need you here tonight. All of you."

I hesitate at the door. I really do want to go home. I want—peace—and no one watching. But one must always do as Mother says when she uses that voice. I sit down again.

Rosalind comes back in the room. She looks from one to the other of us. "Well, what am I going to do with you two?" The question, I realize, is only barely a joke. I frown. I know something has happened to upset Mother, but I can't put my finger on it. It seems I'm to blame. When I can't remember something like this, it usually means I'm at fault somewhere, somehow, even if it's simply because I forget so much. How to fix the thing that's wrong is very hard when one doesn't know what to fix.

Mother seems more perturbed than she usually is with one of my mistakes. Rosalind seems to sense that too, probably because Mother has remained so quiet and so inwardly focused. She seems to be watching us as if we are on a stage, in some sort of play. I feel as though I'm acting most of the time these days anyway: I can never quite remember what should come next. It seems I'm always forgetting my lines, but I shouldn't feel like that in my own life, should I? However, none of my lines come easy any more, that's certain. And not much is certain these days. I wish Mother would speak.

Rosalind goes to her and holds both her hands, so she can no longer twist her wedding band about. Mother looks momentarily bereft, then quickly her face changes, and she smiles up at Rosalind. "I'm all right, my dear," she says. "You needn't worry any more about me. Let's get your mother a cup of tea to wash down all that popcorn." Mother rises, almost majestically, and follows Rosalind into the hallway and down to the kitchen.

I'm alone now, which is what I wanted, yet now I feel deserted, rather than peaceful, as I'd hoped. I am an obstinate thing, I suppose. No wonder Rosalind and Mother don't know what to do with me. I'll go to the kitchen too. Perhaps the children are there. They always provide a distraction. Maybe one of them will let slip what I've done wrong this time. They're still too young to hold their tongues, especially the girl. Sometimes, that is of great benefit to me.

OCTOBER 18, 1982

I think I've been out walking. I had thought to go again, but my shoes are damp and my favourite gloves are wet through. I strain and think, really think, but I don't remember walking. A

The Path to Kitty Islet

walk will help. If I go fast enough the cobwebs will get blown away and I will remember.

I choose another pair of gloves. I close the door. I should lock it, but I can't quite remember how to do so. I'll ask Mother another day. She's always been so much more mechanically minded than I am. Funny that she never sewed as well as me. She could always keep her machine so nicely, though. Well oiled and in perfect condition.

There's a fine mist today. Father liked these kinds of days. No heaviness to the rain, but all is covered in damp nonetheless. My hair is wet and I can feel the cold despite my coat. I'll walk along the waterfront for a little while and then go inland, through the neighbourhoods. Perhaps I'll go north a bit.

Not too many others out. Cold and clammy. Father loved a good Scotch mist. I'm getting hungry. Perhaps I should go home. I stand at the corner and look up at the signs: St Ann and Cranmore. Neither really seems to suggest a direction. I was out for a walk, but I'm away from the water. Had I intended to shop? I've forgotten my purse if I had. If I keep walking I'll get to the water again, I'm almost certain. The movement is calming and I walk with determination. Nothing like a good, brisk walk to clear the head. Not very many out today. It's a fine Scotch mist, though. Damp, but Father would be happy.

Another intersection. Foul Bay and Fort. And the big grocery store, the one Mother hates. What did I need? I am hungry. Perhaps I'd planned to get something for lunch? But why did I walk past the store in the village? I know I'm standing here frowning. The cars are always so fast a body can't even begin to cross—and there they all are, honking now. I try to hurry, to see what they're honking at. So noisy! At least they've stopped. At last. I'm still hungry. I'll just go in and get a little something. The bakery seems warm, and here are some lovely buns, all kinds, in clear bins. I try not to get crumbs on the floor, but I'm so very hungry and the buns are very good. Flaky and quite fresh.

I don't know this woman. She seems to be upset about something. I take another bun and try to go down a different aisle, away from her. She is older too. Usually older women are more polite than this. She's yelling now, something about cashiers and the store manager. I'm sure I can't help her. I turn down a different aisle and bump into a nice young man. He catches hold of my arm to steady me, and, in a very calm voice, he apologizes for bumping me. He seems much more considerate. He even asks if I would like a drink. Once he mentions it, I realize I'm very thirsty as well. The buns have been delicious, but it is a bit dry going without a drink. He still has my arm, just gently, in his hand, and he guides me into the back of the store. Oh, I see, it's a little sitting room for the workers with a table and a fridge and even a couch. He steers me toward the couch and asks what I'd like.

He has the kettle on in no time. He helps me off with my coat and wet gloves and asks if he can put my purse somewhere safe. Trouble is, I can't recollect where it is. I was shopping, wasn't I? Perhaps it is in one of the carts. That other woman is here too. He sends her out to look. At least she's gone and has stopped shouting. He is hanging up my coat now, but has stopped and is looking at it. At the inside of it. I'm curious too. What has he found? I start to get up, but he smiles very charmingly at me, and tells me to wait until he gets the tea made. The woman comes back, but does not have—what? She looks disappointed, but I don't know why.

The man makes the tea and gives the woman a piece of paper. That cheers her up. I'm pleased the tea is steeping. Not long now. Can't remember either of their names. Their kitchen is really not like mine. I guess each apartment is a little different. We do own them, so we can make them over to suit us. How do they manage without a stove? Odd that he's the one in charge of the kitchen, especially with him being so much younger.

He makes good tea. I was very thirsty. She's back now, and much more talkative. I ask them when they moved in. They don't really answer. I guess I must've asked them before. I don't remember, but I know that look. Can't think of their names still.

Ah, here's Rosalind! What a lovely surprise! She does look flushed. Flustered. How did she find me in their apartment?

"It's not Mother, is it?" I ask.

"No, no. She's fine," she says, too quickly.

She's trying to pay the man. How very odd, and rude. "Rosalind," I say firmly, "one does not pay neighbours for tea." She looks like she's ready to cry. I didn't mean to be that firm, but I raised her to know better than to pay for a neighbourly visit. I'll make a gesture in kind instead, perhaps next week. The man refuses graciously anyway. The woman looks around the room, not meeting my eyes. Being older, she knows what a faux pas I have just averted. I wonder if she has children of her own. Perhaps, I guess, but not with him.

Rosalind takes me out to the car. The girl is there, waiting for us. She gets out and moves into the back seat.

"Are we going to Mother's then?" I ask. I don't know why they came in the car. I far prefer to walk.

"Yes, Mommy. We'll go to Grandmama's. Perhaps you can have a rest there. Then I'll take you home."

Ah, yes, the girl calls Mother "Grandmama." It always takes me a minute to remember that. Yes, perhaps we'll be in time for tea. And scones. Mother almost always has scones, with jam. I know that Rosalind and her girl like that too. Yes.

JANUARY 11, 1983

Pictures. All spread out around me, on the floor, the table, and the chairs. I was looking for one photograph, a certain, specific one. Now there are piles all around. There are so many of the view from here. I can see it out my window and also everywhere in the piles: sunrise over Mount Baker, moonrise, sunset, and the water. All the pictures glimmer with golds and pinks and velvety purples. Always the same view.

People too. Some black and white ones. Older, those. Mother and Father and Eliza and Douglas. Agatha too. And finally, pictures of me. Funny. I never looked like Eliza or Douglas. In some families, all the children have a look. I suppose I don't because of Father. Their father was someone else. He died, of course, long ago. But I do look like Mother. She never speaks of their father. Even when I was little and Eliza and Douglas would ask. She only ever said, "He died, in a fire." And that was the end. I wonder now; I wonder if Eliza and Douglas have ever asked again.

Such a lot of pictures and so many the same. I must have taken them. But I don't recall. Of course, I'm looking for something. An old picture. Perhaps it's at Mother's. I think it's in an album. Not loose. If only I could remember. Such a long time ago since I found it. Hiding. I was trying to hide from Eliza and Douglas. I was in Mother's room. All dark and gloomy. Blinds down. Her room was supposed to be private and I knew it. I hoped the older ones wouldn't think of looking for me there. Then I could really hide, for a long time.

I went behind her hope chest and got as small as could be. Dark and dusty. Cool, even though it was a hot day. Quiet. My fingers were on the floor, almost under the chest. They touched something. Scared. But touched it again. A book. Full of pictures. Opened it up and saw Mother. Young and in a big city. Definitely Mother, and with a person who was Eliza, but wrong. Heard footsteps. Closed the book. Rolled out from behind the chest and—did I get discovered? I can't remember.

All these pictures, yet Mother must have that one. I cross over to the phone. Why am I standing here? I put the phone down.

Rosalind must've been here. Look at all the pictures she's left out. I put the old ones in boxes; they're easy to put away, as the sizes of the kids tell the order. These others—the sky—Mount Baker. I push the stacks together. There seem to be hundreds of them. The stacks tip. I put pillows on top and tuck the stray ones out of sight down the sides of the couch.

When did Rosalind leave? I go into the kitchen. There are lots of dishes, but I can't tell if any are from today. Was she here for tea? Was Mother with her? I'm too tired to know. Where are the pictures that go in these boxes? They're empty, but I'm sure they should be full. Where can the pictures be? With Rosalind? With Mother? But why? These are my pictures. No matter how long I look at the empty boxes, nothing changes. They're still empty.

FEBRUARY 18, 1983

Rosalind and Mother. A young woman too. An office. Chairs. Some paintings. I look at the one of the sea. A ship. The front looks like a woman. The young woman is familiar, but I don't think I know her. She whispers to Rosalind. Not polite, really.

A painting. A ship. I go closer. A woman on the front. Perhaps the girl is from the ship, for she is young, just a new woman really, mostly she's still a girl.

Mother has my hand. We walk down a narrow hall. Another room. The girl is here too. No painting. Only a few chairs. I sit and fold my hands. Mother is beside me. I must walk. I start to get up, but the door opens. In comes a doctor wearing his white coat and his doctor's necklace. I can't think of its name. The word won't come, only the doctor's necklace. Father had one. I could use it sometimes, on my dollies, carefully.

I blink. They've been talking. The girl too. The doctor's asking questions and they're all answering. No one's looking at me. I want to walk. Perhaps now I could go? I get up and place my hand on the doorknob. Rosalind is there.

"No, Mommy, not now," she says.

I sit down again, unwillingly.

The doctor finally looks right at me. "Georgie, how are you today?"

I nod.

He persists. "Can you tell me where you are?"

I nod again and smile. Rosalind likes it when I smile.

The doctor smiles back. He has good teeth. "Who is with you today?"

"Rosalind and Mother," I say. That is an easy question.

"Who's this?" he asks, pointing at the girl.

I smile and nod and say, "A girl. From the painting."

The girl smiles at that, but not with her eyes. I look at Mother. She's not smiling and Rosalind looks tired.

"What's today's date?" he asks.

"The day after yesterday's," I say quickly. I know that one too.

The doctor looks a little surprised, and then he pats my knee. "A very good answer," he notes. "Absolutely true."

I nod. I know it myself.

"Who is our prime minister?"

An odd question from a doctor, to be sure: I'm really quite surprised. Father always kept up with politics no matter how busy he got. This doctor can't be a very conscientious man. I quickly look at Mother's face. I don't know what she's thinking. She must be worried about this doctor's credentials.

"Don't you know?" I finally ask.

"I do, but I need to hear you say the answer," he replies. He seems crafty. He wants to make me say it so he won't have to let Rosalind and Mother see his failings.

I consider. Perhaps I should help him. He does seem kind, even if he is a little sneaky. "Pierre Trudeau, of course," I say and picture our PM with his bright red rose.

Mother makes a funny sound in her throat. She always thought Trudeau was flashy. She likes more sedate politicians.

"Now I need to ask you some questions about math and logic," says the doctor. "Just answer as best you can, and take your time. Don't worry if you need to pass on a few questions. That's perfectly all right, if you do."

His voice goes on. I hear some of the questions and try to answer. They are hard, but sometimes the answer pops out of my mouth before I can even taste the sound of the word. Mother and Rosalind sit silently. The girl shifts occasionally in her chair, and her eyes look big and very serious by the end. It's easier to look at her than the doctor. He keeps smiling too much. His teeth are very white, all except one anyway.

I need to walk. He's still talking, but I get up. Rosalind tries to stop me again, but I push past her. The hallway is quite long. I walk to the end and turn and come back. To the end and back. Over and over. It's a rhythm. I feel my fingers uncurl. My breathing feels looser. I keep walking. To the end and back. Again and again. The door to the little room stays open. I can hear voices when I'm across from it.

Mother is being firm. I make sure I stand up straighter as I walk. Mother always stands up so proudly. Rosalind seems sad and unsure. I can't make out the girl's voice. I hear the doctor say something odd. It sounds like "all strummers." Perhaps he is a musician too. Mother always has liked music and is quite interested in instruments of all sorts. I hum a song I hear in my head. I hear it often. I think I used to play it on our old piano. Mother still plays the piano sometimes. I keep walking and hum too. Back and forth. Over and over.

They come out. Rosalind takes my arm and steers me down the hallway and out of the building. The girl is still with us. She has Mother's arm. Perhaps she's a nurse in training. Someone I know did that. Was it me? Mother? No. Rosalind? No. She hates blood. I can see the nurse in my mind's eye with lots of curly hair under her white cap. Big brown eyes, like chocolate pools. I stop humming. Who is she? Maybe Eliza?

Rosalind urges me into her car. It seems new and big. "Is my Volkswagen at home?" I ask.

Rosalind sighs as she helps me with the seatbelt. "No, Mommy," her voice is low and soothing, "We sold it, years ago. Remember?"

Mother and the girl get in. I don't say anything. I don't remember. And it hurts. I fold my hands in my lap and promise myself that I won't ask any more questions of Rosalind. Not ever. The answers make no sense anyway, because I don't remember.

JUNE 21, 1988

Walking. A hand in mine. A girl. She walks fast. She is young, but my height. Sunshine. Quite warm. I turn my face in its direction. A rush of smells; blossoms; grass; salt. She doesn't let go. We are on the sidewalk. I can hear and see the sea. Waves. Boats. Out from shore. Big mountains. Sunshine everywhere. I put my hand up and bump a hat off. I hate hats. It tumbles. She stops. Gets it. But only carries it herself.

Small room. The doors close and the room moves. She still has my hand. The doors open. A hallway. Long and white. She still walks fast. A small room with a bed. Two women sitting on chairs. Look, look.

"Mother!" I see her. The girl walks me over to Mother. Mother's hand is cool, soft, with knobbly fingers. I start to cry. I haven't seen Mother in so long. She strokes my hair. I rest my head on her shoulder. She hums.

The other woman and girl disappear. Mother hums and strokes my head and shoulders. I stop crying. We hum together, and then she just holds my hand. I'm very tired.

The Path to Kitty Islet

OCTOBER 15, 1989

One step, then another. Tippy. A girl on one side. A woman on the other. The sidewalk is very smooth, like glass. No, not outside. Inside still. A hallway.

I laugh. I got it wrong.

The floor bumps and the woman opens two sets of doors. She pushes buttons with numbers. I try to watch. Important. Numbers. My eyes slide to the outside. Leaves everywhere. We walk together. Leaves crunch. The air is cool. I shiver. The woman looks at me. A big look. She squeezes my hand. I squeeze back. She seems helpful. The girl is quiet, but has noisy shoes. They squeak. We walk.

Panting. The woman? The girl? Me. Need big gulps of air to breathe. Stop walking. Press my hand onto my head at the front. Sharp. Pokes. Still panting. More pain. Panting hurts too.

Slowly walk. Breathing through my mouth. Sharp pain in my head. Want to hold it. Cover it. The girl won't let me. The woman won't. Their hands hold mine. They feel warm. My head is warm. My hands are cold, very cold.

Doorway. Numbers. Shiny floor. Polished. Still panting. Hurts. Sit. Lean back. Hurts more. Panting. The girl and the woman gone. All in white and blue now. Lying down. Pain. Breathing hard. Hand across my face. Mine. Pull at my nose. Something there. Pull. Pull. Claw. Not right.

Hands stop me. My hands can't move. Feel them; still cold. Can't move. All white and blue. Smells like Father. Not panting any longer. Breathe. In and out. And again.

AMELIA

NOVEMBER 1989
ONE

I regard him surreptitiously from the side of the window. I'm hiding behind the curtains, though I know he won't bother looking up to see if I'm watching. He puts the last box in the back of the large—too large—van he rented. I wonder why he got such a big rental. Most of the stuff in our apartment is mine. "*My* apartment," I correct myself, wincing. He closes the van's back doors, walks around to the front, and gets in. He doesn't look up. Sometimes my instincts are right.

As he drives away, I close the curtains. Dusk drew in long ago, it being November, and I need to hold on to as much light in my life as possible. Tears are running down my face, but I try to ignore them as I make my apartment mine again. I shift the furniture around in each room, filling any obvious empty spaces, and turn on all the lamps and lights.

It is very quiet, aside from the few thumps I make; Clive took the stereo. In a way, I'm glad. I don't want or need a soundtrack for my sadness. This isn't a movie, though recent events make me feel I've somehow gotten caught up in one, a really badly written one actually. My life has become a cliché—pathetic, hurtful, and oh so ordinary. The only positive is the fact that Clive decided to leave before we got married. Not before we'd gotten engaged,

The Path to Kitty Islet

and not before we'd planned our wedding, but at least before the big day.

"I've got two more weeks to get through," I think. "Two more weeks to cancel everything, send back the early wedding gifts, and send some sort of announcement." Though Clive promised to help, I know I can't count on him for anything. I contemplate calling someone, but I also know deep down that the choices I make in the next while will have lasting consequences. I really do want to make them on my own.

My cat sits at my feet as I stand in the hallway, thinking. He's been with me since before I met Clive and I know he never particularly liked the other man in my life. "Well, old boy," I say, scratching him behind his ears, "it's back to you and me." I walk through the two-bedroom apartment one more time. I've done a pretty good job of making it look as if nothing much is missing. I need to get a few of my pictures up out of the storage locker, but it is remarkable how much it looks like my apartment again.

It's time to go to bed. I'm exhausted, but sleep will be hard to come by. Even though things have been strained between Clive and me for a while, we always seemed to find a way to come back together. I believed that we had the ability to talk through anything, until this. Clive obviously has been keeping things back and not telling me how he really feels. Has he been doing that all along? Has our whole relationship been built on a façade? Is he being honest even now? No, sleep is not going to be easy.

I enter the study and sit down at my desk. I could compose our "non-wedding" announcement. I could do some marking. My school bag is full of student essays and papers that really should get returned to my classes before the start of Christmas break. It is difficult to imagine focusing on anything, doing anything that requires sustained thought. A distraction is what I need; but none of the things I've thought of have any appeal.

If only I could stop thinking, could stop replaying those scenes of the last few weeks. I keep hearing Clive's words, so hurtful and so unbelievable. He said he doesn't love me any longer; he doesn't know why. He tried to make himself do so because we were such good friends, such a good team, so perfect together, but in the end he wasn't able to pull it off. "I really thought I could go through with the marriage," he said. "I know we've been good together, I know we look as if we're good together, and that on paper we should be one of those couples that grows old together, but—well, the reality of us, just us, for the rest of our lives—It just seems so ordinary, so boring. You had it all planned out, and there's got to be more. I need more. It's all so—mundane. I can't do it. You're just not enough for me."

How his blunt words echo in my head. He seemed determined to hurt me, and he has. Maybe he realized that if he angered me, I'd have some protection from what he was doing and how he was choosing to abandon me. But maybe he truly doesn't care at all. That is the scariest thought. Whatever protection my anger offers, it isn't enough. Clive seems to have become such a good actor that I have no idea when he was acting and when he was telling the truth. Perhaps he's acting now? I have no idea. Now, he claims that he'd been thinking about calling everything off for months—even before we'd gotten engaged—yet I didn't notice anything different, anything amiss, until just a few short weeks ago. I feel duped, scared, lonely, and angry all at once.

I turn off the lights in the study, pick out a book from the hall bookcase, and put myself to bed. Tomorrow I will find a way to focus. I will soldier on no matter how much it costs me or how my heart aches. It feels as if it can't break anymore; my heart has become a group of hard stones, loose gravel in my chest, each piece rubbing against the other and anchoring me, at least for the foreseeable future, to all the pain I feel tonight.

The Path to Kitty Islet

A few weeks later, I realize I've done it. Christmas break has almost arrived, and I've survived. I've marked papers like a fiend, and returned every single one to my students. Never mind that I had to ask them to return one set back to me, so as to write down their marks, which I'd forgotten to record in my grade book; I've done it. I cancelled the teacher on call who'd been ready to cover my classes while I was off preparing for the wedding, and I've taught all my classes myself. I've called the church, the minister, the caterers, the string quartet, the singer, the videographer, the florist, and on and on, and I've cancelled all of them. I've forfeited many of our deposits, of course, but I really don't care, nor could it be helped. It is, as everyone reminds me, very late to be cancelling.

I even unbooked our honeymoon flight to Mexico, though Clive suggested he might want to keep it booked for himself and a friend of his. I can't help speculating: which "friend"?

And some part of me wonders. If Clive wanted to come back into my life, all contrite and apologetic, would I let him? Would I trust him? I was hopeful at first. Even a few days after he moved out, I wondered if he might change his mind. However, I've come to realize that he was very self-absorbed in the weeks before he left, and really insensitive. Had he always been that way? Perhaps I've only just noticed what was there all along.

How much of his character did I see, and how much of it was simply invention on my part? I don't know. And that fact really hurts. Betrayal by another is one thing, but feeling betrayed by my own instincts is even more gut wrenching.

Tomorrow is going to be very difficult. It is supposed to be my wedding day: my day to live in a fairy tale and dress up like a princess. I have my dress. It's at my great-grandmother's house, waiting in the closet in the second bedroom. I planned to dress at Grandmama's, so that all the women in my family could get ready for the wedding together. Grandmama and my mom would have had such fun helping me get ready. That part would have been perfect, and then my mom would have walked me down the aisle, to Clive.

The image doesn't quite have the same power over me that it had even a few days ago. It is getting harder to picture myself walking toward Clive, as I'm so angry with him. I can easily see myself in the dress; I can imagine all my family and friends together helping me get ready and then seeing them seated in the church; but then the picture wavers and becomes loose and fluid, like the shimmers on hot pavement. I can't really see Clive anymore. It's both disconcerting and comforting. He is the love of my life, isn't he? Though he has rejected me, I still love him deep down, underneath all my heartache and wounded pride and anger—don't I?

DECEMBER 1989
TWO

Yes, I've officially made it to Christmas break. I can simply drive home, crawl into bed, and stay there for the next three weeks. I can simply collapse. Everyone would understand, and probably even my mom would leave me be, more or less. But although I am exhausted, although I am stricken, I don't think I want to give in to despair completely—at least not yet, anyway.

I was on my way home, driving back to my apartment, but change course slightly, choosing instead to go to my great-grandmother's. I ease the car into the small driveway and turn off the ignition. For a brief moment, I simply sit, hands on the steering wheel, staring unseeingly into the back garden. Finally rousing myself, I let myself in, calling out as I do so, in case my grandmama hasn't heard the car. I should know better. In her late nineties, Minnie Cosgrove still has almost perfect hearing and eyesight. There she is, waiting in the hall to give her great-granddaughter a warm and loving hug.

"School's done now?" she asks.

"All done. Me too," I reply.

"I thought as much. Come through to the kitchen, and let's have some tea."

Avoiding even looking into the second bedroom as we go past, I'm glad I decided to delay going home for a bit. It's so easy being with Grandmama. I'm tired of everything feeling so hard these days, especially being on my own. I've always savoured being alone, but since Clive left, I've felt like all I have is time with myself.

Once tea is poured, Grandmama looks searchingly at me. I brace myself for the inevitable "So, how are you, really?" question that most people want to ask, but don't. But she doesn't ask either; she simply takes another sip of her tea and seems to come to some sort of a decision.

"I'll be right back," she says, and leaves the room.

When she returns, she's carrying an armload of photo boxes. "These were your grandmother's. When she went into extended care, I brought them here. I know your mother wants them eventually, but I always thought I would do my best to get them into some sort of order for her, write on the backs—all the things Georgie and I never did before."

I know my mouth drops open as Grandmama opens some of the boxes. They are jam-packed; photos slip and slide out as soon as the lids are removed.

"Shouldn't you do this with Mom, or maybe even Aunt Eliza or—" I protest. Family history isn't really my thing; it's Mom's.

"Anybody but you," Grandmama finishes, her eyes twinkling. "You're going to need a project this winter, and I'm finally ready to organize these photos. Mine too. You've just been volunteered."

"Voluntold is more like it," I think, but don't say out loud.

Later, as I crawl into bed, I think some more about what she said. These next weeks, months—heck, even years—do seem to loom ahead of me now that I'm no longer getting married. Perhaps I do need a project to focus on—besides work and dwelling on what went wrong with Clive. It might be the very thing.

JANUARY 1990
THREE

The wind is bitterly cold as Mom and I open our car doors and hurry over to the building's entrance. Although it's warm inside, I can't stop shivering. I find it so hard to visit my grandmother here. It isn't that the facility is so awful; it isn't. It's always clean, brightly lit, and as cheerful as it can be. The problem is seeing my grandmother, seeing Georgie, in such a state.

Grandma has gone through various stages of memory loss. At first we assumed it was her usual forgetfulness. Both Mom and Grandmama have lots of stories of Grandma turning up for special occasions on the wrong day or at the wrong hour. I myself can count on the fingers of one hand the number of times my grandmother has actually remembered my name without prompting. Grandma usually resorted to calling me "Eliza," her sister's name, not that I minded all that much. But a few years ago things got much worse. Grandma no longer recognized her own daughter, my mom, and finally she no longer recognized Grandmama, her mother.

Mom and I stop outside Grandma's room. Grandma has a private room now, with a stunning view south to the Olympic Mountains, but she's too unaware of the outside world to appreciate it. Mom looks at me, squares her shoulders, and takes a deep breath. Letting it out, she says, "Ready?" I nod. We go in.

Grandma is on the bed, on her back, eyes open. Her chest moves up and down, and occasionally her hands clutch at the covers. Her wrists still show some faint marks where she'd been restrained. Restraints are no longer necessary, as she's no longer able to walk or talk or even eat. Her breath makes a deep rasping sound and rattles at times, but the only machine in the room, the one evaluating her heart rate, shows that her heart is as regular and strong as ever.

Mom sways slightly on her way to the bed and then takes her mother's hand in her own. "I'm here, Mother. It's me, Rosalind. Amelia's here too."

Grandma doesn't respond. Neither Mom nor I expect her to, but there's still a small part in each of us that hopes for something. Though the doctors have finally been very clear about the natural progression of the disease, it hasn't affected that minuscule grain of hope that rubs against each of our hearts, making us hold our breath, just for a moment, whenever we re-enter Grandma's room and take her hand.

I make my way round the bed and grip my grandmother's right hand. The long, slender fingers, so very like my own, are paler than I've ever seen them. Grandma always spent so much time outside, walking in all sorts of weather, that her hands and face have always been quite tanned. "That's part of the problem," I think as I look down at her face. "She's too pale." The other problem is the fact that her face is devoid of expression. Its wrinkles map so well what used to be laugh lines and a very expressive mouth, but there's no longer any animation.

Grandma's rasping breathing continues. The sound fills the room and eddies around us. Unable to look at her any longer, I turn to gaze through the window and across the Strait of Juan de Fuca. For the millionth time, I think how nice it would've been if there'd been a room available that looked east, toward Mount Baker, the same view Grandma enjoyed for so many years from her Oak Bay condo. But what does it really matter? As soon as I think that, I feel guilty, but Grandma's inability to notice anyone or anything is all too clear.

Looking across at my mom, I realize she's crying silently. Tears slip down her face and drip inelegantly off her nose, but Mom makes no move to wipe them.

It's hard enough for me to visit my grandmother and see her like this. I pray Alzheimer's will never strike my mom. But how can I help my mom now? How can I ease the sorrow of visiting a person who's barely more than a shell, a person who never recognizes anyone, but who has a heart as strong and rhythmic as the ocean itself? It's horrible to wish for death, to hope for it, so that we can all be released.

At least I've managed to convince Mom and Grandmama to take turns. When Grandma first slipped into her almost comatose state, both visited every day, staying for hours. Now, Mom often comes on her own one day, then I bring Grandmama down the next. Neither of them stays long. It's simply too hard.

Grandma's noisy breathing continues. After a while, I look over at Mom again and notice she's stopped crying. She's stroking Grandma's fingers and humming very softly under her breath. That has become part of the visit too, sort of a goodbye ritual. I can never quite make out the tune, and I haven't been able to ask. Funny, Mom and I are so close and such good friends, yet I feel as if I'd be intruding if I did.

Mom straightens up, pats Grandma's hand three times, looks over to me, and nods. Bending down, I press my cheek against my grandmother's. We leave the room, closing the door carefully behind us. Away from the intense sound of Grandma's laboured breathing, our own breathing seems much lighter. And, back outside in the brisk wind, I feel energized. At the same time, we both say, "Let's go for a walk." Grinning at each other, we start off, straight into the wind, toward the water.

The Path to Kitty Islet

FEBRUARY 1990
FOUR

    I drive my great-grandmother to the care home so that she can check on Grandma. Her condition has weakened. We decided, as a family, to avoid giving her a feeding tube, but it's hard to watch her already slender frame diminish day by day. She now has an oxygen tube in her nose, just to ease the rasping and to make her breathing a little easier. Grandmama pauses at the doorway, taking it all in. She has never wavered in her determination to honour her daughter's wishes, and though both Mom and I have had second thoughts about the feeding tube, Grandmama has been adamant. "Her spirit is already with Stuart and her father. We need to let her body go too."
    She enters the room and pulls a chair close to Grandma's bed. The ornate walking stick she carries, for show really, she hangs over the chair's back. She looks up at me. "Could you please get me a drink of water? I'm parched."
    I nod and leave. It's extremely unusual for Grandmama to send me out for anything. In the past, she's gone herself, in order to "stretch my legs and connect with the nurses." I have a feeling that Grandmama has a reason for this request, but I have no idea what it is.
    I return, glass of water in one hand, and I grasp the doorknob with the other so as to open the door wider. Before I actually move the door, however, I hear my great-grandmother talking.
    " ... so you see, it all came right in the end, didn't it? I'm just sorry I couldn't tell you before. But I couldn't even tell your father. I tried a dozen times, managed to share bits, but never managed to tell him all the truth. When he died, I thought it would be easier to tell you. But still, I had Eliza and Douglas to consider. It was always so complicated."

My hand is clutching the doorknob tightly. When I make myself relax my hand, the doorknob suddenly releases and makes a squeaky, sproinging sound. Grandmama stops talking, and I force myself to walk in casually as if I've heard nothing. But, in reality, what have I heard? What on earth has Grandmama kept secret from her husband? And from all her children? It almost sounds—I don't like the direction my train of thought is taking, but it almost sounds as if Grandmama had an affair—as if Grandma is not Grandpapa's daughter! Could that be possible? Surely I'm imagining things, or jumping to the wrong conclusion.

I look carefully at Grandmama, who is thoughtfully sipping the water I brought her. Beautifully dressed, completely cogent, and physically fit, Grandmama still works in her own garden, goes out for walks, and attends church. Her eyesight and her hearing are better than those of many fifty-year-olds. She really is a remarkable woman, so much so that her age hasn't diminished her vitality or her character. Because she's been able to keep both her health and her wits about her, it isn't difficult to imagine her at twenty or thirty. But to imagine her as Grandma's mother, wondering how to tell her husband she'd been unfaithful? No, I must have misheard or misunderstood.

I force myself to look away from Grandmama and to focus on Grandma instead. It's very hard to see how frail and skeletal she has become. It's impossible to look closely at the figure in the bed and imagine her as a young mother, or even as she was when I was a child. Alzheimer's has taken her memories, destroyed her abilities; but it's unable to kill her. An infection or illness will have to do that. Meanwhile, we must all wait.

FEBRUARY 1990
FIVE

Mom calls at precisely 6:30 a.m. Knowing my routine, she knows I am about to step in the shower.

"Your grandmother died at about three a.m. this morning. One of the nurses was with her; she said she'd just had a feeling it was time." Mom sniffs a bit, and then continues. "She said it happened quickly. Amelia, she's gone." With that, she starts to weep.

"Oh, Mom; I'm sorry. I'll call in to work and get a TOC. Have you told Grandmama?"

"Not yet. I called you first. I haven't called Michael or Eliza or Douglas either."

"Okay, don't worry. I'll come get you in about forty-five minutes and take you over to Grandmama's. I can phone Eliza and Douglas and Michael from there. We'll tell Grandmama together. Then Eliza and Douglas can phone their kids."

A few more sniffles, then a soft "Thank you" and a click.

I put down the phone. We've waited for so long, known for so long. I hadn't expected to feel so surprised.

—

Though it is only eight a.m. when Mom and I walk up Grandmama's front steps, it is unseasonably warm. Grandmama's garden, lovingly designed by Grandpapa so many years ago, is a gentle riot of early spring colour, a joy to behold on a bright February morning. I knock and wait. I'm about to pull out my key when I hear footsteps; Grandmama must have looked out and recognized my car in the driveway. The door opens, and she says, "My girl's gone, isn't she?"

"Yes, Grandmama. She's gone," Mom says quietly.

"We need tea," Grandmama turns and walks, more slowly than usual, down the hall.

Once the tea is steeping, she reaches for Mom and envelopes her in a hug. Both of them are crying.

"To outlive a child," Grandmama pauses, swallowing hard, "is not the natural way of things, no matter how old one may be. Georgie was my little girl," her voice breaks and stops.

I don't know where to look or what to say. This is grief, pure and true. Although we lost Grandma's self long ago, little by little, there has always been hope. Foolish perhaps, but it sang out, a wind-beruffled tiny bird, as Emily Dickinson put it, hopeful despite all the medical facts. But now that hope is gone. Lost in thought, I realize that my sadness over losing Clive is in another, lesser category altogether. Losing my grandmother, and watching my mother and great-grandmother deal with her death, puts the demise of my relationship with Clive into perspective.

"Amelia?"

I realize I haven't been paying attention. "Yes?"

Grandmama and Mom both look at me searchingly.

"Are you all right, pet?" asks Grandmama.

"Yes, well, yes." I sip my tea, giving myself some time to return to the present. "We haven't called Eliza and Douglas yet." I reach for the phone. "Are they likely to be home now?"

Grandmama nods. "Neither of them likes to do much very early."

I call Eliza first, then Douglas, and finally my own brother, Michael. No one is shocked, but I can detect the same sense of surprise among them that I still feel. I hang up and decide to make more tea. Mom and Grandmama have moved into the front room. As I enter, Mom comments on the photo boxes.

"Grandmama, what's all this?"

"They're your mother's, mostly. I've roped Amelia into helping me organize them and trying to make sense of the chaos. Georgie never really had a comprehensive system, especially lately, so we've been trying to, well, sort of merge them with mine. Unfortunately, my own system's not much better, and there are dates on precious few."

Mom shakes her head. "Well, I'll be." She looks from Grandmama to me in amazement. "You don't care about ancient history."

"Mom, that's not quite true," I say, probably sounding defensive. "I never have cared as much as you, and I've never had time, to take it all in properly, but now," I shrug.

Mom stands up and gives me a hug. "Thank you," she whispers in my ear and pats my back. "Mom would be so pleased."

MARCH 1990

SIX

Douglas splurged and rented a large limousine complete with driver. It seems ridiculous—three elderly people and four younger ones, riding in a car generally used by twenty delirious high school grads or tipsy wedding parties, but Douglas was adamant. "We should be in one vehicle, and no one should have to drive." Neither Eliza's nor Douglas's children could make it. They all moved back east years ago, and as Eliza pointed out, they all said their goodbyes to Georgie when they'd last seen her.

At least the limo is silver, not black, and the driver seems happy to keep to himself. I sit facing forward, my window rolled down a bit. I don't do well riding in the back of a vehicle, no matter what the circumstances. Grandmama sits in state in the centre of the back seat, with Eliza beside her. Douglas and Mom sit on the side, but face backwards. Michael, my older brother, and his wife, Suzanne, sit across from me. He is holding Suzanne's hand in his. I take care not to look at the cardboard box resting on Grandmama's lap.

Victoria's scenic waterfront drive is winding and quite bumpy. I start to feel queasy and have to roll my window down lower. I know we don't have much farther to go, but my stomach is going to have to hang on while the car rocks its way up and around

Gonzales Hill, past the viewing terrace, and down to the east side of McNeill Bay.

We talked about where along the route we should ask the driver to stop. At first Grandmama and Eliza were focused on Turkey Head, one of Grandma's favourite places to walk—a spot visible from her condo and offering a jaw-dropping view of Mount Baker. I pointed out that it was such a scenic spot that it would be very difficult to complete our task without attracting attention—spreading ashes in a public place isn't exactly encouraged. So Douglas suggested Kitty Islet, reminding everyone that Grandma loved to walk here as well. She clambered out onto the rocks as a child and, taking advantage of the Adirondack chair someone placed there more recently, often sat there in the sun as an adult.

Everyone agreed with Douglas's suggestion. Mom and I went out to the funeral home and picked up the ashes. We didn't purchase a fancy urn or even a metal box, but simply accepted the cardboard box they gave us and drove to the car rental place. The others were there, waiting.

The limo eases onto the widened shoulder and parks. The driver comes around and opens the back door, helping each of us out in turn. It is a grey March day. The wind is up, and the darkened sky threatens showers; it looks as if we'll have the point to ourselves. We've all worn sensible shoes, and Grandmama takes Mom's arm once they each make their own way down the concrete steps. The rocks on the beach could easily sprain an ankle. Douglas carries the box, while Michael brings up the rear.

Once we reach the rocky outcropping facing across the strait to Trial Island, Douglas puts the box on the weathered chair. Grandmama steps forward and unhooks the self-hinging lid. Inside is a clear plastic bag filled with a greyish powder. Standing with her hands in her pockets, Mom looks as if the last thing she wants to do is go closer to that box. Eliza, too, looks drawn in on herself.

For a few moments, none of us move. We are surrounded by the cries of seagulls and the low whoosh of the waves moving in and out. What an odd tableau this is: I remember the day, last year or the year before, when I rounded this very point on a run and inexplicably heard the strains of "Amazing Grace." Sure I was imagining things, I stopped running, caught my breath, and then realized that a piper was standing on these rocks, cradling his bagpipes and playing that haunting melody for the wind and the sea. Seeing him again in my mind's eye and hearing the tune in my head, I step forward and dip my hand into the box.

Turning so I can't see any of the others' faces, I take a few steps across the rocks and let the powder trickle through my fingers, down onto the rocks and water below. "Goodbye, Grandma," I whisper. "I will always think of you the way you used to be. With your walking shoes on and your hair wind-blown and your cheeks flushed with colour." Then, more fiercely, "I know you knew who I was, even if you almost never remembered my name."

When I turn around, I see that everyone has followed suit, even Mom. They've each taken a handful and gone closer to the water's edge, committing Grandma's ashes to the ocean. As I get closer to the box, I'm amazed to see how full it remains. Taking a deep breath, I take another handful. We all do. And another. Almost overbalancing in my zeal to keep up with Michael, I let out a giggle. Catching my eye, Michael guffaws and as soon as Grandmama, Mom, Douglas, Eliza, and Suzanne return to the box, we burst out laughing together.

We've each taken handfuls, cast them into the wind, into the water, and across the rocks, and still there are more. Mom wipes her eyes. "I knew I would cry while we were doing this, but I didn't think they'd be tears of laughter," she says, looking around at our family. "My heart is aching; I've missed her for so long and it should be over, but the damned box is still half full!"

"It certainly doesn't take a minute or two, like it does in the movies, does it?" agrees Michael.

With that, we are solemn once more. Douglas clears his throat, "Mother, I think we should pray and perhaps say a few words now. Then maybe you could pour the rest out. Just there, near the beach?"

Grandmama nods. Her voice starts ours as we all then say the Lord's Prayer together. One by one, we each say something about Grandma or to Grandma. None of us manages to say very much. My throat is thick, and I'm only able to say, "God bless." Michael, the last to speak, blurts out, rather puzzlingly, "I've never forgotten the ice cream."

Wordlessly, Douglas picks up the box. We mourners make our way off the rocks and down onto the small beach that is one side of the narrow isthmus that forms part of the point. At high tide, these rocks are almost an island. Grandmama takes the box in one hand and, using my mom's arm for balance, they make their way to the water's edge. Taking the plastic bag out, she lets the cardboard box drop to the ground. Tilting the bag, she holds it like a pennant, and the wind, catching at it, helps disperse the final grey ashes. It is done.

My eyes full of tears, I can hardly see where to place my feet as I turn to go back to the car. The rocks of the beach are all an indeterminate grey blur—all except one. It is an incredible, glowing orange. It looks like a piece of the sun washed up on the beach and landed at my feet. I bend over and pick it up. The rock is oval and smooth, and somehow almost warm to the touch. I put it in my pocket, but my fingers can't leave it alone. Riding downtown in the limo, I continue to gently rub the stone.

The Path to Kitty Islet

MARCH 1990
SEVEN

It's quite late. I have the school's staff room and, more importantly, the photocopier to myself. I'm running off packages for my Advanced Placement students. Once we return from spring break, it will be full steam ahead to prepare for the AP exams. If they do well, the students can register for second-year college or university courses, skipping the straightforward first-year ones, saving both money and time. If I get all the packages done now, I won't have to come in to school during the break and I'll have two weeks almost entirely to myself.

Then I start thinking. Perhaps it's been a mistake to push myself so hard this last quarter. I've thrown myself into teaching with unmitigated zeal, and my students have responded in kind. Now, however, instead of needing the break to do my usual marking and prep, I'm finished my work before it's even started. If Clive were still around—I clamp down on the thought before it takes hold. I know I've been using work as an escape.

Finishing up the photocopying, I lock away my packages and supplies in the filing cabinets, and turn off the lights. I walk down the stairs and through the main office, calling goodnight to the administrative assistant, who can't lock up until everyone is gone. As usual, I am one of the last teachers out the door.

When I get home, my answering machine is flashing. I listen to the message, and then play it again. Unbelievable. My brother and his wife have signed me up for a dating service, a supper club. I'm supposed to meet up with two other women and three men for dinner and conversation at a local restaurant this weekend.

Of course, Michael and Suzanne are worried about me. They know I'm lonely and miss Clive. What they don't know is how raw I still feel, months afterward. I'm not even sure I can ever contemplate being with someone else, let alone going on a group date with a bunch of strangers. It might be nice to eat out for a change, though. I stir my soup thoughtfully. My cat winds himself around my legs and purrs. He seems to agree.

Because of the impending group date, much of Saturday becomes an absolute write-off. Deciding I have nothing appropriate to wear, I spend part of the morning shopping. Then I go for a long run to clear my head; at least that is productive. For the two hours after my shower, I try on outfit after outfit, going through almost all of my belongings before settling on the first combination I tried, composed only in part of what I purchased this morning. I'm pleased, though, with the way the new black pants make the sparkly but low-key emerald top stand out. Shoes then become the issue. Like all the women in my family, I'm tall, and most men don't appreciate being shorter than me. Though I don't wear really high heels, I do like wearing a bit of one, especially when going out. Such a silly dilemma. I pick my favourite two-inch heels. I might as well start as I mean to go on.

That makes me pause. I look at myself in the mirror. How do I mean to go on? I'm not so lost that I can't contemplate living or anything as dramatic as that. I'm not that depressed—not over Clive, or about my life in general. It's more the metaphysical aspect of it. John Donne's "no man is an island" echoes in my head. Teaching English literature can be helpful at times. What's most hurtful about Clive's leaving is that I believed we had a real connection—that we spoke the same language of the heart—that we had a future together. It's traumatic to have all those beliefs destroyed by your best friend and lover and to be ripped away from him at the same time.

But I do mean to go on. Definitely. I haven't even phoned my brother yet to yell at him about putting my name in for this group date. I've come to realize that my life is going to develop in ways I haven't planned. As I apply some light makeup and choose dangly gold earrings, I think that perhaps it doesn't really matter if my plans actually work out. They offer me comfort and give me dreams to work toward, but if they need adjusting, I can do that too. I'll find a way. And if that way means making my brother and sister-in-law happy by trying out a supper club, so be it. I can do that as well.

I pat my hair back one more time and give myself a serious talking-to in the mirror. "You're going to enjoy this dinner. You like meeting new people. Nothing has to mean anything. Just go out, eat good food, and listen. You can do this."

The restaurant has a beautiful view over much of the city. Though new development continues in the downtown core, most of the buildings are fairly low and architecturally pleasing. I meet another woman, Meryl, who arrives at almost the same time. We decide to sit together side by side, facing the view, "just in case," as Meryl puts it. She's about my age, perhaps a little older, and so full of energy that she can hardly sit still. Luckily, all three men and Sarah, the other woman, arrive quickly. In no time we are chatting together amicably: two artists, two teachers, one lawyer, and one shop owner.

The evening passes swiftly. There's a lot of laughter and not much awkwardness among the group, but once dessert is done, silence falls over us. I clear my throat. "Well, it was lovely meeting everyone." I nod across at the three men, each nice enough but not special, and smile at the other two women. "I'll just go to the restroom and then make my way home." Rising from the table, I realize that both Meryl and Sarah seem eager to follow me. When the three of us get into the restroom and Sarah closes the door, we burst out laughing.

"It was fine; they were fine," Meryl gasps, between giggles. "But how were we supposed to leave?"

"I thought I'd have to order another dessert," Sarah says. "I couldn't think what else to do."

"Thank heavens you spoke up, Amelia," Meryl says, "or we'd have been here all night. Instead, we're in the bathroom together, like high school kids."

"Did anyone meet Mr Right tonight? Or at least Mr Maybe?" Sarah asks.

Meryl and I shake our heads.

"Not me either," Sarah sighs. "I've been doing this for a while, and I've met some lovely women. I've even met up with one or two of them again. Not dating, of course," she says quickly. "Just as friends."

Meryl smiles conspiratorially. "Sometimes I think it might be easier to find the right woman."

—

I let myself in to my apartment. The evening went much better than I expected, but it was still depressing. There are no easy answers. I met two bright, beautiful women who are lonely too. And the men? Well, they'd been fine. Just fine. No magic. No sparks. Just fine. I get ready for bed, feed my cat, and choose a book for companionship. "It's going to be a long two weeks, cat of mine. A long two weeks."

MARCH 1990

EIGHT

Squinting up at my great-grandmother through the warm sunshine streaming in from the windows and illuminating millions of dust particles, I cough.

"Yes, dear. It's dusty. I do realize that, even without the benefit of your fake coughs," Grandmama says dryly. "I hate dusting."

I have to be careful not to knock over any of the pictures or albums piled all around me on the floor.

The Path to Kitty Islet

"What should I tackle next, Grandmama? The blue photo boxes?"

Much to our surprise, Grandmama and I discovered that years ago Grandma had developed a system for organizing her pictures. Once we'd gone through the most recent boxes, which were in no order at all, we'd found that the earlier ones were arranged by decade or by family, and we'd been able to sort through those and even identify and date some of them fairly efficiently. It helped that Grandmama's albums were in good shape, despite her disparaging comments, because Grandmama and I were able to cross-reference some photos, add extra pages, and slot pictures into the appropriate spots. I was able to build piles of pictures, mostly in order, to pass on to Mother, as well as Eliza, Douglas, and Michael. And I had a lovely pile of extras for myself.

Shifting onto my haunches, I reflect that my great-grandmother is astonishing. She lives on her own. She's outlived two husbands, a son, a daughter, and a son-in-law. Her mind is still frighteningly sharp, only slightly less so than her tongue can be, though she tends to be dry and sceptical, rather than mean. But if someone says or does something foolish, she'll notice and comment, for she is also incredibly observant. Not much gets past her.

"Grandmama, how'd you do it?"

"Do what?"

"Leave England with a new husband and come to a strange country? Live in an isolated hamlet like Grande Prairie? Have your babies pretty much on your own? And then survive the fire? And come here and start again?"

An odd look comes over her face as she listens to my tumble of questions.

"What are you really asking, darling? Do you want the facts of the story? You've heard those a hundred times."

"I know—I guess I want to hear the story again, but I really want to listen to the part about starting over. I know I've got it easy, so easy really. Clive and I weren't even married yet, and we didn't have kids. I just keep thinking it should be easier. I've got a job I love, I have you and Mom and Michael and my friends. I just—I just can't seem to get started somehow. I can't stop feeling sad and angry. And then I feel silly because I'm still so lucky," my voice trails off and I start crying.

Grandmama reaches into her pocket, pulls out a handkerchief, and passes it to me, now busily snorting and crying and laughing all at once. All I want Grandmama to do is to enfold me in her arms, but she seems far away and lost in thought. Snuffling and coughing a bit, I make good use of the handkerchief as I mop myself up.

"It never feels easy," she begins, "and starting again can never really be starting anew. I think that's the hard part—one of the hard bits, anyway. There's that saying—is it Buddhist? I can't remember now, but it's something like 'Wherever you go, there you are.' Perhaps Clive has not learned that yet." Her voice takes on a hard edge. She looks down at me, still crouched on the floor. "You get up, you put one foot in front of the other, you keep breathing, and you make it up as you go along—all those clichés. And, you hurt. Nothing feels easy. Your emotions keep ricocheting around in your head, and you bang into sadness every time a good thing happens. At least that's how it has often seemed to me. Then you get old. And you have no real answers."

She gets up. "But you have tea, and stories—and some old pictures. And, if you're really lucky, you have someone who wants to listen to the stories, look at the pictures, and wants to see how they all make sense together. I'll just go put the kettle on." And with that, she's gone.

I slowly unfold myself and stand up. I wish Michael and Suzanne would start a family. My stomach knots. In a way, it

The Path to Kitty Islet

will almost kill me, because I'd thought maybe Clive and I and Michael and Suzanne could all start having babies at the same time. On the other hand, Grandmama isn't getting any younger, and perhaps it's time to see people added to our family instead of subtracted. I miss my grandmother. I miss my father. And I miss the man I believed Clive was.

After our tea break, Grandmama and I settle back into our spots in the front room and continue to go through the photo boxes. We are both working on boxes of black and white photos, mostly taken between the wars—lots of pictures of Grandma as a baby, and of Eliza and Douglas with her or individually. I hold one up of all three kids. Eliza and Douglas are gangly teenagers, and it's striking how similar their features are. Grandma still has that slightly plump toddler look, though her fingers are long and slender already.

"Look, Grandmama. Douglas and Eliza look so funny as teenagers. It's easy to see it's them, even though they're both so much older and greyer now. It's interesting to see how different Grandma looks. The older two must have taken after their father, and Grandma seems to be a combination of you and Grandpapa, don't you think?"

She stops writing on the back of her stack of photos and takes the photo from my outstretched hand. She studies it for a long time, sighing a little as she does so.

I decide to ask a question I have long wondered about. Though my great-grandmother has told me about the fire in Grande Prairie, the facts of it, and though she said that that fire took her first husband's life, she never really talks about what happened. And no one in our family has ever really heard much about the son she lost in the fire. Mom told me the little bit she knew about him when I was a teenager. Apparently, Grandpapa once told Eliza and Douglas that they'd had an older brother and how he'd died; but he hadn't told them, or they didn't remember, what the boy's name was, or even how old he was when he died. If I can get Grandmama to answer some questions about the fire, perhaps I can also ask about what I'd overheard the day I was outside Grandma's room. My speculations can't possibly be right, but maybe I can find out what to make of those words.

So I take a deep breath and blurt out. "In the fire, what happened?"

Grandmama looks at me quickly. I'm glad to see that she is neither upset nor angry.

"Well, you finally asked again. I wondered when you might."

"Again?" I'm confused. I'm fairly certain I've never asked before.

"Oh yes. You asked when you were a teenager. I didn't answer."

"Why not?"

"I don't exactly know," she says carefully. "Lord knows, I've gone over and over that day in my head a million times. When I first came to Victoria I would have nightmares constantly, so I didn't want to talk about it in the daytime too. I tried to put it behind me, make it a part of someone else's life somehow. Eliza and Douglas were both so little they didn't remember a thing, it seemed, so that helped too, and made keeping silent appear to be the right thing." She sighs. "But when I fell in love with Thad he was curious, and I felt he should know, but it took a long time for me to tell him. It seems sort of silly now, but I didn't want him feeling sorry for me and I didn't want him thinking that that tragedy had marked me in any way. Of course it had, but I made myself believe that I had forgotten the worst of it, just as the children had."

Her fingers are twisting her wedding band around and around. "I told Thad the story just once. And I never told the children. Not even when they asked. And not even after your grandpapa had told them. I'm glad he did, but I just couldn't look at them and tell them. I couldn't bear it. I couldn't."

"Can you tell me?" I ask. I really want to hear her tell it. I know the story isn't mine; by rights it should be Eliza and Douglas here instead, but every inch of me needs this story. The hair on the back of my neck is tingling, and I can feel my heart beating faster than usual. There's something here, something I need to know, something that Grandmama learned from the destruction of that part of her life.

She leans back in her husband's favourite chair and closes her eyes. "The story really starts in the spring. I was alone in the house, and the baby came. She was too soon, way too early, and too small. The others were scared. I had to cry out because of the pain—but John and Eliza were frightened. She was so tiny when she was born. Like a little bird, Callie said. Callie came that very day. She found me and the children and took us to the hospital. She was so very kind and worried. The baby died. Little Amelia Anne."

Grandmama opens her eyes when she says that, and watches my face. I'm shocked. I didn't know about the baby, and I definitely didn't know that we shared a name. Grandmama stops her story for a moment and pats my arm. "I never told Grandpapa about the baby. Only the fire. Your mother never knew either. And then she named you. A new Amelia. Amelia Emily. It was hard at first. Very hard. But you made it all right. You were big and bonny and your very own self. It was a miracle. Really."

I'm having trouble swallowing the lump in my throat. Of all the names in the world, my mother just happened upon that particular one? How can that be possible? "Are you sure you didn't tell Grandpapa? Or Grandma? Or Mommy? Are you positively certain?"

"I'm sure. I only told Thad about John." She clears her throat. "He was the other boy. My son. Eliza and Douglas's older brother. He was almost five when he died. He and his father burned and my best friend too." Her voice is low and quiet, but steady. "The fire swept across the prairie. July is very dry sometimes and the winds come up. The sod on the roof caught, and the barn; the horses got away, but not Harry, not John, not her." Here her voice catches and she stops. "They didn't make it out."

She looks directly into my eyes and says, "We heard them inside. For a long time, it seemed. And then we were alone, except for Lady, the mare. Eliza and Douglas and I were alone all night. I never felt the cold that night, but for a long time after I could never get warm."

"Callie died too?" I ask.

"No, not Callie," Grandmama says, in a low voice. "My best friend from London; she'd come out to visit. She—she perished that day too."

I look away and shiver. I can picture the scene, though I know I can't really imagine it. To stand by and hear and see and smell—my stomach recoils, but I make myself finish the thought—my husband and my son and my best friend die, all in one fell swoop, only a few months after losing my baby—I try hard to keep my tears in check. But as I glance at Grandmama again, I realize her eyes are full of unshed tears too. I reach up and clasp her slender hands. "Thank you for telling me," I whisper. I don't know what else to say. I'm still stunned by my connection to that wee baby, that other Amelia, who, had she survived, would have been my great-aunt. I still think that my mom, Rosalind, must have known. Certainly she must have. Perhaps Grandmama has forgotten telling her.

"I didn't tell anyone about Amelia," she says as if reading my mind. "I couldn't. Not until this year. I told Georgie, right before she died, but she didn't know what I was saying. Maybe I needed to tell her first to practise telling. When I told Thad about the fire, it felt as if I was telling someone else's story. It was the only way I could do it. And he had to tell Eliza and Douglas, as I said, for I couldn't. He did it to save me pain."

She pats me again, and then sits up tall, straightening her shoulders. "It's finally out. For good or for ill, it's told. I don't know why I kept it to myself for so long. It's your story now, Amelia. I hope it won't be a burden for you, darling. I've let that other Amelia go, long since, and you helped with that, whether you knew it or not. And it doesn't need to be a secret any longer. You can tell your mother. You can tell Eliza and Douglas. Or not." She smiles sheepishly. "I'm glad you know now. It's time I let my stories go, I think. They deserve a life of their own; perhaps that's what they should have had all this time." Her eyes are soft and unfocused.

I feel as if I've been sitting at her feet for decades. It seems a good time to stand up and stretch. The room tilts a little as I rise, but soon rights itself. "I'll be back," I say. She doesn't appear to hear me, and I leave the room. In the bathroom, I splash cold water on my face before looking at my reflection long and hard. Everything feels different. My mom unwittingly gave me the same name as Grandmama's premature baby, who died so many years ago.

"Well," I think, "you wanted something to keep your mind occupied this spring break."

MARCH 1990
NINE

I walk home in the late afternoon, keeping my chin down inside the collar of my coat. The wind is determined and cold: my nose is quite frozen, and I know it will run like a faucet once I get into my apartment. I quicken my steps, but can't stop replaying Grandmama's words in my head: about the fire and about baby Amelia. There's no way I can keep the story to myself, so I'm glad Grandmama didn't ask me to; however, I still don't know how I feel about it. Flummoxed. The word just pops into my head. Yes, exactly.

Until I found out about the other Amelia, I had no idea how much import my name has for me. Having my name attached to that other soul, even briefly, changes its weight and feel. Had I always known about little Amelia Anne, and had Mom chosen Amelia as a name for her daughter to honour that child who died too soon, I likely would give it nary a thought. It would just be a fact of life, like my height and hair colour. But to find out now is—well, it's odd, like being placed on a boat with no opportunity to develop sea legs. I unlock my apartment door and shrug out of my coat.

As I put it away, I start thinking about my mom. If I find this new information so discombobulating, how will she take it? On the one hand, I can imagine she'll be pleased and feel as if it were meant to be. On the other, Mom will no doubt be annoyed that Grandmama never said anything to her, especially once she started talking about naming her child Amelia. Perhaps a visit rather than a phone call will be best to pass on the story.

At that moment, as if summoned, the phone rings. I jump.

"Hello?"

"It's me."

"Of course," I think. "The one day he isn't front and centre, he calls." Out loud I say, "Oh. Ummm, yeah—why are you calling? It's been—months."

Clive pauses, seemingly searching for the right words. "Uh, well—could I maybe come over? I'd rather not, uh, not do this over the phone."

"Not do what?" I'm not really trying to be difficult, though part of me is screaming that I should hang up. "Clive?"

"I'm here." He pauses again. "Can't I just come over? I could be there in ten minutes."

"No." My answer is instinctive.

"Don't be like that," Clive pleads. "I just—I just need to see you. Can't we still be friends?" He pauses again. "Please?"

The Path to Kitty Islet

"I'll meet you at the café. Ten minutes. Don't be late." I slam the phone down into its cradle. Now why hadn't I simply said no again? Because I'm a glutton for punishment, that's why.

I get to the café first and choose a table toward the front, where more seats are crowded together and where I feel there might be safety in numbers. Folding my coat over the back of the chair, I go to the counter and order a plain coffee. I hate coffee with a vengeance and never drink the stuff, but I'm counting on its vile taste to keep me honest. I'm afraid of what Clive is going to say to me, afraid of my response, and afraid of how much damage this meeting might do to my fragile sense of self. Having to drink that wretched stuff should help dispel any romantic ideas my heart might have. My head knows better.

He arrives a full ten minutes late, raising his eyebrows at my choice of table, especially given the many empty chairs in the back. But he doesn't comment. Taking off his coat, he leans down as if to brush my cheek with his lips—I bend forward to adjust the table leg, avoiding his touch. He smiles wryly.

"Right. I'll get a drink."

I study him as he stands in line. He seems to be his usual self—no dark shadows under his eyes, no new worry lines or extra wrinkles, no evidence of any emotional trauma. I wonder if the same could be said of me. I can detect traces of distress in my face, but perhaps that's because I know where to look. Or perhaps because I want to see proof of what he's done to me.

Holding his very tall cup out in front of him—carefully, using both hands—Clive sits down opposite me.

"Well, isn't this nice?" His voice carries barely a hint of sarcasm.

I shrug. I take a tiny sip of my coffee. It's truly foul.

"My mom wants to see you," he says quickly. "She always liked you, you know, and she misses you."

For the third time that day, I feel stunned. First I learned about the other Amelia, then Clive called, and now this.

"I don't understand. You call me out of the blue. You want to see me, but only because your mother wants to see me? You're kidding, right? Is this some sort of weird joke?" My voice gets dangerously high as I ask the final question.

Refusing to meet my eyes, Clive swirls his coffee around his cup. Then he splutters, "Oh, all right. Yeah, she'd like to see you, but mostly she just wants to get the earrings back. More important than that even, I wanted to ask you if you'd co-sign a loan with me. I want to get into a condo and stop renting like we'd planned to do after our wedding, but on my own I have a lousy credit rating. You were always the financial whiz, and bankers love people like you. You wouldn't have to do anything, just sign—just as friends, for old time's sake," he wheedles.

I'm dumbfounded. Clive broke off our engagement two weeks before the wedding, and now he wants me to co-sign a loan? I have to steady myself. I want to slap him and walk away, but even that won't give me enough satisfaction. After taking another sip of my disgusting coffee, I clear my throat and am about to say something when suddenly Clive starts talking again.

"I knew you'd agree! Mom thought it would be better if she called you and asked about the earrings, though she was quite embarrassed about how I'd left you. I guess it wouldn't surprise you to hear that she thinks I've been a jerk. Anyway," he waves his hand airily, "you've obviously forgiven me, which makes this meeting even better. Mom will feel as if I've done my penance by facing you, she'll have her earrings back—their being family heirlooms and all—we're friends again, and I'll have my loan. What could be better?" He leans back in his chair, clearly self-satisfied, and grins his little-boy grin. "You always were completely reliable; that's one thing I really miss about you."

I start to giggle. I can't help it. My shoulders shake, and soon I'm convulsed with laughter. Everyone nearby turns to stare, and I can feel Clive's dismay emanate from across the table, but I don't care. What a huge relief! Truly, I don't care. Coming on the heels of Grandma's death and Grandmama's revelation, Clive's demands are farcical. Finally, I stop laughing and start hiccupping. I wipe my eyes and, holding my breath to try to stop the hiccups, look at Clive and shake my head.

"Are you saying no?" Clive demands. "To the loan? To the earrings? To both? Are you seriously going to be that much of a cow?" All his pretence of being contrite and amiable is gone. "So much for being friends!"

I shake my head again and finally manage to speak. "Tell your mother she's welcome to the earrings. I'd forgotten I had them. I'll drop them off at your office building tomorrow or the next day.

"But co-sign a loan? With you? My ex-fiancé? How self-centred can you get? Are you kidding? You're an idiot, Clive; you really are, you know. Thank heavens even idiots make good decisions sometimes. Much as your leaving hurt, I'm so grateful we're not married, because now I know how much I would have come to despise you. Don't even think about calling me again. Ever. The same goes for your mother. We are done.

"Enjoy the rest of your coffee—and your life. I'm off." I stand up and intentionally bump the edge of the table so that coffee sloshes out of both our cups. Once I'm sure Clive is left with a swampy mess in front of him, I exit the café.

On my way home, I practically skip down Oak Bay Avenue. I feel free—utterly, completely, and light-heartedly free. True, I'd messed up. I'd thought that Clive was "the one." I'd believed that his inability to save any money was due to bad luck rather than poor management. Worse, I'd overlooked his inability to make any real long-term plans, thinking he was a "live in the moment" kind of guy. Today I understand he is the type to "live off the girl of the moment," and then some.

A few months ago I'd never have believed that Clive's decision was a good one. Now I realize I've had a narrow escape. I remember the look on his face when he thought I'd sign a loan with him. Smug, self-satisfied. Yes, I'd misread him, badly, for years. I'd trusted him. I won't be that foolish again and I certainly have no desire to be with him any longer.

Once home, I dig around in my jewellery box and find the earrings. I put my coat back on, and jump in my car. Pulling up in front of the high-rise building where Clive works, I stop in the loading zone. The night security guard comes to the entrance and opens it after I gesture wildly, showing him the box. "Please make sure it gets delivered tomorrow," I plead. I scribble Clive's name and office number on the top of the box, and the guard promises he'll deliver it safely.

In a flash, I'm back in the car, driving quickly to Mom's. All at once, I feel I'm inhabiting myself and my name fully, now that I know about the other Amelia and now that I'm completely free of Clive. For the first time in a very long time, I'm one hundred per cent me.

MARCH 1990

TEN

Mom is surprised to see me, and even more surprised to see me so flushed and animated. She lets me in the house and follows me to the kitchen. I wonder if she's noticed that I'm back to my old pre-jilted, wry self.

I start to get the tea things out. Now that I'm here with Mom, I'm not sure how to get to the point. I need to share Grandmama's story with her, but realize I don't know how to frame it. Probably an honest, straightforward account would be best.

"Mom, Grandmama told me something today that I need to tell you. It's kind of shocking, but it's not bad news or anything. She's not sick. That's not what it's about. It's—well, she—" I start.

"She adopted Grandma?" Mom interrupts, bustling about.

"What? No!" I protest. "What makes you say that?"

"Well, your grandma always looked so different from Eliza and Douglas."

"I know she doesn't look like either of them," I say, "but she definitely looks like a combination of Grandmama and Grandpapa; trust me, all I've been doing lately is looking at old black and white pictures of everyone, and she is not adopted." But I have a niggling doubt deep inside—what had I overheard Grandmama telling Grandma at the care home? Was she just telling her about baby Amelia or was she saying something else? I believe absolutely that Grandma is Grandmama's child; I wish I felt more positive that Grandma was Grandpapa's too.

"No, Mom. Grandmama told me about the fire in Grande Prairie. But she started the story by telling me about the spring before the fire, the spring that she'd had a baby. Another baby—a daughter named Amelia Anne."

"She had another baby? A baby daughter—a daughter called what?" Mom sits down. "What exactly did she say?"

I repeat the story as best I can. I tell my mom about the premature baby, what Grandmama said about the fire and what she'd heard, and about losing John and Harry and her best friend. Mom shakes her head, and mutters, "I had no idea."

"I know," I say. "It really is—unbelievable—isn't it?"

"And the baby was named Amelia? Amelia Anne? You're sure?" Mom asks again.

"Yep. Amelia. Just like me."

"I had no idea. I—she never told me. She never said a word. I'd talk to her about baby names all the time. She never breathed a word. My goodness." Mom stands up and starts pacing back and forth. "Why didn't she say anything? It must have been—it must have been painful to hear the name Amelia, mustn't it? I mean, out of all the names—she could've just said she didn't like it, or that it sounded odd with our last name or something—anything." She stops speaking for a moment. Then, looking quizzically at me, she asks, "How do you feel? Is it odd?"

"It was—shocking—at first. I kept thinking exactly what you said, 'Of all the names,' but Grandmama said that I made it okay. She said I was so big and so different, I guess, from that other Amelia, that it was really okay.

"And, well, today has been the weirdest day all round. I just— Clive called and we saw each other. He's—he's an idiot, really, and I'm glad, but I feel so stupid and yet so relieved. His mother, well, she wanted the family earrings back, but was afraid to ask, while he wanted me to co-sign a loan. I laughed at him, and then it all came on top of Grandmama's story, and well, that's it."

I stop babbling and am reduced to tracing the knotholes on the kitchen table with my fingertip. It has been a crazy day, all in all.

Mom returns to the teapot, obviously trying to make sense of what I've just told her. "Why don't you tell me all about it, Amy? But go slow, so I can keep up. Go on."

My mother hasn't called me Amy since I was thirteen and stamped my foot and declared that Amy was a name for dolls and babies. I've been Amelia to everyone ever since. But, on this craziest of days, it feels comforting to hear that name. It feels right to have all the pieces of my past, and my family's past, come together all in one place. So I begin at the beginning and continue long enough for us to have two cups of tea each.

When I'm done, I feel an overwhelming sense of rightness and freedom. Clive's asinine behaviour today seems to have released me from the worst of my pain, and for that I'm grateful. As for the rest, somehow knowing about Grandmama's other baby makes me feel closer to my great-grandmother, even though I myself have not had such a heart-rending experience. The fact that Grandmama told me, now, feels significant. I realize the revelation wouldn't have touched me the same way if I'd always known it or if I'd learned about it even a few months or years ago.

"Mom," I ask, "does it bother you that Grandmama never told you about her baby?"

My mother drains the teapot into her mug and slowly adds milk and sugar. "Yes and no. I don't really like secrets, and I still can't believe that I chose the same name for my own daughter, but I also have to respect Grandmama for letting your father and me pick the names we wanted for our children and not interfering.

"She never did interfere, you know. Mother always said the same thing. Grandmama wouldn't meddle in important things like that—but that could be hard too, because you didn't really know what she thought unless you flat out asked. So, yes and no. But, in many ways, I guess it's right that she told you first and waited until now to tell you. Somehow it seems to complete the circle. Are you going to tell Eliza and Douglas? It will likely be odd for them too. After all, she is their mother, and Amelia Anne was their sister, however briefly. Yes, it might be even harder for them," her voice trails off.

"I don't know. Maybe I should ask Grandmama if she'll tell them?" I really don't want the responsibility and I don't want to hurt them. "What do you think, Mom?"

"Do what feels best. I have a feeling that if you ask her, Grandmama will do it. She obviously felt relieved after telling you; she may want to feel even more relieved. At least, that's how I'd try to pitch it to her, if I were you!"

I go round the table and hug my mother from behind. "Thanks, Mom. For everything, especially since Clive."

Neither of us is able to say anything else—our tears are close. Luckily, my hug speaks for itself.

APRIL 1990
ELEVEN

For the rest of spring break, I immerse myself in my family's history. Most days, I walk over to my great-grandmother's and put in a full day's work. The two of us go through all of Grandma's photos, sorting, labelling, dating, and organizing. Grandmama manages to put all the photos together with her own, so that each album becomes the definitive edition, holding all the known pictures for that set of years. Mom went through her family photos and mementoes as well, and Grandmama and I made a few copies of things that we felt needed to be in the main albums.

At almost the end of the two weeks, we have come to a crossroads. We need to decide if we're done—if anyone wants to look for a specific photo it will be easy to find, but if we want extra prints of significant photos so that Grandmama, Eliza, Douglas, and Mom will each have their own copies we'll need to keep going. "If we do that," I think, "I'll have plans for the summer. I'll be knee deep in family history again."

I realize I don't mind the thought at all. Working with Grandmama has proven to be fascinating. She tells me about various pictures and reminisces about how things used to work or where shops and merchants used to be located in Victoria. Although she has never been reticent about most of the past, this project seems to have put her in the mood to square away all the bits and pieces, including her stories. I wish I were brave enough to record one of her memory sessions on tape. I want to hold onto everything: both her stories and her voice telling them.

Surveying the albums now neatly lined up on shelves in her front room, Grandmama says, "Before you have to go back to school, I think we should have a celebratory dinner to mark all our hard work and explore our summer plans. We'll invite your mother, Eliza and Douglas, and Michael and Suzanne. You haven't told Eliza and Douglas about their sister, have you?"

I shake my head. "I told Mom. We thought maybe you should tell them. They might think it odd not to hear about her from you."

Grandmama sighs. "I know you're right, dear, but I had hoped you'd just rush over and tell them. They'll have more questions, and they'll wonder why I waited all this time—Never mind. Perhaps if I cook some of their favourite things for dinner, it will take a bit of the sting out of the surprise. One can only hope."

—

Two days later we all gather in Grandmama's front room. Grandmama and Mom are in charge of dinner, so from time to time one of them leaves the room to check on things in the kitchen. I, meanwhile, am showing the others the newly reorganized and very full albums. Eliza and Douglas are enjoying all the pictures from their childhood. Though Grandma is missed, everyone seems to be making a point of fleshing out her part in the stories being told so that it is almost as if she were still here with us. When we're seated at the table, the recollections continue and I find myself getting a little nervous. Grandmama has yet to mention anything about Amelia Anne, and it seems to me that several golden opportunities to do so have already come and gone. I keep telling myself to be patient. "A secret that has been kept this long can keep for just a little longer," I think.

Finally, Grandmama looks round the table and winks at me. "I know this will come as a bit of a shock," she says, "especially to you two." She gestures toward Eliza and Douglas. "But the truth will out eventually, and there's no reason not to tell it now. There was no real reason not to tell it years ago, save that I was too proud and stubborn— and most of all, scared."

Her voice goes on, never faltering. In much the same way that she'd told me, she tells the others about the wee baby Amelia Anne, and then she talks about the fire. She stops a couple of times, almost as if she expects one of us to comment or ask a question, but no one does. On she goes, describing the move to Victoria, how she settled in, how she met Grandpapa.

"And that complicated everything," she admits. "I always believed it was necessary to be truthful in a marriage, but—," she braces herself. "But I wasn't truthful myself. Or at least I was never able to tell Thad the whole truth. Not about myself, not about my husband, my boy, John, my dear friend, and not about the baby, Amelia." She's not looking at her immediate surroundings; she is looking far back in time, seeing the past again, all in her mind's eye.

"Not telling becomes a habit. At first, I was sure I was doing it for all the right reasons: to protect the children, to protect myself from reliving all of it, to protect Thad. Later, I wasn't so sure, but by then it had been such a long time; I convinced myself it didn't really matter, if I didn't tell all of it. I'd told Thad pieces, here and there. More than I realized I think. I don't suppose it really matters if I told him everything. Or does it?" Suddenly Grandmama looks directly at Eliza and Douglas. She looks very young somehow, young and unsure.

"I remember the fire," Eliza says flatly. "I always have."

Grandmama is clearly surprised. She looks a question at Douglas, but he shakes his head.

"My earliest memory is this house," he says. "Playing in the back yard with Eliza, and tripping and almost knocking a tooth out on one of those big rocks back there. I don't remember Grande Prairie at all."

Everyone turns back to Eliza. She too is very far away. "I remember a man chasing a horse. He was yelling and his face was black—with smoke, I guess—he was very angry. I remember thinking it was my fault. There were screams. I always thought it must have been the animals. I guess when I was young I couldn't let myself understand that people—could sound like that." Her voice is a thin thread.

"When I was older and Thad talked about it with us a bit, I realized that all the animals got out. The man was my father. And it was him—my father and John and your friend. I remember John a bit too. He was bigger than me; he always liked to chase me, and he'd pull the cat's tail. I used to cry about that." Eliza's voice stops.

"You never said you remembered," Grandmama says, gently.

"I always knew you hoped I didn't," Eliza replies. "Even as a child I knew that. Besides, I'm still trying to understand what it is that I can remember."

Michael lets out a big breath. That seems to be the signal for all of us to shift in our chairs, clear our throats, and breathe properly again.

Before Eliza can say more, Douglas interjects. "Why tell us now, Mother? I mean you could've just carried on. There aren't any pictures of the baby, are there?" He looks from Grandmama to me, and back again, as we shake our heads. "We'd never have found out. How could we? And, perhaps I'm callous, but why dredge all this up? It must bring back painful memories for you, but it doesn't really change things for us. It's not as if she is still alive somewhere out there or something. She didn't go missing. She died when you were just a young mother, stuck out in the middle of nowhere. It's a wonder any of us made it."

Mom shuts her eyes. Douglas's practical view doesn't leave much room for subtlety or anyone's finer feelings. He still has an affinity for creatures of all sorts, but he is occasionally too blunt-speaking for his fellow humans. I note my mom's look of concern, but no one else seems to share it, except perhaps Eliza, who looks pained—the rest seem to appreciate Douglas's straight shooting, especially Grandmama.

Grandmama laughs before speaking, "It's a wonder that you made it—as you put it, Douglas—you were always getting into scrapes. On the prairie I worried that you'd wander off so far that I'd never find you! Once we moved here, I was sure you'd tumble into the water and drift out to sea, all in the name of adventure. Raising you two—and Georgie, of course—that was plenty of adventure for me.

"As for telling you now, well, looking back at all those pictures makes it all come up here again," Grandmama pats her chest, "and not in a bad way either. I decided to tell Amelia, given her name and all. It just seemed—natural finally. It did give me a bit of a turn when Rosalind and Brian chose the name—like an echo come back years later, but it wasn't really painful. Names take on a life of their own, whether you have certain people in mind to start with or not. And it's a beautiful name.

"Amelia thought I should tell the rest of you. I told Georgie too, not long before she died. I don't imagine she really had any idea what I was saying; her mind had been gone so long already, but knowing I was losing her—kind of loosened my tongue, I guess. I never told Thad about the baby. Too proud, as I said, and I didn't want him having any more reason to pity me. There were too many already.

"Did you know I actually refused him at first? He wanted to court me, and he couldn't ask my father for permission, so he asked me, and I said virtually nothing. I let him think that I couldn't, that I just couldn't, and let him go. Such a little goose was I!

"Thank heavens for my dear friend—his sister, your Aunt Agatha. She threw us together again, no doubt tired of listening to each of us moan about being lonely. And I was lucky; Thad was willing to take me on, to be patient with me, to put up with what I couldn't or wouldn't share. Truth be told, I kept trying to tell him more of my story, and, somehow from the little pieces I managed to share over the years, I always felt that he may have guessed much more of the truth than he ever said. I know that he forgave me for not actually telling him outright. That was one of the last things he said to me, bless his heart—that he never minded not knowing all of my past." Thoughtfully, Grandmama shakes her head. "He was such a good man."

Rousing herself a bit, she looks at each of us in turn. "And now you all know the story. Yet—," her voice stops.

Mom and I exchange glances. Neither of us knows what is coming next. Grandmama stands up and holds tightly to the back of her chair; her knuckles are very visible, and deep emotion plays across her face.

"Mother?" Eliza puts up her hand and touches Grandmama. "Are you all right?"

Absently, Grandmama covers Eliza's hand with one of her own. "Yes, yes; of course. Just thinking about what a mountain I made of a molehill. All because of pride and youth." She turns and walks away from her seat, patting Michael's shoulder on the way by. "Don't let pride get in your way, Michael. Pride makes for a very cold bedfellow." Grandmama leaves the room and makes her way down the hall.

Michael looks from his wife to Mom and then to me. "What did I do to deserve that?"

Grandmama's voice carries down the hall: "You worry too much about how things look; isn't that right, Suzanne?"

Suzanne and I start giggling while Michael looks confused and hard done by. "What's so funny?" he demands. "What did Grandmama mean?"

This time, there is no comment from the hall. I stifle my laughter and try to explain, "I think Grandmama just used you as her exit line. We enjoyed it anyway. Didn't we, Suzanne?"

"Huh," my brother replies. Michael is left at the table as everyone else rises and starts to clear away the dishes. That job done, we join Grandmama in the front room. Michael comes in last.

"Amelia and I, and Rosalind too, are going to put together family history packs for everyone this summer," Grandmama announces. "Amelia needs a project and I need to organize all of my past. I've got some documents too, and a few other odds and ends." There are raised eyebrows as Grandmama says that, but no comments. "Eliza, Douglas—if you two have anything of significance to us all, please make copies—see to it that we get them before the end of June. We want to get started as soon as Amelia's school year ends. When we're done, we'll have another dinner. Do look at the albums more, if you'd like. I need some air." She brandishes her cane and makes her way to the door.

LATE JULY 1990
TWELVE

The summer speeds by, and our project continues. Occasionally, we have help: Mom comes by frequently, and once in a while Douglas or Michael will drop in "just to see how it's progressing." Eliza occasionally drops off some old pictures and school reports that she'd taken when she moved out. She never stays, though; ever since she admitted that she remembered the fire, she's seemed distant. I can't quite figure out why, nor can Mom offer an explanation. At that first dinner, before the "revelation," as Michael calls it, Eliza had seemed eager to look at all the old photos and to tell the old stories. Now, she doesn't seem to want to get too close.

Although Grandmama and I never discuss it, I know my great-grandmother has noticed Eliza's behaviour and is curious about it. I am too, and I keep hoping for an opportunity to speak to my great-aunt on my own. So far, no such chance has materialized. Perhaps the end of summer dinner will provide one. The last family dinner certainly had its moments.

"We've really done it now," Grandmama interrupts my train of thought. "Everyone has a complete family history to take home, and the master set of photos and papers has been catalogued. Our family history is as well organized as an official archive. Quite an accomplishment for an old lady and a broken-hearted teacher."

I grin. "Funny, I don't feel quite so broken-hearted anymore. I think Clive actually did me a favour, Grandmama. His leaving made me take a long look at him—and at myself. And, looking at all these pictures, hearing all the stories, reminded me of the things that really last, that remain important. I know myself now, better than I did before, and better than Clive knows himself I think. He was always so busy trying to look the part: the perfect boyfriend, the perfect son, the perfect employee, the perfect fiancé, and the perfect whatever. I don't know if he will ever find out who or what he is behind all those façades."

Suddenly feeling self-conscious, I pause to gather my thoughts. "I'm obviously not a psychologist or psychiatrist, and I'm probably not making much sense, but," I take a deep breath, "but I feel like there was a lack there, a place inside him that was—that is—empty."

Grandmama, sitting in her favourite chair, watches me closely. Her brow furrows in concentration, and she nods.

I continue. "I know we all act differently at different times and with different people. We all put on different roles. 'Ms Thate,' the teacher, is different from Amelia, your great-granddaughter—but no matter my name or my position, I always feel as if the core of who I am remains the same. There are parts of the young Amy still here," I tap my forehead, perhaps a little too hard, "and they inform how I act when I teach or when I meet strangers or when I have dinner with my family. It's like the roles all come together, all—converge at one point, in my heart or head or psyche, and that's me. That's honestly me, and that always comes through.

"I never saw that happen with Clive. I thought I did. I assumed that I did, but thinking about it, I know that it never really happened. His roles didn't come together. He's very good at each role, but, looking back, I can't find any evidence of that convergence. Some part of him is missing or empty. And I would've spent a lifetime trying to find it or fill it."

The realization surprises me. "I never understood it like that until I just said it out loud. Do you know what I mean?"

Grandmama nods. "I don't know that I can verify your interpretation of Clive, darling, but I do like your theory of self. It's like putting all the threads of your life through the eye of one needle; if you know who you are—all the roles—all the threads can come together at one point, in one place. All the dark ones and light ones and broken ones—and splayed out behind that needle, each thread goes to its spot on the tapestry. That picture becomes your whole life—

"I've been thinking something similar for the last few years. Yes." She keeps nodding. "Yes, and each person can choose to hold that needle or not. And to look at the completed tapestry or not."

Both of us are silent. I have no idea what my great-grandmother is thinking, but, for my part, I know I've found an answer of sorts to the whole Clive episode. Maybe it isn't the right answer; maybe Clive would scoff at it or completely deny it if he knew, but for me, the truth of what I've said hums inside my skin. As I explained to Grandmama, I hadn't known what I was going to say until I said it, and yet each word seemed to drop into place as if it were a piece of a puzzle that could only be attached to that exact next piece. For me, the words sing with truth.

The Path to Kitty Islet

JANUARY 1991
THIRTEEN

Six months later, Mom and I are at the Monterey house. Grandmama died there, peacefully, in her sleep, two weeks earlier. She hadn't been ill, to our knowledge anyway, so we'd had no warning other than her advanced age.

Douglas stopped by for a visit in the morning only to find her in her bed, not awake and not breathing. He'd called the ambulance, but it was clear that she'd died hours before. By the time the rest of the family arrived, he was in shock. He clung to Eliza and wept like the little boy he'd once been.

Eliza too reacted unexpectedly. She cried, but she also questioned everyone over and over about Grandmama's last days. She asked me repeatedly if Grandmama had said anything more about Grande Prairie. She behaved more like a private detective than a bereaved daughter, yet there were moments when she'd be overcome by a storm of tears the likes of which I've never seen before, not even in the teenage boys and girls I teach. Losing the family matriarch was taking its toll on all of us, and because of her indomitable spirit, we'd all convinced ourselves that somehow Grandmama would indeed outlive us all.

As Mom and I root around in the low basement, I ask the question I've been mulling over.

"Mom, what do you think really killed Grandmama?"

Without a moment's pause, Mom replies, "She was ready to go. She'd decided. Besides, she was almost a hundred."

"But what about what the doctors said? Whatever the heart thing was called?"

Mom shrugs. "Maybe that's the scientific way of saying that she chose. They have to give it a name. Have a label. But we know what really happened. It was her time. And when Grandmama made up her mind—" she looked up at me expectantly.

"Everyone did as she decided," I finish.

"Especially her own heart," Mom adds. "Well," she continues, "there isn't really much down here. We'll get Michael and some of his friends over to move the old trunks. Douglas can supervise. Once we get them upstairs, we can look through them and decide what to do with the contents. I think at least one of them has some really old Christmas decorations in it. Maybe people could choose some to keep if they'd like. Or not." She wrinkles up her nose. "Everything's dusty; the contents probably are too."

Returning upstairs, I put the kettle on. Though Grandmama's will was quite straightforward, there's still a lot for us to do and to decide. Michael and Suzanne think they might like to buy this house on Monterey; if so, they'll have to buy out Eliza, Douglas, and Mom, and they'll likely want to do some renovating first too.

But before that can happen though, all of Grandmama's belongings and papers have to be gone through. Anything the family doesn't want is to go to recycling or charity. It's going to take a while, even though Grandmama and I had finished with the photos and family history things. Grandmama's will also mentioned two special boxes, boxes that no one in the family remembers seeing. Both boxes have been left to me, with specific instructions that I am to share the contents only if I think that best. "And no one is to pester Amelia about them," Grandmama instructed.

I can hear her voice saying those words, even though the lawyer read them out. Everyone turned to look at me when he did, and Mom immediately asked if I knew what was in the two "green and gold" boxes, as they're called in the will. I was honestly able to say that I have no idea. Grandmama's will gave no indication where the boxes are, or what's in them, or even what size they are; they're simply to go to me, unopened, when they are found.

Since the family heard the reading of the will, each member has come up with some idea for the location of "Amelia's treasure," as Douglas has christened the boxes. We've looked in the attic, the basement, the separate garage, and both spare bedrooms. They haven't come to light yet. Originally, we assumed that the boxes must be large; however, as we've searched the obvious spots and come up empty-handed, I've started to believe that they must be fairly small. Mom is now certain they're jewellery boxes; if so, they'll likely be in Grandmama's room. It does, however, make the job of sorting through all of Grandmama's belongings a little less sad and even a tiny bit exciting, since we're always on the lookout for my "treasure."

Finishing our tea, Mom and I decide it's time to tackle Grandmama's bedroom. We've saved it for almost last, so we haven't really gone in it much yet. I've been both dreading and looking forward to this. Of all the rooms in the house, Grandmama's bedroom is the least familiar to me. As a child, I had permission to explore every room, including the basement and attic, as long as I kept out of her bedroom. It was a mark of my respect for my great-grandmother that I always had. Curious though I had been, I'd never gone into her room without her being there and giving me permission to enter—and that permission hadn't been given very often.

Mom pushes open the door, and I realize again that my great-grandmother isn't simply gone for the day, even though her dresser looks as if she has just gotten up from it; her comb is there, alongside a pair of favourite earrings, a watch, and a lace handkerchief. A few of her clothes are draped over the armchair in the corner. The closet door is ajar, allowing a glimpse of the clothes and scarves inside. On the bedside table is a stack of books: an Agatha Christie mystery, a biography of Elizabeth I, a collection of short stories by Alice Munro. The lamp has a soft pink shade with an elaborately beaded fringe. I turn it on despite the bright sunlight coming in the window, and admire the warm pool of lamplight it creates at the head of the bed. Though Grandmama's room is simple, it's also warm and comfortable.

"It's like a little den, isn't it?" Mom observes. "I can still picture Grandmama curled up in this bed, reading."

I sit on the edge of the bed, stroking the multi-coloured afghan that is draped over its foot. "I wanted to sleep in here with Grandmama when I was little. I begged and begged, but she only let me do it every once in a while. It seems funny, because she'd give in to so many other suggestions—things you'd never let me do—but she didn't let me spend time in her room very often. I wonder why?"

Mom stops opening and closing the bureau drawers. "I only got to sleep in here on the odd occasion too. Funny, I hadn't thought about that in years, but it's true. I was quite afraid of the dark as a child, and Mother would always let me come and snuggle with her. But Grandmama rarely would."

"Maybe she snored," I suggest. "Maybe she didn't want any of us to know. Or maybe she talked in her sleep. I wish we could ask Grandma, although I imagine Eliza or Douglas must know too. Since we haven't found the boxes anywhere else, they must be somewhere in this room, don't you think Mom?"

"Um hmm," she says, somewhat distractedly, as she has her head part way in the clothes closet.

I sit down at the mirrored dresser and open the ornate jewellery box sitting on top of it. It isn't large, and though it holds many of Grandmama's favourites, no green and gold boxes are among them. My eyes mist over as I pick up a few pieces. Grandmama had a beautiful blue cameo that she liked to wear on special occasions, and it looks oddly bereft, here in the velvet of the jewellery box instead of being pinned to one of Grandmama's boiled-wool blazers. The pearls, the tiny gold fan earrings, and the dainty silver cross too all look orphaned. Mom comes and stands behind me. "I guess we'll have to figure out how to let

The Path to Kitty Islet

everyone have something out of there. I do hope it won't cause any disagreements."

She moves on to Grandmama's cedar chest while I decide to open the tall sweater armoire. It has two long vertical doors on top, each side carved with roses and leaves intertwining, and then two drawers at the bottom, running the full width of the piece. Opening the doors exposes neatly piled sweaters in a rainbow of colours. Pulling open the first drawer reveals one green and gold box, and then when I open the second, I find the other. I gasp. Mom immediately comes over and watches me pull each one out of its drawer, gently. The boxes are exactly the same size: two feet long, about a foot wide, and perhaps eight inches deep.

I lay them side by side on the bed. They look old, but they're in perfect condition. The boxes are a deep green colour, with gold trim, and golden-coloured reinforced edges and corners. I can't tell if they are made of thin wood or very thick cardboard. Regardless, here is my "treasure." Holding my breath, I open the first one. Inside are a very old and very ornate-looking photograph album and an old Bible.

"Have you ever seen these before, Mom?" I ask.

Mom shakes her head. "I don't think so."

I open up the album, discovering page after page of ancient black and white photos. Most are portraits, taken inside a studio. The people in them are in very set, unnatural positions. Some pictures show large groups of people, outside, gathered together for various events. A couple occupy centre stage in a few, and the dresses and small bouquets indicate those must be wedding pictures. Finally, toward the very end of the album, on each of the last half-dozen pages, are one or two pictures of a very young Grandmama, but none of the other people look familiar.

Tucked under the album and Bible are several bundles of letters. I undo one, and choose a letter from the top. "'Dear Emily,' it says," I read, scanning quickly. "And it's signed 'God bless,

241

Minnie.'" I squint at the handwriting. "These are letters from Grandmama to someone else, to Emily Somebody or other. But the writing looks different—I guess that's how she wrote when she was younger?" My voice echoes the perplexity I feel. "Maybe they were written by someone else named Minnie? Another Minnie? Because—well, the handwriting is all wrong."

Mom picks up another letter. She shows it to me. It, too, has the same kind of handwriting: thin loops and whorls, and bits crossed out here and there. It is nothing like Grandmama's tidy copperplate, which had nary a mistake, spelling or otherwise. Neither Mom nor I can figure out what we've found. Putting the letters aside for the moment, I open the second box.

Right on top is an envelope, in Grandmama's own beautiful script, addressed to "My darling Amelia Thate." Glad that I'm sitting down, I look at my mother, turn the envelope over, and take out the letter. It is beautifully handwritten and dated a month or so before her death.

> *To my darling Amelia,*
> *my beloved great-granddaughter,*
>
> *This is not an easy letter to write, nor will it be easy to read I'm afraid. Let me begin by saying how very proud I am of you and how much I have enjoyed all the time you've given me over the last year or so. I've finally had to acknowledge that time is not something I have much more of, not here anyway, so I thought I'd best finish what you and I, and your mother, started.*
>
> *As far as you knew, we had finished the family history. Although we talked about researching more about the Cosgroves and the Worthings and the Sinclairs, I never really encouraged you to do*

so. Perhaps you wondered about that, though I'd like to think that I was so casually offhand about it that you never really noticed.

The truth is—

How funny it feels to even write that phrase. I have spent long years of my life guarding against telling the truth. I have denied myself opportunities, all in an effort to keep the truth hidden. I never did tell my poor dear Thad the whole truth. I believe he guessed much of it, and I know he forgave me for not sharing. I do wish that I had had the courage to tell him, though. I loved him. As I grew older, I realized he would've loved me no matter what, but I couldn't trust in that before. I just couldn't. I did tell Georgie, but only at the end, when it was really too late. And there were a thousand moments when I wanted to tell your mother or you, but I couldn't bring myself to actually say the words, even all these years later. I can only write them.

The truth is, I am not Minnie Cosgrove.

But that too is a lie. Perhaps it would be better to say I began life as Emily Anne McCrindle, born in London, England, on May 12, 1893, to William McCrindle and Nellie Pawluk. My very best friend in all the world was a wonderful light-hearted girl named Hermione Abigail Sinclair, but we all called her Minnie. **She** *married the dashing Harry Worthing, Jr., and she went to Canada in 1908. I was left behind in London, pining for my best friend and wishing for adventure. We managed to keep in touch, and foolishly or not, I kept many of* the letters all this time. They are included here for you to see—and to hear—the real Minnie's voice from all those years ago.

I stop reading. My hands are shaking. I put the letter down and look at my mother. "Mom? Can it really be possible? Is Grandmama someone else?"

Mom looks and sounds the way I feel: disoriented and breathless, as if she'd just hurried up a long flight of stairs. "I don't know," she says. "It seems so farfetched, so unbelievable. What else does she say?"

I pick up the letter and read on.

> After my mother died, I decided to go to Minnie. My father was a hard and distant man and I was afraid of who or what I would become if I stayed with him. I ran away. I stole the family Bible and photo album, plotted with a neighbour, and got myself to the New World. I wanted a new start.
>
> It took forever to get to Minnie. The country was so very big, and travel was a lot more complicated then of course. And I was a young lady alone. I spent some time with Harry's parents in Ontario first, waiting for the worst of winter to be over. Harry's family was kind to me, but I could see why Harry and Minnie were determined to go out west. They had many traits in common with my father, did Harold Sr. and Jane Worthing. I sometimes fear my later actions were unkind to them. I never contacted them, and perhaps they weren't as bad as my twenty-year-old self judged them to be. But I never considered that until later. And by then it was much too late.

> When I arrived in Grande Prairie, Minnie was sorely changed. No one knew what to do for her—especially not me, still basically a child myself. The death of her baby, Amelia Anne, had affected her mind, though it seemed she had been unwell even before that. Harry was also failing to cope and he had been mistreating her. I imagine nowadays both would have been treated for depression at the very least. I did all I could, but it wasn't enough. What follows is a copy of what I wrote in my diary when I got to their homestead. (My diaries too are tucked inside this box; they are yours now.)

APRIL 1914
GRANDE PRAIRIE

Minnie seems so broken and so damaged.

It seems that she told no one, not Harry or Callie, or the Worthings or me, that she was again with child. She delivered the baby herself, alone in the house save for the other three children, and it seems that it was born far too soon. Callie came by later that day to visit, only to find Minnie in quite a bad way and the baby in even worse shape. She decided to hitch up the wagon, as she could not see Harry anywhere, and take Minnie and the little baby girl to Montrose, the local hospital. It was cold—as it is still, especially at night—and Callie fretted the whole way that perhaps she'd have been better to try to care for Minnie and the babe at home. By this time, Minnie was more coherent and kept asking after little Amelia Anne by name. The other three children, John, Eliza, and Douglas, seemed to realize the enormity of the situation and were well behaved and pliant.

Minnie stayed in Montrose for almost two weeks. She slipped in and out of consciousness and often woke in hysterics. The two nurses did what they could for her and the baby, but Amelia was very small and very weak. Callie was hopeful that another miracle could be worked, and she called on Mrs Clifford to ask for her help. A few years before, Mrs Clifford had managed to keep tiny Frank Bezanson alive though his mother died just after his birth and he was only a mere two pounds himself. But not even Mrs Clifford could perform a miracle this time. Amelia Anne died, aged a week and a half, in her mother's arms. I was still on my way here at that time so I could bring no cheer. She was buried in the Flyingshot Cemetery, poor wee girl, and Minnie's heart was buried with her.

—

You may read the rest for yourself. My diary became my friend after that, because poor Minnie just wasn't herself any longer. There were glimmers, but she never fully recovered.

—

The fire happened as I told you, except for one crucial omission. Harry went into the house to try to rescue his son, John, **and** his wife, Minnie. All three of them perished. It was their screams that Eliza remembers: the screams of her parents and her brother, until they were overcome by smoke, and silenced.

When Eliza was little, she told me she remembered the "sad lady" and the sea of grass. The sad lady was her mother, though I kept trying to tell myself, and Eliza, that it was Callie, even though Eliza hadn't yet been born when Callie suffered from her depression. I tried to rework that piece of history for my own ends, you see. Eliza never told me, until this past year, that she remembered anything of the fire. It unnerved me to discover that, and I've wondered if she's remembered more. I wish I could ask, but I am so very frightened to know the answer. I worked so hard, for so long, to build a life, for Eliza and Douglas and myself, that didn't have at its heart an even deeper yawning cavern of tragedy. It's terrible enough to lose one parent in a fire, but two? I never wanted them to know they were orphans. I fought against that all the rest of my life.

Out of the ashes of that fire, "Minnie" was reborn. She was happy and determined, and I tried, God as my witness, to take the best of me, and the best of Minnie, and become the mother those two children deserved. I was selfish. I knew that, but I refused to give them up. I had found a purpose and a place in life, and I took it on willingly. I pulled all the threads together, Amelia, and I took hold of that needle in both hands. And it was done.

Everything else happened the way I've always said. I brought "my" two children to Victoria, met Thad, pushed him away, but eventually gave in and let him love me, for I loved him so myself. When Georgie was born, I felt so fortunate. I'd chosen to mother Eliza and Douglas, chosen freely and fiercely, but Georgie felt like a gift, a blessing, and a child for me and my dear Thad. After all that tragedy, in both Minnie's life and mine, I was so happy here in this bungalow on Monterey. But, as the years went by, I felt the weight of what I had done. I had abandoned my own father and brother, and I never let the Worthings see their grandchildren. Even if Harold and Jane had come looking for them, Thad adopted them and we changed their last name. I suppose they could have found them, but I certainly never made it easy.

Amelia, you are my own flesh and blood and I am sorry I could never summon the courage to tell you, or your mother, or Eliza or Douglas, or even Georgie before it was too late. I still don't know if I have done right by you, or by Eliza and Douglas especially, to write this down now, and to leave you with the burden of telling. Knowing you as I do, especially after being so much with you over the last year, I believe that you will tell them and will do so with all the grace and compassion you offer so freely to the world. More than anything, let my dear Eliza and my sweet Douglas know how very much I loved them, each and every day that I was their mother. I never could imagine leaving them, so I never did.

To you, Amelia, my own Amelia Emily (your mother, my darling Rosalind, must have some sort of second sight to have given you **those two** names), I give you my whole true story and my love. You have given me so much, more than I can ever thank you for. As for Rosalind, I hope she knows how very precious she has always been, and how, from the moment she was born, she brought light and love into a home that so desperately needed both, because her father was so far away and then never got to come home to his wonderful wife and child.

There is no way to end a letter such as this. You are reading it because I am gone. We cannot talk things over and I'm sorry I didn't have the courage to do that with you. I believe you will always carry a part of me in your heart, and, in the stillness and the quiet, you may hear me the way I've often heard my own darling mother, my dear, dear Thad, and my best friend, Minnie. When you need me, be still, and I will endeavour to come, God willing.

With all my heart, and from the best of us both,
Minnie/Emily

Mom and I sit in stunned silence. I root around deeper in the second green and gold box, opening diaries and flipping through the pages until I come across the one dated 1913 to 1914. Shifting on the bed so that I am as close to my mother as possible, I open it to the entries for Grande Prairie. My hands start shaking again. I skim the first few pages, then stop and read one out loud, in as unemotional a voice as I can muster.

JUNE 1914
EDSON

The prairie is so beautiful, so beautifully cruel. I had thought my world ended when dear Mama left me—but I continued. And it seems my destiny is to be witness at endings. Minnie's Grande Prairie world was incinerated, and I saw it all.

And once again, I have acted precipitately. But it was my decision. I made it. And I will live by it.

But the rest—needs telling once. And I need forgiveness, once. Then, it is over. For I cannot and will not undo my part in it.

The house was ablaze. Minnie followed John into the burning building. I don't know why John went in. I couldn't stop any of them—I could not. Did I try hard enough? There is only one answer to that which gives me permission to live.

Minnie went in after her son. Harry followed them trying to save them both, but it was too late. The roof collapsed soon after he ran in.

I do not know whose screams I could hear—it could have, may have, been Minnie, or the boy, poor little John. I thought I heard Minnie calling for Amelia, and John. Later the sounds did not seem human—and it seemed to take a long time for them to stop.

In my head, they echo still.

Harry had released the horses, and when the smoke died off they came back.

I held Eliza and Douglas to me. They never left me. We stayed that way, quietly.

And finally, the release of darkness. Lady, the old mare, came close for comfort. Only then did Douglas start his unintelligible monologue. Lady stayed with us.

Everyone in Grande Prairie knew Harry, but Minnie had kept to herself. If I could win Callie over, if I could avoid the nurses, Mrs Clifford, and the minister, I could be Minnie. If I left—Minnie had only ever been the woman waving from a distance, really.

Before I even understood it myself, I had made my decision.

In the early morning, in the cold grey light, I let the children sleep on with Lady. I found what was left of Minnie. I could not think—could not let her be that—I cannot and will not describe her. I will never forget the sight of her—it will haunt me I know.

Poor, poor Minnie's ring—gold does not burn. I took it. I reached down, removed it, and left her there.

I washed the ring with water from the wretched rain barrel. There was still water left—but never enough. I almost retched then—but the children—the poor darlings, my poor, dear darlings.

Tim and Callie came first. Callie saw the ring. Our locked eyes knew—her eyes dropped first, and then the hugged forgiveness came. I very nearly cried, but couldn't. The fire had touched their farm too, but not their buildings or many of their crops.

Others came slowly. Callie and Tim stayed silent. They stood behind me, backing me. The others consoled Minnie—me. The children slept.

Callie clasped me tightly once the neighbours left, and made sure I had this diary, the album, and the Bible. Why was I driven to keep them all tucked away in the cold cellar? She will be the last one to look into my own eyes. I miss her vision already, but it would be too dangerous to try and stay in touch.

We were bundled into a wagon, and we left. Lady will go to Callie. The other animals will cover the debts in town. Our farm is destroyed. I must use the right words now, evermore. I must be careful.

Minnie would not—I would not—want Harry's parents to have Eliza and Douglas. A new start, not anger and recriminations and lost, damaged hopes. It is too heavy a price. But my cost?

Eliza calls me Mother already. Douglas is his usual self. These selves that I will guard. To their own selves be true. My motto now.

And this diary. Whose needs does it serve? Which self? The last step. This and the photographs and Mama's Bible. All mine. But to keep? To destroy? It is a burden for now. That burden—and the sadness—are mine to bear, and to keep.

ROSALIND

1991
VICTORIA, B.C.

I can't even pretend to explain how my Amelia was named "Amelia Emily." I never knew about Minnie's premature baby, Amelia Anne. And I certainly had no idea that Grandmama was actually not Minnie at all, but Emily. How did my husband and I land on those two names? Brian and I simply liked each one of them, that's all.

Is it, though?

Grandmama joked that perhaps I had second sight; I must confess that I feel like there was something other worldly involved. I mean, of all the names we could've picked, we chose—well, really I chose and Brian agreed—those exact names. And Grandmama never said a word. For over twenty years, she never said a single thing about our decision.

Now that her secret's out, it's no wonder that she chose Amelia to work alongside her as she got all of our family's old photos organized. Amelia embodies both Minnie's and Emily's pasts in a way no one else in our family does.

Grandmama loved telling stories and loved literature her whole life. I know that Mom used to tell me about the way Grandmama and Aunt Agatha had long discussions about all kinds of novels and poems. Grandmama used to write herself, even, funny little sketches or poems for birthdays and special occasions. She read aloud to all of us, from her favourite books, and she herself was almost always reading multiple books at a time, voraciously devouring words.

Because of this, I firmly believe that she must have relished the symbolism of giving my Amelia the whole story: all the pieces of Minnie's life and her own—Emily's story—that she'd never been able to share with anyone else.

I may never fully understand all of her decisions, but I feel that I understand this one, at least. As a lifelong spinner of stories, there was no other way for Grandmama to do it.

EPILOGUE

ELIZA

1991
VICTORIA, B.C.

It took a long time for me to come to terms with what Amelia learned when she found those green and gold boxes. That it was the truth, I knew immediately. That Mother couldn't tell me herself was very difficult to accept, at first, especially because I had always known.

As a child, I couldn't figure out what I knew. I just knew that Mother was very different after we left Grande Prairie. As an adult, I started to piece together the fractured memories I had of those days. They were like a patchwork quilt, with some of the most important squares missing. So, for a few years, I would put the quilt blocks in this order, and try to make a pattern. Then, for the next few years, I'd try another, but I was never satisfied with the result. By the time of the family dinner when Mother told us about Amelia Anne, I'd just about decided that my memories must be creative reconstructions or poorly remembered childhood nightmares, because I couldn't find a way to make a coherent whole.

Once I'd heard about my sister Amelia, though, I knew my memories—at least most of them—were probably accurate. And then I was really frightened. What I believed I had seen did not correspond with the story Mother told of the fire. I was certain, in the core of my being, that I had seen my own mother go into the house; I believed that she had purposefully walked into that burning building. And I could not remember her coming out. Yet, all along, "Mother" had been with me, with me and with Douglas. But I always got caught there too. The mother Douglas and I had after Grande Prairie was a new person. She was not a person bowed down by tragedy, mourning the loss of a husband and child, but a woman full of life. Even as a child, I understood this. I knew it didn't make sense, but I couldn't explain it.

And I couldn't trust the flashes of memory that appeared so real, but didn't match what I thought was true, what Mother had told us was true.

I also remember the wagon ride with Callie and my birth mother to Montrose Hospital. I remember Amelia Anne's small face, her tiny, fragile body. I can remember my birth mother, rocking absently in her chair, rarely able to play with or smile at me. And I remember Emily, my second mother, or my always mother, as I have taken to calling her. She was so full of fun and laughter, and I know I clung to her even before the fire.

I do remember that terrible day too, quite clearly. Minnie, my birth mother, did seem to choose to go into the house, and she never came out. My father went in after her, and I now know that John had gone in first. Minnie had been trying to save him. She had roused herself enough—perhaps she really was getting better?—to try to save her child.

As I said at the dinner, I remember the sounds of the fire and the sounds of my family as the flames trapped them. Try though I might, I could never remember seeing my birth mother come out. And Emily, my always mother, looked unscathed when I pictured her on that day. I always wondered if perhaps I had mixed up two days. Now it makes perfect sense. My birth mother never did come out, and Emily, my always mother, never got too close to the flames and the soot. She kept Douglas and me safe and protected. And I know that's what she did, or wanted to do, for all those years that she pretended to be Minnie. I can see how, at the time, she would have felt that she had no other option, and in many ways I am deeply grateful. She was a wonderful mother. She and Thad gave us an amazing life here in Victoria, and I never, ever, felt any sort of want or lack in my life; I know I was treasured, and loved, and never alone.

But—there is a but. Reading the letters from Minnie to Emily has been difficult. The voice of that Minnie is all I have of my birth mother. It is no wonder that no one really ever saw Mother's face or features in me. No wonder that my own son and daughter look nothing like Rosalind or her children. We are not related by blood. That sounds so harsh and final, but it's true. All the ties that bound us, that bind us still, were—are—ties of love, not of shared genetics.

However, all of this has brought Douglas and me closer than we've been for years. He has decided to try to contact our birth mother's family, to see if there's anyone left in London. He has also, for the first time in his life, decided he wants to try to contact the Worthings in Ontario, hoping that perhaps our father had siblings who had children we can meet. It is interesting how anchored we felt by Mother and how unimportant our father's family was until we found out that we actually have no shared genes with the woman who raised us so carefully and loved us so deeply. I have been encouraging Douglas in all this and have determined that I will travel with him if he decides to go back east or even to England in order to track down our own blood relations.

In the meantime, all of this has taken its toll. I feel as though Rosalind and Amelia, and even Michael, are feeling guilty because they are just as much Emily's kin as they were Minnie's. For even though their grandmother/great-grandmother was named something else, all the other aspects of her remain the same. Her smile that we remember, so similar to the one we sometimes see on Amelia's face, is still her smile, whether she's smiling as Minnie or as Emily. They know from whence they sprang.

It is a different story for me and for Douglas. And it is really quite odd, at this stage in my life, to discover that I don't really know the first thing about my own birth mother. At least Douglas and I can make this journey of discovery together.

No matter what happens, I am determined to make this all come right in the end. Douglas is in his seventies and I am eighty. For decades, we were fiercely loved by an independent and resourceful woman who refused to abandon us. She carved out a new life for all of us and never made us feel inferior in any way to her own flesh and blood child, Georgie. She was my rock, and I only wish I could tell Mother now, knowing all of the truth, how very much I love, admire, and thank her. Her solution wasn't perfect, but there is no doubt in my mind that she did what she thought was best. And perhaps it was.

On most sunny days, I walk down to McNeill Bay and go out to Kitty Islet. The blue Adirondack chair is still out on the rocks, though it gets moved around at times—the better to take advantage of the sun, I think—and I still love to settle myself against its weathered wood and contemplate the sea and the sky.

That's when I really let myself drift, in and out of the past and present—when I let myself remember all those languid summer and fall afternoons when Mother was pregnant and I would bring her a biscuit and her tea. That was in fact her first pregnancy, I realize now. How hard it must have been for her to stifle her very natural joy and fear, and pretend that it was all old hat. But she did; she did it for me—for me and for Douglas, and for Minnie, her dear, dear friend.

Today I sit on the chair and look across at the Olympic Mountains. The waves lap against the rocks below. I remember coming here with Georgie when she was a small child, and I remember the day we all came here to spread her ashes and wish her Godspeed, with Mother here then too.

The sun is warm on my face, and the breeze is light; I close my eyes. Almost unconsciously, my fingers play with the two small stones some child has left on the arm of the chair. One is soft and curved, smoothly sensuous to the touch. The other is rough still, and a bit jagged on one corner, where a piece has broken off. I open my eyes and look carefully at both stones. They are each exactly as they should be: two grey-blue sea stones, lying together beautifully in my palm.

~

Minnie's Family Tree according to Amelia's first set of notes
(Based on the family photos and research they worked on together)

Ephraim Sinclair (born 1859) marries **Amelia Lockyer** (born 1867)

Children:

1) Albert (born 1889)

2) Edward (born 1890)

3) Elizabeth (born 1891)

4) **Hermione (known as Minnie) Sinclair (born 1892)**

5) Malcolm (born 1904)

Harold Worthing, Senior (born 1840) marries **Jane Tarry (born 1863)**

Children:

1) **Harold (known as Harry) Worthing, Jr.** (1879)

2) Sarah (born 1881)

3) Arthur (born 1883)

4) Anne (born 1886)

Minnie Sinclair marries **Harry Worthing, Jr.** in June 1908 (London, England); they move to Grande Prairie, Alberta

Children:

1) John Harold (born 1909)

2) Eliza Jane (born 1911)

3) Douglas Ephraim (born 1912)

Minnie (formerly Minnie Sinclair) Worthing marries **Thaddeus Cosgrove** (born 1885) in November 1921, in Victoria, B.C.

Child:

1) **Georgina (known as Georgie) Anne Cosgrove (born 1923)**

Georgie Cosgrove marries **Stuart Prentice** (born 1919) in 1941, in Victoria, B.C.

Child:

1) **Rosalind Anne Prentice** (born 1942)

Rosalind Anne Prentice marries **Brian Thate** (born 1937) in 1962, in Victoria, B.C.

Children:

1) Michael Theodore Thate (born 1963)

2) **Amelia Emily Thate (born 1965)**

CPSIA information can be obtained at www.ICGtesting.com
Printed in the USA
LVOW08*0349080616

491630LV00005B/23/P